THE RILEY COLLINS SERIES | BOOK ONE

a DANGEROUS *Year*

KES TRESTER

$16.99

A Division of **Whampa, LLC**

P.O. Box 2160

Reston, VA 20195

Tel/Fax: 800-998-2509

http://curiosityquills.com

Cover Art by Eugene Teplitsky

http://eugeneteplitsky.deviantart.com

ISBN 978-1-62007-906-5 (ebook)

ISBN 978-1-62007-907-2 (paperback)

10.2017

With love to Fred, Luke, Jordan, and Robb
And to Mom, always my first editor

BENSON'S RULE #1

LEVEL THE PLAYING FIELD

Please, don't let them take me!"

I knew enough Urdu to understand the girl's desperate plea.

The scrawny little thing clutching my arm was like any other twelve-year-old in the crowded Karachi marketplace, her hair covered with the traditional hijab headscarf, and her soft brown eyes wide with fear.

"It's okay," I said, betting she'd understand the tone if not the actual English words. My eyes darted about, attempting to pinpoint who or what was about to destroy the peace of a sweltering September afternoon. I'd heard enough horror stories to know if a young girl turned to an ambassador's daughter for help, it had to be a matter of life or death.

The American embassy was only three blocks away, but we couldn't walk there directly. A labyrinth of tiny stalls offering everything from used books to live chickens hemmed us in. Each booth butted up against the next, forcing shoppers to navigate a jostling gauntlet through a rabbit warren of sights and smells. It was one of my favorite places in the city.

I took her hand as we pressed through the crowd. I too wore a hijab, and though I normally tried to walk respectfully with head bowed, her panic was contagious. For once I didn't care who caught sight of my bright blue eyes, a dead giveaway of my foreignness.

A glance back revealed three bearded men shoving people aside with careless brutality. They were dressed in loose tunics and trousers, but it was the sight of their turbans, a squashed version of what most men wore, that sent my heart racing. Benson once told me the local extremists sported the odd style as a badge of honor and were to be avoided at all costs.

A shout told me we'd been spotted. It also warned the other shoppers there was trouble brewing. As the crowd magically thinned, I knew with absolute certainty we were never going to make it to the embassy before our pursuers closed the gap. The girl's fingernails bit into my skin as she realized it, too.

I searched the stalls as we raced, hunting desperately for something I could use as a weapon. Benson said the local group wasn't well armed, but in his mind, that meant they probably wouldn't have guns. Knives and clubs were another matter.

Inspiration struck when I spied the music man.

He always sat perched on a big, colorful pillow as he played one of the many musical instruments filling every square inch of his stall, his dark eyes twinkling as if we shared some secret. I hoped he'd forgive what I was about to do.

Five or six tall wind instruments resembling overgrown rhaitas, the flutes popular with snake charmers, stood in an orderly row at the front of the open-air shop. I grabbed the nearest one, about six feet in length and surprisingly heavy. The mouthpiece and flared opening were both fitted with metal coverings, but the rest was a solid shaft of gleaming wood. It was perfect.

What I was about to do broke every rule, but the men bearing down on us left me no choice. I shoved the girl behind me and stood my ground.

The shoppers cleared a path as our pursuers slowed to a confident pace. A cluster of old men cackled as they placed bets on how long I could fend them off, and how many blows I could land before I succumbed.

The trio came to a halt, kicking up a cloud of dust. The guy in the center regarded me with contempt as I bounced on the balls of my feet, the staff balanced in my hands. He appeared to be in his late twenties, but his two young companions were only a few years older than me.

"Go home… girl." He spit out the last word as if it were dirt in his mouth. English was the second language of Pakistan, but he spoke it better than I would ever manage Urdu.

"No problem," I said evenly. "I'll just take my friend and go." I didn't dare turn to look, but she still hovered behind me.

"No. She has offended Allah and shamed her family. We will take her." He took a threatening step in my direction, but I held firm.

"What has she done?" The kid looked barely strong enough to walk to the dinner table.

"This." Her high voice piped up as she stepped forward, her stance defiant as she held up the forbidden object causing all the commotion. A book. "I have been going to school." Her English was clear and precise, her words ringing with pride.

Oh, shit. As far as these guys were concerned, she might as well have announced she danced naked with sheep. The traditionalists in this part of the world were hell bent on keeping their girls ignorant and subservient. There would be no walking away from this one gracefully.

The old men holding wagers were getting impatient. One of them called out a taunt, egging the trio on. The leader took the bait, but I was ready for him. A quick flick, and the staff smacked him squarely across the face, shattering his nose. My stomach clenched at the sight of spurting blood.

Benson's voice rang inside my head, directing my movements as I followed with a hard jab to the ribs and an uppercut to the jaw. My shocked opponent sank to his knees before passing out cold on the dusty street.

Cheers and catcalls arose from our audience. They didn't care who won or lost; this was the most fun they'd had all day. It also fueled the righteous anger of the remaining two, one of whom pulled out a gleaming knife. He nodded to the other and they broke apart, intent on circling me. I couldn't let that happen.

"Benson's rule," my dad's security chief would say. "Level the playing field." The knife had to go.

I feinted toward the guy with the weapon, and he fell for it. Off balance, it was a simple matter to sweep the staff behind his knees and whip him off his feet. The other guy attacked. Fortunately, he fought like an untrained schoolboy and clumsily swung a fist in my general direction. I dodged it easily and sank an elbow into his exposed throat. His windpipe was probably fine, but he was suddenly a whole lot more worried about breathing than he was about messing with me.

The guy with the knife lurched back to his feet and came looking for blood. The chatter from the sidelines grew as bets were doubled, maybe tripled. I danced just out of reach, counting on his anger to make him reckless. I was shaming him in front of his people, something my dad would surely ream me for later.

The swiftness of the girl's movements surprised us both. Like a cornered kitten, she launched herself at him with arms raised. She viciously slammed the book down on his knife hand. The weapon skittered away and so did she, beaming as she cleared the field. I immediately swept the staff into the sweet spot between my opponent's legs, and his eyes glazed over as he sank to the ground.

I glanced at the spectators, worried an uncle or cousin of one of the fallen would feel honor-bound to enter the fray, but they were all too busy arguing over their wagers.

"Let's go," I urged the girl, pausing in front of the grinning music man to return the dented instrument and empty my pockets of every last rupee. I hoped it was enough.

"Thanks!" I yelled back as we dashed away.

BENSON'S RULE #2

EXPECT THE UNEXPECTED

The ticking of the antique grandfather clock in the corner, a relic from British colonial days, echoed in the silence of my father's office. He'd been stewing as he worked for twenty minutes, one of his favorite tactics for drawing out a punishment. I stood on the carpet, supposedly to consider the error of my ways, but I had no regrets. The only difference between the girl in the marketplace and me was simple geography.

The room was appropriately grand for the office of a United States ambassador. It could also be shrugged off as impersonal, with very few items belonging to my dad on display. With a new posting every two years or so, he deemed it imperative to travel light.

On his desk sat a beautiful black and white photo of my mother, a smiling Italian woman who was nothing but a hazy collection of stories in my mind. He also had a bronze camel paperweight presented to him by a former prime minister of Madagascar, and a prized chess set he'd won in a heated match with the late South African president, Nelson Mandela.

A detective trying to analyze the personality of Joseph Collins would have little to go on.

"You can't rescue every child in every country," he said, breaking into my thoughts. His pale coloring was no match for the noonday sun, and today's outing to meet with a council of warlords had left him flushed. "Remember what happened in Yemen?" He meant to be stern, but there was a note of compassion in his voice.

"You see a pattern, I see a problem-solver," I replied. "Who knows what would have happened if those camel jackers had gotten hold of her?"

He cast me a scolding glare, but I didn't back down. Those guys deserved to be called every nasty slur in the book.

"You probably saved her life," he admitted. "But you've also just complicated yours. Those men will not forget what you've done. The streets are no longer safe for you, even with Benson and your mandatory security detail."

I plopped down in one of the chairs fronting his desk. "I know, but come on. I've heard what you were doing at seventeen, and you sure weren't walking around with a team of armed guards." He'd grown up wild and undisciplined on the streets of Boston until his parents threw up their hands and sent him to military school.

"That was a lifetime ago," he said, impatience creeping in. "Hell, even Pakistan of ten years ago was a different world. Do you think the new rules don't apply to you simply because you don't like them?"

"Somebody's got to stand up to the religious police who want to take this place back to the Dark Ages," I said. "That girl is somebody's daughter, too."

His expression softened. "Maybe it's time we rethink this life," he said, but that's as far as he got before we both jumped at my name being bellowed from somewhere within the embassy.

"Riley!" We both knew the voice, and worse, *that* tone.

"Save me," I begged.

He turned back to the computer screen with a sigh. "Nope. I can't keep you in line. Maybe he can do something with you." He glanced at me again over his wire-rimmed glasses. With his wilted white polo shirt and wrinkled khakis, he was more like a forgetful English professor than a player on the international stage. "Go meet your fate."

"Fat lot of good you are," I muttered, rising to my feet.

"Riley!" I was out in the hall when the summons came again, this time echoing up the enormous marble staircase. I could envision the blood vessels popping out on Benson's wide forehead as he hunted me down.

"I'm coming," I called out, defeated.

Benson stood at the bottom of the next flight of steps with arms crossed and lips compressed into a narrow line. The nostrils of his crooked nose, the result of being broken one too many times, flared with anger. The white button-down he wore on duty barely contained his hulking frame, and I paused two steps up so I could meet our resident giant face to face. I'm not short, but he topped out at six-foot-five.

His Australian accent was as thick as the day he and my dad met on a joint military mission decades ago. They'd become close friends, and after my mom's death Benson had signed on permanently as my dad's security chief – and my unofficial jailor.

"Bloody hell! What were you thinking?" He raked a meaty hand across the bristle of his closely cropped hair. It had once been jet black, but now it was liberally sprinkled with gray. "I know you can handle yourself, but what is the first rule of fighting?"

"To avoid a fight. But Benson—"

"And going out without your security detail? After what happened in Yemen? Do I need to put a blasted bell around your neck?"

I opened my mouth to protest, but in all honesty my excuses were totally weak. He was right. Once again I'd been overly confident and foolish, and I really had no defense. But what did he expect? My only friends were guys like Martinez and Brady, who worked under Benson. There were no girls my age to hang out with, most of my shopping was done online, and my entertainment was limited to books or my computer.

"I'm sorry," I said at last. "It won't happen again." Since I would most likely have a price on my head after today's run in, it was an easy promise to make.

He regarded me suspiciously. "Just like that? The girl who'd rather die than admit she's wrong just apologized?"

I shrugged. "What I did was wrong."

The badass melted. "Oh, darlin' girl, you scared the hell out of me today. What if something had happened? Why do you take such awful risks?"

"It would have been fine if it hadn't been for those jerks," I said, unable to stay repentant for long. "I know this city, Benson, and I know these people."

"No, you don't," he said. "We are divided by much more than a flag and twenty-foot walls."

"Only if we want to be! How will they ever come to know us if all we ever do is drive past them in armored vehicles?"

It was true there was an element of danger on the streets; beneath the mask of a modern city there lived a people in turmoil. But it was also a place where the world's best fried pakoras and spicy chai were as close as the nearest café, the hours of the day could be marked by the melodious cry of the muezzin calling the faithful to prayer, and holidays found thousands joyously tossing food to the birds and fishes.

He growled in frustration. "How can a girl raised in every hot spot from here to Egypt be so ignorant about the world?"

"Not ignorant," I disagreed, "just not afraid. There is a difference."

"Not if it gets you killed," he said. "You can speak their language, you can dance in their homes, but you will never be one of them."

I had no comeback because he was right. As much as I yearned to belong to the world outside our gates, it was too dangerous, for them and for me. People would notice if I spent too much time with any particular family, and neighbors would talk. Gossip reaching the ears of close-minded men could mean trouble, and I couldn't do that to the kindly people I'd met. It left me in the lonely position of outsider, never allowed any true friends.

Benson gave me a reluctant smile, probably debating whether he was done being angry. "Are you hungry?"

I expelled a breath and nodded. If he was thinking about food, we were good again.

"Then let's go downstairs, and see what Nadira has to eat. Did you really take down three of them?" He hooked an arm around my shoulders, and by the time we'd reached the kitchen, his face was suffused with pride as I regaled him with all the gory details.

The girl's name was Farida, and she was an orphan. Her school had been firebombed last year and though her uncle had forbidden it, she'd been attending classes held in secret in a teahouse basement.

"The uncle has agreed to claim he married her off to some distant cousin," my father said a few days later over lunch in the embassy's communal dining room. No one would question it, I thought with a shiver, because child marriages were not uncommon in this part of the world.

"The rainy day fund sure took a hit, though," Benson grumbled. "That bugger of an uncle bargained like the girl was the bloody Queen of Sheba."

"What happens to her now?" I dug into the vegetable korma before me, one of my favorite dishes. Our chef Nadira had been going out of her way to serve foods I loved ever since the incident in the marketplace. At least someone was happy with me.

"A relief organization out of London picked her up about an hour ago. They'll get her to England and place her with a sympathetic Pakistani family." Benson picked up his iced tea and held it up for a toast. "To new beginnings."

We all clinked our glasses and echoed the sentiment.

"Mr. Ambassador?" Mrs. Parks, my dad's middle-aged executive secretary, approached. "There's a State Department envoy here to see you. I put her in your office." Her eyes cut in my direction. "She said it's about Riley."

Dad and Benson immediately locked gazes. This could only mean trouble.

"Thanks, Carol," my dad said. "We'll be right there."

As the clicks of the secretary's sensible heels retreated, I squirmed under the stares of the two men. "I didn't do anything, I swear. I mean," I said, backtracking, "nothing you don't already know about."

I sat through the rest of lunch with the air of the condemned, barely tasting the food. Whatever punishment there was to be handed down for my lapse in judgment had arrived. Disgraced diplomats were usually transferred to the most miserable outposts, but how much worse could it get than a country on the verge of tearing itself apart? Though I personally loved Pakistan, it sure as hell wasn't Paris.

Benson led the way to the executive wing and surprisingly, into the ambassador's offices. He didn't usually sit in on my dad's meetings, but then I normally was not the topic of discussion.

The woman taking tea at the small conference table stood at our approach. About the same age as my father, her round face had the serious look of a woman too busy to bother with makeup. She must have come directly from the airport because no sane person would wear the navy wool suit she had on in this heat.

She thrust out her hand to my dad, gripping his in an efficient greeting. "Mr. Ambassador, I'm Natalie Abramowitz with the Washington bureau. I apologize for turning up uninvited."

"Natalie, please call me Joe." Eliminating titles was a negotiating tactic meant to bring both sides together quickly, and my dad did it unconsciously.

"And you must be Riley," she said, sizing me up in much the same way Nadira did when buying a leg of lamb from the butcher.

"And I'm Special Agent Benson." He stepped protectively between Natalie and me, having also picked up our visitor's unusual scrutiny.

My dad gestured for everyone to be seated. "It must be something important to bring you all this way," he said.

"Yes." She hesitated. "Perhaps you'd like to have this discussion in private?"

He waved away her concern. "These two will know everything we discuss before you've even checked into your hotel. We might as well save everyone time and trouble."

"I see," she said. "Your daughter's file landed on my boss's desk and I must say, it's quite impressive." She turned to me, resting her folded arms on the table. "I was also interested to learn you've been part of the political life at all the embassies your father has been posted to."

I'd been a baby when my mother was killed fighting for her purse in a Beirut alley. When I got to the age when most other diplomat's kids were shipped off to boarding school, Dad made token noises about sending me, but his heart wasn't in it. He'd fought in combat, stared down rebels, and done a ton of other scary things I'd never know about, but he said losing me was more than he could handle.

"She's been a great asset, which is one of the many reasons I've kept her with me," my dad said, feeling out the situation. "She's fluent in Arabic and is often included in conversations among the wives at embassy parties. They tend to reveal things their husbands never would."

"Don't forget to mention she's a crack shot, and she took down Martinez last week in hand-to-hand," Benson cheerfully volunteered, only to be met with my dad's withering stare. "Well, she did," he added, not letting Dad have the last word.

"I see," Natalie murmured with quiet amusement.

I risked a peek at my dad. This woman was way too friendly for someone planning to transfer us to Timbuktu, but something was definitely going down here.

"Riley," she said, "do you know who Stephen Frasier is?"

Probably the better question was: who didn't?

My dad answered for me. "What does a tech billionaire have to do with my daughter?"

"Stephen Frasier is developing software with the potential to revolutionize intelligence gathering," she said. In other words, more efficient ways to spy on each other. "He has agreed to sell it to the U.S. and our allies, and no one else."

"I'm not sure I understand why you're telling us this, ma'am," I said.

"Stephen Frasier has a daughter, Hayden, who's the same age as you." She reached for the pretty china teapot Mrs. Parks always set out for guests. "She's a student at The Harrington Academy."

Whoa, even I'd heard of that school. It was a swaggy place somewhere in Connecticut catering to children of the rich and fabulous. We'd spent Christmas in Washington a few years back where I'd met some senator's kid at a holiday party. He thought he was all that and bragged about going to Harrington.

A shadow of concern passed over Natalie's features as she sipped her tea. "The girl's safety has been called into question. They've recently implemented new security protocols at Harrington, but if the young lady had someone on the inside, who could perhaps accompany her where traditional bodyguards could not, it would add an extra layer of security."

"Let me guess," Dad said in a tight voice. "Our government must guarantee his family's safety from less-ethical competitors, or the deal's off."

She leaned back in her chair and shrugged; she was just the messenger, after all. "In a nutshell, yes."

The subtle shift in my dad's pose signaled it was time to get down to business. "I assume you're telling us this because your superiors are interested in Riley?"

Natalie set down her cup, recognizing her opening. "Your report regarding her encounter with the three militants in the marketplace was factual and correct?"

He gave her a sharp nod.

"Then yes, we would like to offer her a place at Harrington."

BENSON'S RULE #3

DO WHAT IS RIGHT, NOT WHAT IS EASY

You can't send me away!" I frantically paced the carpet. Natalie had tactfully withdrawn, leaving the three of us alone to hash over her offer.

"I know it's earlier than we planned, but you'll be leaving for college next year anyway," my dad pointed out, still seated at the table with Benson. "There are people who would kill to get into that school."

I halted in my tracks. "My tutors say my grades are good enough to get me into a really good college... *next year.*"

"Grades aren't always enough," he said. "Right now, the only extra-curriculars you can list on a college application are street fighting and instigating international incidents. Don't you think you could use the clout being a Harrington graduate will give you?"

"But look what I'd have to do for it! Those people aren't like us. The minute I don't know which fork to use, they'll skin me alive!" I flailed about for excuses, and from the looks on their faces, they both knew it.

"I think you would really benefit from a year spent with your peers," Dad said, overriding my protests.

He looked at Benson, and though no words were exchanged, they did that thing where they packed an entire conversation into a single glance. Sometimes it made me want to scream.

Benson picked up his cue. "What your dad is trying to say is maybe what we've been teaching you isn't the most useful of skills for a teenage girl. You need to spend time with girls your own age who are interested in… whatever they're interested in." He loved and respected women, but made no secret of the fact he considered us a separate species.

Being raised in hostile foreign lands by a diplomat and his commando sidekick wasn't exactly normal, but I was turning out okay. Thanks to years of tagging around after Benson I might know more than the average girl about combat sports like jiu-jitsu and kickboxing, or be able to assemble an AR-15 assault rifle blindfolded, but there was nothing wrong with that. And I chose my clothes more for modesty and freedom of movement than to adhere to the latest trends because you never knew when you'd have to fight your way out of a popular uprising or a military coup. I'd like to see Hayden Frasier do that while tottering around in stilettos or lugging a purse the size of carry-on luggage.

"The timing couldn't be better," my dad said, warming to the idea. "The school year is just about to start, and you'd be going in as a senior. Sounds pretty good to me."

"Then you go to Harrington," I huffed. "I'm staying here." Pakistan was my home, and these two men were my family. I wanted the extra year I'd been promised.

Once again they did the silent mind meld thing, and some sort of decision must have been reached because Benson nodded.

"There's something else you should know," Benson said, facing me squarely. "The cost of your fight in the marketplace has just been named. One of our friendlies tells us you're now on a list of approved targets."

I propped a supporting hand on the back of his chair to keep my knees from buckling. "I've been marked for death?"

"It's not as dramatic as all that," he said matter-of-factly. "It's not like they'll be popping up in the loo. But you can be sure there's some bloody Terry out there hoping to make his bones by slitting your throat."

I'd lost count of how many times I'd attended receptions just like the one we were hosting for a local artist, but this night held a measure of desperation as I clung tightly to every detail. The insistent thrum of guitars, the high-pitched laughter of people determined to forget their troubles, and the hearty clink of crystal as if a toast to happiness guaranteed a bright future. The country was changing, and once I stepped into my new life in America, I would be changed, too.

I retreated to a corner facing a colorful painting of three Arab women in traditional dress, barely noticing how the artist daringly made his subjects look like runway models. I'd spent the last three days coming to grips with how quickly my fate had been sealed, and how fast the time had slipped away until there were mere hours to go before it would be time to say goodbye.

Benson, in a black suit and tie that made him look like the world's largest undertaker, appeared at my elbow. "I don't know much about art, but even I know that would look better painted on velvet." When I didn't needle him back about his taste being all in his mouth, he said, "Cheer up, darlin' girl, or you'll have me weepin' in my beer."

He might weep, but there were no tears left in me. If I cried one more time, I would shrivel up and blow away.

"I'm afraid," I admitted for the first time, even to myself.

"What?" he roared. "Of a princess with an unlimited credit card?"

"No," I said, though that wasn't completely true.

As the daughter of an American diplomat, my life in Karachi had value and meaning, but who would I be in Connecticut, a place as foreign to me as the moon? I would be abandoning voiceless girls like Farida, and for what? To obsess over whether I had the same jeans as the latest celebrity? Here I worked at bridging the gap of two unlikely allies, even if it was simply having a casual conversation with a local student over a cup of tea. There I would be forced to bow to the culture of conformity because fighting it would bring more loneliness and isolation.

"I'm afraid," I said at last, "of forgetting who I am."

"Who you are," he said, after contemplating the painting in front of us for several more moments, "is someone who will always choose to do what is right rather than what is easy. I should know. There wasn't a gray hair on my head before I met you." He grinned, rubbing his hand over his prickly scalp for emphasis.

I sighed. "But am I ready?"

Benson put his arm around me, and I rested my head on his shoulder.

"How many recruits do you reckon I've trained as your dad's security chief? Two hundred? Three hundred? And I'll tell you what: no matter what I do, no matter how well prepared they are to go into the field, when the bullets start flying they either duck and run for cover, or they stand and fight. There's nothing I can do to change who they are."

I squinted up at him in confusion. "And...?"

"And nothing," he said. "You've already been tested by those men in the marketplace. You know who you are, and nobody is going to change that—least of all some snot-nosed ankle biters barely out of nappies. Are we clear?"

He thought that settled matters, so he led me to the next painting, where he insisted the addition of a few dogs playing poker would be the only thing that could save it from the garbage heap.

"How much am I worth anyway?" I asked. At his raised brow, I added, "The marked for death list. What's the price on my head?"

He cleared his throat and tugged at his tie. "Er, two goats and a chicken."

"That's it?" I was worth at least two camels and a mule.

It appeared my options had been whittled down to one of two choices: go to one of the most elite schools in America, or stay in Karachi where my life could be traded for a large family meal.

My dad eased himself away from a nearby group and joined us. "Up for a game?" he asked me.

There were at least fifty guests still milling about the embassy. "What about the party?"

He smiled. "For once I'm going to pull rank and do what I want to do. Right now, I'd like to play chess with my daughter."

Benson squeezed my hand in farewell. He knew I couldn't say no to a match with my dad.

"Don't worry about a thing," he said to my dad. "I'll toss these freeloading blighters out soon enough."

"*Guests*, Benson, they are our guests," my dad said with an exasperated sigh.

"To-may-to, to-mah-to," Benson mumbled as he strolled away.

A few minutes later, Dad and I met in the family room of our private quarters, both of us having changed into T-shirts and shorts. The alabaster chess set had been my mom's wedding gift to her new husband, and sat ever ready on a small, round table with two leather armchairs stationed nearby.

He'd been a minor chess champ back in the day and still played a wicked game. We'd been playing together since I was old enough to understand the rules, but I didn't win my first match until I was twelve. After that, my record of wins steadily grew to the point where now we were evenly matched. It wasn't really the competition that drew us back to the board week after week, year after year. Here was where we talked. Sometimes I was pissed at him for being so preoccupied I needed an appointment to get his attention. Other times he was annoyed because I happened to bend a few unimportant embassy rules. Occasionally we were happily in sync, and he would tell stories about my mother that kept me hanging on his every word, trying to imagine the black and white photo on his desk coming to life.

In one of Benson's more brilliant moments, he dubbed it chess therapy. And we were both painfully aware tonight was our final session.

"Natalie Abramowitz called me today," my dad said, opening the game and the conversation. He was playing white tonight.

After we'd accepted her offer, Natalie hadn't even bothered to spend the night before hopping the next plane back to Washington. I countered the move and waited for him to continue.

"I'm afraid it's gotten a bit more complicated than we expected," he said, putting a second pawn into play.

"Doesn't it always," I muttered, sending one of my own pawns into battle.

He pretended not to hear me. "Hayden Frasier has a history of slipping away from her bodyguards." He tapped a finger on one of his knights, deliberating. "Natalie said it would be best if Hayden didn't know why you were there." He committed to his charger and sent it into the field.

"Won't she wonder why I'm following her around?" The word "stalker" came to mind, but Dad hated sarcasm. It came from years of having to watch every word and nuance so a sarcastic retort didn't result in World War III.

"Not if you two are friends." He frowned as I marched a rook toward his front lines.

"Yeah, 'cause we have *so* much in common," I said, unable to resist.

He looked up from the board. "Why do you think I reach out to all the local players when we arrive at a new posting? Think about it."

I scowled, and decided he deserved an all-out attack. I unleashed my bishop. "You make it sound so easy."

"Easy?" He let out a laugh. "No. But it's time to decide what kind of life you want. Do you want it to be big and exciting and worthwhile? Here's your chance."

"And you think Harrington's going to do that for me?" I took down one of his pawns.

"No, you're going to do that for you. You're my smart, strong-willed daughter who understands that sometimes the best opportunities are the ones you never see coming." He moved his bishop into an offensive position.

We played in silence for a while as I pondered his words. Finally I asked, "You don't really think Hayden Frasier is in any danger, do you?"

His hand hovered over the board as he considered my question. "I wouldn't let you go if I thought you'd come to harm." He set his queen down in front of my king. "Check."

"You didn't exactly answer my question," I pointed out, slipping out of the trap.

"I'm an ambassador. I don't have to directly answer any questions," he smiled, feigning a superior air.

I almost fumbled the rook in my hand. "Dad, are you being sarcastic?"

"Don't get used to it," he joked, neglecting to protect his king's flank.

"Fine," I said. "Checkmate."

BENSON'S RULE #4

PREPARATION IS EVERYTHING

The scent of rotting garbage and jet fuel clung to the stagnant air. Benson fussed like I was a shiny five-year-old heading off for her first day of kindergarten, while my dad retreated behind a stoic façade.

"Now if there's anything you need," Benson said, straightening my collar for the third time, "call me, day or night. That includes dumping the bodies of any randy blokes who even think of laying a paw on you."

I gave him a watery smile. "Yes, Mom."

Dad grabbed me into a hug that would have gone on forever if my military escort hadn't impatiently cleared his throat. The transport to Germany would leave with or without me, so with a final nervous glance at the two men who were my unlikely parents, I dashed across the hot tarmac to a C-27 Spartan revving its engines.

Twenty-two hours later we touched down at Wheeler-Sack Army Airfield in upstate New York. I'd caught a ride with a 10th Mountain Division platoon at the end of their tour, playing chess with a handful of guys all the way across the Atlantic. We'd played for pocket change, and I happily swept the winning pot into my purse as we taxied to a stop.

"Are you sure you're only seventeen?" The good-natured staff sergeant with a Tennessee twang had lost five bucks to me.

With a lot of fist bumping and calls of good luck, the soldiers filed off the transport and into the arms of excited families waiting with new babies and homemade signs of welcome. Shouldering my travel-weary duffle bag, I trudged down the ramp and into my future.

It took only a moment to find my ride; she was impossible to miss. The woman impatiently waiting next to a black town car looked like she could wrestle alligators and win. Standing almost six feet tall, she was a solid mass of muscle with a square jaw, copper skin, and tight black curls sculpted into a helmet rising a good four inches above her scalp. Her dark eyes swept over me, and by her sour expression, it was apparent she'd pulled the short straw for this assignment. Now I knew how new recruits must feel when meeting Benson for the first time.

"Riley Collins?" she asked in the no-nonsense tones of a native New Yorker. "I'm Karen Jones with the State Department. I've been assigned to check you into Harrington tomorrow, and by the look of things"—she pursed her wide lips at my travel-stained clothing while I shivered in the cold breeze—"I've got my work cut out for me."

She launched right into my briefing. By the time we reached the city, my head swam with images of Harrington's blueprints, employee lists and backgrounds, and even the names of the VIPs who sent their kids to the school.

"I doubt you're going to need any of this, but you never know," Karen said, pulling out a file marked HARRINGTON–FOOD VENDORS. Did they think Hayden was going to be poisoned by a lunch lady in a hairnet?

We'd come straight to Beau's, a Mecca of beauty in the heart of Manhattan. The dull roar of blow dryers, ringing phones, and people shouting over the din greeted us as we entered a cavernous room of sparkling white and gleaming silver.

Karen delivered me into the hands of Diego, the first guy I'd ever seen in real life wearing eyeliner. His assistant, a sullen girl around my age who was dressed for a funeral, handed me a white cotton robe and ordered me to strip.

My hair was then smothered in fragrant oils and wrapped in plastic, my skin steamed until I was ready to be served with drawn butter, and they had performed an "extraction." In my world, that meant a black ops team going into dangerous territory to recover a lost man. Here it involved squeezing every pore on my face until I would have willingly confessed to anything.

"Hold on, princess, this may sting a bit." White bits of cloth were ripped from my eyebrows along with about six layers of skin. Tears sprang to my eyes as he tilted my chin to get a better view of his work. "Gorgeous," he breezily pronounced in a Spanish accent. Reaching for a glass jar with contents the color of pistachio ice cream, he said, "This is an exfoliating mask, which you simply must have or die."

I supposed painfully losing another layer of skin cells was preferable to death, but not by much.

Karen sauntered back in as I admired my first ever mani-pedi. Yet another assistant gently dried my newly lustrous ebony curls. My hair hadn't been cut in ages, but despite the healthy trim, it still cascaded halfway down my back.

She inspected me critically before turning to Diego. "Make sure she has all the right makeup and products a Harrington girl would have, will you? I don't want to get sloppy with the details."

Someone thrust a fussy sandwich of tomatoes, mozzarella, and basil into my hand during a session with the makeup artist. Running on nothing but nerves and jet lag, I bolted it down while learning how to paint on a smoky eye.

Our next stop was Barney's on Madison Avenue, where a small army of clones awaited. Petite, perfect, and all dressed in black, the sales clerks marched me to a spacious, mirror-lined dressing room where a rack of fabulous clothes awaited. Tags with names I'd only gawked at in fashion magazines—Prada, YSL, Chanel—dangled from wool crepe skirts, cashmere jackets, and silk tops. In the corner towered a mountain of shoeboxes from Manolo Blahnik, Gucci, and Jimmy Choo, along with stacks of flannel-wrapped handbags from designers like Céline and Chloé.

"Holy cow," I said, forgetting I'd barely slept in the past twenty-four hours. This was a reality TV dream come true... until I glanced at a price tag and gasped. "This would feed a family of four in Karachi for a year!"

"Welcome to New York," Karen said in a weary tone, trying to make herself comfortable on an unyielding white sofa. "What a ridiculous piece of furniture," she muttered, accepting a bottle of designer water from one of the smiling young women.

She pulled out an electronic tablet and became immediately engrossed while one of the attendants slipped the first piece off the rack and held it out expectantly. Buying a wardrobe appeared to be a group activity. Self-consciously, I stripped down to my plain white cotton bra and underwear.

"One of every bra and panty you've got in La Perla," Karen ordered, barely flicking her eyes up from her pad.

"Who's paying for all this?" I whispered when the sales clerk glided off, presumably to relay Karen's order.

"If I drop you off in that Land's End special you were wearing, those Harrington kids will think you're one of the gardeners," she said.

I gritted my teeth but said no more, standing half-naked in front of strangers as dressers zipped and buttoned, laced and fastened. Karen signaled her approval over each purchase with a queenly nod.

"Get the navy Louboutins to go with those jeans," she barked. "Have you ever discharged a firearm at a human target?" Her finger hovered over the pad in expectation of my answer.

"Um, no," I said, whiplashed. "I did get shot at, though, when a militant made it over the embassy walls. At first I thought the thing that buzzed by my ear was one of those nasty sausage flies, but it turned out to be a bullet. Usually assassins bypass the living quarters and go right for the main offices, but this guy didn't get the memo." The girl returning with the requested shoes listened in horrified fascination.

"We'll take it from here," Karen said to the clerk, who thrust the heels into my arms before quickly making her escape.

I regarded Karen anxiously. "That story was on CNN. It's not like it's classified or anything, is it?"

She acted as if I hadn't spoken. "Have you been informed of your mission?"

My job was to babysit a rich girl, sure, but mostly, as my dad kept saying, I was going to a top school and finally getting to make friends with people who didn't carry AK-47s. "I'm supposed to hang out with Hayden Frasier. What else do I need to know?"

She stood and checked me out in the full-length mirror, and for a surprising moment her face reflected empathy. "Are you aware of the software Stephen Frasier is developing?"

"We were told something about spyware." I peeled off the jeans and traded them for floral cigarette pants.

"It's been classified as the Rosetta project," she said, stepping closer to zip me up. "It's supposed to be the ultimate encryption-breaking software, able to decipher any written message in any format in less than a minute."

No wonder everyone was so jumpy. Whoever controlled that software would also be able to monitor every electronic communication the world over.

"The delivery date is sometime within the next twelve months," she added.

The pants were awesome, but they were so tight, sitting down might not be an option. I never wore anything I couldn't run in.

"Okay," I said, "so we need to keep his daughter safe for the next year. I get it."

"Intel says there currently isn't any heat on the Frasier girl, but if other interested parties can't get her father to open up the bidding, it'll just be a matter of time." She picked up a taffeta crop top. "Try this."

I eyed her suspiciously, wondering why she was suddenly being so nice. "But I'm just the babysitter, right?" I slipped the shirt over my head.

"We've brought in a new security chief who has installed her own team at the school, so you're in good hands." She came up behind me and wrapped a Chanel belt around my waist. It totally rocked the outfit, though the girl in the mirror was a stranger to me.

I slipped on a white leather trench coat so buttery-soft you could sleep in it. "What are you not telling me?"

She met my eyes in the mirror. "I won't lie to you. Every precaution is being taken to protect Stephen Frasier and his family. But keeping this technology exclusive to the United States and its allies is more important than my life... or yours." Her gaze swept my figure. "Love the coat."

A knock on the door announced the arrival of a smiling woman carrying a neatly folded stack of pastel silks and boldly printed cotton, which turned out to be sleepwear. Karen directed her to the growing pile of approved purchases while I waded back into the pool of clothes and tried not to worry about what had just been said.

Finally, after an appalling amount of taxpayer's money had been shelled out, they let me out of the dressing room. Leaving behind instructions on where to send everything, Karen checked me into an elegant hotel facing Central Park. She left me alone with instructions to order dinner from room service before I keeled over from exhaustion.

Freshly showered and wrapped in a fluffy white robe, I parted the curtains on the picture windows. Evening had fallen, but the scene below pulsed with activity. Horse-drawn carriages jockeyed for position as hybrid taxis honked in annoyance. Antique streetlights of vintage milk glass illuminated the hotel doorman in his time-honored cap and overcoat as he spewed out rapid-fire directions to Arabic tourists in flowing white robes.

It was an uneasy jumble of old and new, of tradition and trend. I'd left behind a world steeped in rituals and customs dating back thousands of years, where change could be measured in centuries rather than heartbeats. Ahead was a social media wasteland where materialism and popularity was the coin of the realm. Add in the vague warning that trouble could arrive as unexpectedly and as deadly as a sand storm, and I was as unprepared as Dorothy when she was unceremoniously dropped into Oz.

Ten hours and roughly seven thousand miles separated New York from Karachi, but I suddenly longed to bridge the gap. I booted up my computer and put in a Skype call. It might wake my dad, but I needed the assurance only his familiar voice could offer.

He sounded alert, though that was no surprise; he could be jolted from sleep and be battle ready in about five seconds. His image appeared at the same time his bedside lamp switched on, looking about the way you'd expect if you'd been woken at four in the morning.

"Sorry to wake you, Dad."

"No, I was awake, trying to decide if I should toss and turn another dozen times, or just give in and call you." His hair stuck out in every direction, a testament to his sleepless night. "How's New York?"

"Different, but the same." I remembered the feeling of wide-eyed wonder on my previous visit. The city still had the power to captivate, but I saw it now through a grittier lens.

"You belong there. You just need to give it time."

I cracked a rueful smile. "Do I look that pathetic?"

He laughed. "No, you look beautiful. I like your hair." He grew wistful. "You look like your mother." He didn't say it often, but I knew there were times he saw her face when he looked at me.

I twisted the belt on my robe. "What was it like on your first mission?" I still hadn't come to grips with the term, but there was no getting around the fact I had a job to do.

"Same as you," he said, propping up a pillow and settling in. "I was young, green, scared, and made a ton of mistakes, but deep down I could survive whatever they threw at me."

"What if I'm not like you? What if I'm not ready?" It had been way too long since I'd had any real sleep, and my emotions simmered just below the surface. I couldn't prevent the tears from spilling down my cheeks.

"Hey, hey," he soothed, touching his fingertips to the screen. "Do you think I would've agreed to this if I didn't think you could pull it off?"

"But what if I hate it?" My second biggest fear. I'd rather crawl through fifty miles of scorpion-infested desert than be the loser no one wanted to eat lunch with.

His smile was bittersweet. "Every time we moved you acted like it was the end of the world. Remember how much you fought me over Karachi? Give it time. Maybe we'll find out this is where you belong."

My mouth went dry. "That's just it, Dad. What if I love it?"

Because that's what frightened me most.

BENSON'S RULE #5

SHOW NO FEAR

Abusiness-like rap on the door the next morning woke me from a fitful sleep. I staggered out of bed to admit my chaperone.

"Here." Karen thrust a garment bag and a gorgeous Louis Vuitton tote into my hands. "Hit the shower. Breakfast will be here in thirty, and we leave at ten-hundred."

"Good morning to you, too," I groused, stumbling to the bathroom. My body might be living in New York, but my internal clock insisted it was still in Karachi. Add in the fragments of stress dreams assaulting me throughout the night, and I was like the walking dead. One squint into the bathroom mirror confirmed I looked like it, too.

The coffee from my breakfast tray kicked in about the same time I tried using a bit of makeup to stave off further zombie comparisons. The shade was pretty good, but the clothes were another story. For years my wardrobe had been chosen to hide my femininity with the pleasant side effect that everything was worn loose, so I didn't die from being cooked alive.

The clothes Karen dropped off were like a stage costume. The flirty wool crepe skirt made my thighs itch, the cropped sweater outlined boobs never before seen, and the high-heeled boots were like walking on stilts. If this was what the natives wore, this was a society in decline.

I teetered downstairs to find Sutton, the black-suited driver, wrestling my duffle and the fancy new tote into a trunk already jam-packed with several expensive pieces of matching luggage. Karen looked up from the sheaf of papers in her hands.

"Stop looking like you sucked a grapefruit for breakfast," she commanded.

I glared at her flowing tunic and relaxed trousers before gesturing to my outfit. "Wanna trade?"

"Hell, no," she retorted. "Now get your skinny ass into the car. Your new life begins in two hours." She wasted no time. "It's time for a final rundown of the players."

My father had weeks to get familiarized with the key political figures of a region before a transfer went through. A boarding school didn't hold the same potential for an international incident—hopefully—but the blinding speed of my recruitment and deployment had the air of last minute planning.

The car lurched into traffic, practically throwing me to the floor. Climbing back on my seat, I reached for a seatbelt.

"The Head of School, Mrs. Gretchen McKenna, is a real piece of work." Karen flashed me a color photo of a starched woman in her early sixties, her silver hair cut short in a style framing her angular face. "It took a mandate from Harrington's board of directors to get her to allow the upgrade to her school's security team. We didn't dare tell her you worked for us. Getting you in was a minor miracle."

Surely McKenna had seen my excellent transcripts, which hopefully noted my fluency in Arabic and French, as well as my ability to curse in six different tribal dialects.

"Don't take it personally," Karen said, catching my scowl. "When they say this place is exclusive, they mean it. Besides, McKenna doesn't think security is a problem because no one would dare enter her hallowed halls without an engraved invitation."

Benson had shown me a patient and creative approach could breach even the most sophisticated of defenses. Each time we landed at a new posting, he always delighted in poking holes in the security protocols. I wondered if he realized it was his training that allowed me to discover ways to sneak out of each embassy without ever getting busted. After all, those places were built to keep people out, not in.

We skidded to a stop, and Sutton leaned on the horn. If he ever got tired of driving limos in New York, he'd fit right in as a cabbie in Cairo.

Karen reached into her handbag and came up with a white envelope, plain except for my name typed across it. "Here, this is your get-out-of-jail-free card."

I ripped it open and found an ID card bearing my name and picture. It also said I worked for the State Department. "How did you pull this off?" I couldn't imagine too many people my age running around with one of these.

She shrugged as if it were none of her concern. "Your father made it part of the deal. Now raise your right hand and repeat after me."

Something told me I'd regret this, but I obeyed.

"I, Riley Collins," she prompted, which I dutifully repeated, "do solemnly swear that I will support and defend the Constitution of the United States against all enemies, foreign and domestic; that I will bear true faith and allegiance to the same; that I take this obligation freely, without any mental reservation or purpose of evasion; and I will well and faithfully discharge my duties. So help me God."

My final words hung in the air. I recognized the oath as a version my father and his entire staff took when they entered service, but the gravity of it suddenly struck me.

Next came a transparent zippered pouch, the kind you kept pencils in, but its contents were a whole lot more interesting.

"There's five thousand dollars in there, and a platinum American Express card." She dropped it in my lap.

"Holy shit," I murmured.

"Yeah, I know. I could pay my rent for almost two months with that kind of cash," she said. "It's for show so spend it only when someone is looking. Don't let me find any charges for pizza delivery or Hulu, and save your receipts." She did everything but wag a finger in my face.

As the car swerved in and out of Manhattan traffic, she filled me in on my cover story. "Your father and Stephen Frasier are old friends. Frasier did some work for the defense department years ago, so it's plausible. That should help break the ice with Hayden. Here's her file."

I was skeptical as she passed me a thick manila folder. Opening the cover, I quickly thumbed past the photos I'd already seen online. Photographers stalked Hayden Frasier like prey, in part because she was a blonde-haired, blue-eyed clone of her famous actress mom, Tory Palmer. Like her mother, Hayden had perfected that faintly bored, untouchable look mere mortals could never hope to achieve. She was famous for stepping coolly out of a limo with the season's must-have handbag on her arm and strolling the streets of New York as if she'd come straight from the pages of Vogue. Compared to her, with my Irish-Italian heritage, I was the guttersnipe Eponine to her angelic Cosette.

It was in the middle of the file where things got interesting. About a dozen tabloid pages were clipped together, all stamped UNAUTHORIZED. One shot captured Hayden dancing, arms thrown out in abandon; another showed her gazing off with the unfocused look of a girl who'd had one too many. A quick skim of the other photos revealed similarly private moments showing the heiress more human and more alive than anything snapped by the paparazzi.

"What are these?" I asked.

"A problem. Those were all taken at school functions with no sanctioned photographers. Someone is selling unauthorized photos of her to the tabloids."

I didn't see what the big deal was. Seeing her like that made me like her better.

Noticing my bemusement, she explained, "Whoever is following Hayden Frasier around with a camera could also be selling pictures of the campus grounds, the security systems, the schedule of the guards' shift changes... are you getting it now? We need to find out who's playing paparazzi." She left no doubt when she said *we,* she meant *me.*

Handing over a school schedule with Hayden's name at the top, she said, "This should help you keep track of her."

The car picked up speed on the Parkway, leaving Manhattan behind. I glanced out the window as the city faded from view, wishing there'd been time to visit the Empire State Building or take in a Broadway show. There was zero nightlife in Karachi. The city's only entertainment at night was eating, giving it the totally disgusting nickname of the "city that eats itself to sleep".

Karen pulled out another glossy photo from her stack of papers, and I reminded myself to pay attention. "You won't be alone at Harrington. This is Major Grace Taylor. She's the school's new head of security. She alone knows you're coming, so you should meet up with her ASAP."

The picture showed a dark-haired woman in an army uniform posed stiffly in front of the American flag. Her steely-eyed gaze made her look as if she could reach through the lens of the camera and beat you to a pulp. The career military women I'd met attained their rank by being twice as sharp as the men around them. I had no doubt Major Taylor fell into that category.

All signs of city life disappeared, and we traveled down two-lane country roads. I had never seen so many trees. Before long the car made a sharp right turn and braked. In front of us was an imposing entrance of ivy-covered walls, faded brick, and boatloads of wrought iron. Karen expelled a shaky breath as if she was the one facing down her worst fears. "This is it."

We'd reached Harrington Academy way too fast. My fingernails left divots in the soft leather seat as a uniformed guard scanned an electronic tablet for my name while a German Shepherd sniffed around the outside of the car. It was like entering a foreign embassy.

Massive gates swung open, and another guard waved us through. I twisted in my seat to watch the portal slam shut on everything I'd ever known. Reluctantly facing forward, I was immediately struck by the impression we were driving into a postcard, the kind you'd send to the friend who was always trying to outdo you.

The sprawling campus ahead appeared warm and inviting. Lining the road were leafy trees decked out in the earthy colors of Benetton's fall catalogue. On one side, a gently flowing river peeked through the foliage, and as if on cue a uniformed rowing team streaked past. On the other, an endless white picket fence fronted a distant barn as sleek horses lazily nibbled at the emerald grass.

So why was my heart racing? Why could I not accept my fate and try to make the best of it? Maybe because it was all so radically different from everything I'd ever known. And maybe it was because just like Pakistan and Yemen and Cairo, I would once again be an outsider, never allowed to reveal my true self to anyone. The trendy outfit I wore here was as foreign to me as the hijab back home.

My growing panic verged on full-scale hyperventilation. Karen must have noticed the sheen of cold sweat on my face because she none-too-gently grabbed the back of my head and shoved my face between my knees.

"Breathe," she ordered.

"I don't think I can do this." My words fell flat on the plush carpeting between my feet.

"You can, and you will. You're going to put one foot in front of the other, and you're going to get through this. You are now a sworn agent of the United States of America. Don't you forget that." She pinched the back of my neck for emphasis. No sympathy there.

When at last I hauled myself upright, we were nearing the main campus where stately buildings all shared a common bond of red brick, white trim, and weathered roofs of slate gray. Built more or less in a massive oval, the structures all fronted a welcoming, park-like space with graceful trees, a duck pond, and graveled walking paths.

The fall term started the following day. According to Harrington's website, almost a thousand students attended the coed high school and of those, only a small number went home after class. The rest lived on campus during the school year.

Clusters of people darted about. Many carried boxes and backpacks with parents trailing behind. Others had already settled in and played a game of pickup soccer or lounged about the grounds.

We came to a stop in front of Harrington Hall, a particularly imposing building featuring quite a number of chimneys jutting into the midday sky, dating its origins to a time before central heating. Built in a T shape, white Georgian columns supported a graceful portico and sheltered the massive entryway. Casement windows shot up three stories and rambled endlessly in either direction, while French doors on the ground floor had been thrown open to admit the light breeze. It had probably been the showplace home of some Connecticut statesman when both it and the country were young.

Karen looked faintly ill herself as she stared at the great hall. Turning away, she reached into her bag and pulled out a sleek smartphone, an advanced model not on the market. I forgot for a moment to be freaked out. Mine was two years old with a cracked screen, and I coveted the device in her hands like Benson craved the next *James Bond* movie. I had to stop myself from reaching over to touch it.

Then a miracle happened. "This is for you."

"Shut the front door! Are you serious?" All thoughts of death by social anxiety disappeared as I powered it up. I couldn't wait to see what games had been preloaded, and check out the latest sites, and...

"Riley." She laid a hand across the phone. "This is important. My number is in there under Aunt Karen."

She returned my faint smirk with one of her own. I'd always wished for more family, but a less warm and fuzzy aunt I couldn't imagine.

"It's also loaded with photos, texts, and all the other stuff you'd be expected to have. You need to look like you had a life before you got here."

"I did have a life before I got here," I said.

She let out a humorless chuckle. "Not like these kids have."

Unable to resist, I checked out the photo roll and found pictures of me Photoshopped with beautiful people I'd never seen in photogenic places I'd never been. A quick check of my texting history showed fabricated conversations with girls named Naomi and Becca. I was now Riley Collins, Rich American Teenager.

"Well," Karen said, nodding once in farewell, "good luck."

"Wait, what? You're just leaving me here?" I didn't expect her to hold my hand, but surely she wouldn't just dump me on the curb.

"Your mission begins now. Go to McKenna's office and pick up your schedule. Sutton will deliver your luggage to the dorm. Just remember who you are and what your objective is, and you'll be fine." She sounded as if she was trying to convince herself as well as me.

It was like she couldn't get away from me fast enough. Or was it something else? After a few moments when neither of us had budged, I asked, "Why were you the one who got stuck with me?" I knew how things worked. Chauffeuring some kid to school wasn't exactly a career-maker for anyone.

She stared out the window for so long, I thought she didn't intend to answer. Abruptly she reached into her purse, coming up with a gold ring emblazoned with the Harrington Academy crest. She handed it to me.

"I don't understand," I said, turning it over to catch the light.

"It's mine. I earned it," she said, as if challenging me to disagree. "It was four of the most hellish years of my life, but it's part of me now, and no one can take that away."

I stared at her for a moment. "You graduated from Harrington?" Why was she just now telling me? There were a hundred questions I would have asked her.

"That's why I drew this assignment. They wanted me to tell you this place is all kittens and rainbows," she huffed, shaking her head in disbelief. "But I saw your file, and I know where you're coming from. They may not kill you here, but that doesn't mean they won't try to eat you."

She must have seen my stricken face because she dialed it back a notch. "I don't mean to scare you, but don't trust anyone, especially McKenna. She was head of school when I was here, and she thinks she owns the place. Look, just watch over the Frasier girl, study until your eyeballs fall out, and you'll get by. Understand?"

I thrust the ring at her, almost glad we were parting company. If she was supposed to be my handler, I sure didn't feel handled. "That's it?

You went here for four years, and all you can tell me is if I'm lucky I won't get my soul sucked out?"

She looked as if she already regretted being so forthright, but figured why stop now because she said, "Nothing I've ever done, before or since, has been as hard as getting through Harrington, but that's not the point. What matters is who you are at the end of the day, and if you're proud of the choices you've made. Just don't drink the Kool-Aid, know what I'm sayin'?"

I took a deep breath. With a defiant glare at Karen, I opened the car door and stepped out into the light.

BENSON'S RULE #6

START AS YOU MEAN TO FINISH

I entered the great hall's soaring foyer and looked about in hopes there'd be some sign pointing the way to admissions. Standing like a rock in the middle of a stream, students flowed past me, their excited chatter only slightly muffled by the banners hanging overhead. Made up in the school colors of navy and white, each banner proclaimed one of Harrington's lofty ideals: Honor, Achievement, Character, and so on. I noticed none of them said anything that might be remotely helpful, like Run For Your Life.

I stood there open-mouthed long enough for someone to notice. The guy who stopped had a boy-next-door quality. Not the kind to make you forget how to string a sentence together, but cute enough. His wiry frame and mop of floppy brown hair reinforced the impression of friendliness.

"You must be new here," he said. "Need some help?"

I couldn't help returning his smile. "It's that obvious, huh? Can you tell me which way to Mrs. McKenna's office?"

"It's on the second floor." He gestured toward the wide, hardwood stairs anchoring the center of the great hall. "C'mon, I'll show you. It's easy to get turned around if you don't know where you're going. I'm Von, by the way. Fredric Von Alder the Fifth, but everyone calls me Von."

"I can see why you need a nickname." I grinned. "I'm Riley Collins."

He glanced around, curious. "You're all by yourself?"

"Yep," I said, hoping that wasn't too weird. "My dad lives overseas and couldn't get away." It was a small fib, but I couldn't remember the last time I'd lied. I didn't always tell Dad or Benson everything, but rarely did I ever make stuff up.

He didn't find my solo status unusual. "Are you a junior?"

He matched my slower pace as I concentrated on climbing the stairs in heels without falling on my face.

"No, a senior."

"Really?" That got a reaction. "Harrington doesn't admit seniors."

"Oh, um, I guess they made an exception," I said, mentally cursing Karen. What else had she neglected to tell me?

At the top of the stairs he turned down a wide hallway. Numerous opaque glass doors with names and department titles stenciled across them in gold lined the path leading to Gretchen McKenna's office, centered at the end.

"You can go on in," he volunteered. "Her assistant is usually there."

"Thanks a million," I said, taking a moment to pull it together. I was no stranger to hostility. Whenever I left the embassy with a bunch of uniformed Marines, we were often on the receiving end of suspicious glares, but I never took it personally. They weren't judging me, but rather a symbol.

McKenna's outright disapproval toward me was different. She had presumably seen my transcripts but still found fault. It was harder to shrug off the rejection this time, but hopefully I could just grab my schedule and run. If I was really lucky, maybe I could avoid her until she handed me my diploma next spring.

Von still hovered behind me. "Are you okay? Do you want me to show you around? I can come find you later."

I'd learned early on in my dad's postings each embassy had more than its fair share of backstabbers, connivers, and users. Before you got friendly, it was best to figure out who was trustworthy versus who would sell you to a camel trader if it would advance his career. I had a feeling high school was no different. It would be safer to check the place out on my own.

"I've already taken enough of your time," I said, with some regret. "Thanks, though."

Entering the office was like walking into a command center. Phones rang, a couple of printers hummed industriously as they spewed out pages, and calmly chatting into a phone while furiously typing away was a woman who was an explosion of color. Between her unnaturally red hair, a blazing orange blouse, and turquoise glasses hanging from a string of purple beads, I barely knew where to look first. A brass nameplate on her desk identified her as Ms. Portman.

"May I help you?" she asked sweetly, the phone still cradled against her cheek.

"Um, hi, I'm Riley Collins. I'm here to pick up my schedule?" I hated sounding so unsure.

She intercepted another phone call and clacked out a dozen more rapid-fire words before saying, "Mrs. McKenna is expecting you. You can go on in." She nodded toward the closed door at the other end of the office.

My feet froze to the floor. I glanced around for a camera, wondering how the head of school knew I'd arrived. This wasn't part of the plan. What if there'd been a mistake, and they weren't admitting me after all? Fear, along with a kind of desperate hope, flashed through me.

"Dear, are you going in?" Ms. Portman regarded me curiously.

I gave her a smile that came out as more of a grimace and trudged forward. Should I knock or just walk in? *Start as you mean to finish,* Benson often said. I grasped the doorknob, took a deep breath, and pretended a confidence I didn't feel.

The spindly woman who rose from her desk was a career politician; I'd met her kind before. Armed with a professional smile that welcomed me without a hint of warmth, she wore a well-chosen, sky blue skirt suit that said, "I may be female, but I can still kick your ass."

"Riley, what a pleasure to meet you," Mrs. McKenna said insincerely, extending a boney hand. "I'm sure we're going to get along well."

I immediately went on high alert. When my dad negotiated a deal where he had the upper hand, he always opened with the conclusion. He said it made it easier for his opponents to come to the same realization. This woman wanted something from me, and she expected to get it. She gestured for me to take the small chair facing her desk as she reclaimed her own.

Her office was a fortress of antique cherry wood furnishings, the sort that were super expensive because they'd once belonged to someone like Ben Franklin. On the wall behind her, an old man in scholar's robes scowled down from an oil painting. Beneath it was a credenza displaying several photographs of the administrator posing with the rich and famous-discreetly displayed, of course. It subtly informed visitors she moved in high circles, and you'd best not forget it.

"I was rather surprised to get a call from the chairman of our school board insisting a student, especially a senior, be admitted," she said, her tone deceptively casual as she took in every detail of my appearance. "It was even more surprising to then be informed she must be roommates with Hayden Frasier."

At least that explained how I was supposed to keep an eye on Hayden without being served with a restraining order. She hadn't asked a question, but I still felt compelled to answer. "Yes, ma'am."

"You and Miss Frasier are close friends, I presume?" Her smug smile told me she already knew the answer.

"No, ma'am," I said.

"Really? How curious." Flipping open a file on her desk, she skimmed through it. "Your father is a well-regarded ambassador, though without any remarkable connections or fortune to speak of. Your transcripts are acceptable, but by no means exceptional. You've never experienced a traditional school environment, and your file doesn't contain a single letter of recommendation." She dismissively flicked the cover shut. "There is nothing in here that qualifies you to be a Harrington girl. Surely there is something I've missed?"

She definitely had a talent for stripping it down to the nubs. Sitting back in her chair, she stared me down as she fingered the heavy set of pearls at her throat. "Who are you, Riley Collins?"

I dropped my gaze. Who was I? At home I was a girl who walked the streets of Karachi without fear, who didn't back down when one of Benson's team challenged me to spar, who dined with sheiks, played soccer with street kids, and drank endless cups of tea in the local cafes. Who was I, she wanted to know? I raised my eyes to meet her cold, knowing gaze. If I was going down in flames, it wouldn't be without a fight.

"I'm the girl who learned how to shoot in case we had to fight our way out of Cairo *again*, the one who smuggled school books to a teacher in Yemen who was forbidden to have them, the one who stood at her father's side while he draped American flags over the coffins of Marines who were my friends, and the one who deserves to be here just as much as anyone else. That's who I am."

I didn't know how I expected her to react to my speech, but it wasn't with dead silence. As the seconds ticked by, I began to wonder if anyone had ever died while sitting in this particular chair. I wouldn't put it past the old witch to have placed it over a trapdoor with a caldron of boiling oil underneath. Even now she was probably reaching for the release button under her desk.

Death would be preferable to showing my face in Pakistan again anyway. This time my dad really would be transferred to someplace punishing, like Siberia. I should probably start working on my Russian.

"For twenty-six years this has been *my* school," she said at last, her voice low and threatening. "I decide who is admitted. I decide who has the character and background necessary to prepare them for a future of leading our institutions, our governments, and our world." Her eyes narrowed. "And I decide who is out of her depth, who has no business in my school, and who will be dismissed the moment I learn she is not who she pretends to be. Am I making myself clear?"

My whole body clenched in anger. It was high-handed people like her who thought they had the right to impose their judgments on everyone else. She didn't know me. Maybe a little sand and grit would do the bluebloods here some good. Until that moment, I'd had one foot on either side of a dividing line ready to be swept in whichever direction the prevailing winds took me. No more. I was here at Harrington, and I was here to stay.

I leaned forward in my chair and pinned her with a stare. "Not everything that makes a person valuable can be found in some file. I might be different, I might not have a trust fund or a pedigree like some overbred poodle, but I matter." I flashed briefly on Farida and hoped she was doing better in her new life than I was doing in mine. "So unless you're planning on hauling me out in the square and having me stoned, I'll take my school schedule now."

She glared at me. I did my best to glare back, but she had years more practice, and I started to waver.

"If for one minute you don't live up to the standards we expect of our students, or you make trouble of any kind, school board or not, I *will* send you straight back to the middle of nowhere. Do you understand?"

I felt like repeating her words in Arabic and asking if she understood, but I knew when it was time to shut up and run. I nodded curtly.

She turned to gaze out the window as if she'd already put me from her mind. "Go see Ms. Portman out front."

My ridiculous footwear prevented the graceful exit I would have liked, but at least I didn't fall flat on my face. My knees shook as I stood in front of Ms. Portman again. She barely took her hands off the computer keys as she rolled her swivel chair over to a nearby cabinet and plucked out an envelope.

"There you are, dear," she said, the phone still plastered to one ear.

Staggering out to the hallway, Von kicked off the wall where he'd been leaning, obviously waiting for me the whole time. He peered intently at my face. "Are you okay? You look like you've seen a ghost."

Merely a dragon, I wanted to tell him. I didn't miss the irony that here in my own country I was being treated little better than Farida had been in hers. There were no death threats, of course, but this business about deciding who did and didn't deserve to be educated was frighteningly similiar.

"It's just been a while since I've eaten." My stomach gurgled in agreement.

"There'll be snacks at the dorm. Have you checked out your schedule yet?" He cast a pointed glance at the sealed envelope I'd forgotten was in my hand.

"Um, no," I said, not sure how much to share with my new friend. He decided it for me by casually sliding it though my fingers.

"Wow," he said, as he looked over the first few pages. "Who *are* you?"

"*Excuse me?*" I snatched my schedule back.

"No, I mean, not just anyone rooms with Hayden Frasier," he quickly explained, raising his hands in surrender. "I think they have to be interviewed and go through a background check or something."

Fabulous. I hoped she didn't kill me in my sleep.

I turned toward the stairwell, ready to clomp my way to wherever I might be able to find food and a chance to regroup. Von tagged along.

"Hey, I noticed we're in the same equestrian class, though," he said cheerfully, as if that was supposed to smooth over our rough patch.

"Equestrian?" I stopped and desperately scanned my schedule, praying he'd made a mistake. "I can't take an equestrian class. No way."

He looked pained, realizing he'd said the wrong thing again. "Didn't you know riding is a requirement? Our founder made it part of the school charter."

"Was the founder a freakin' cowboy or something?" My voice rose in panic. "Horses hate me. It's like the horse underworld got together and marked me for death."

His jaw clenched as he tried not to smile. "Don't worry. A lot of kids have never been on horseback when they come here. You'll be fine."

I had serious doubts about that, but I was also hungry, unsettled, and missing home. Maybe I'd reached my quota of misery for the day, and everything would be fine from here on out.

"C'mon," Von said, beckoning me down the stairs. "Let's find you something to eat."

BENSON'S RULE #7

KEEP YOUR HEAD IN THE GAME

That's Watson Hall, the upper girls' dorm." Von pointed out a building across the commons the size of a small hotel, similar in style to the place we'd just left, its many windows sparkling in the autumn sunshine.

"Guys are allowed in the common rooms until ten o'clock," he added, like I should expect to see him hanging out there a lot. "Further down is Hale Hall, which is where I room." He pointed to another large structure not too far away.

We took a gravel pathway cutting through the park. Von kept up a running patter, which I listened to with half an ear. I tuned in when he tugged open the front door of my new home and said, "There are vending machines on the top floor. I recommend the Doritos dinamita mojo criollos." I didn't know what language he spoke but nodded anyway. "Check in with your house mother, and she'll take you from there."

The moment I'd been dreading most, meeting Hayden Frasier, had arrived, but there was no putting it off any longer. "Thanks, Von. I really appreciate all your help."

He held the door for me, looking pleased.

I stiffened at the high-pitched shrieks and laughter bouncing down the stairwell and into the busy lobby. I felt like a bird who'd fallen out of the nest and been raised by another species. Suddenly, my cage door had opened, and I was expected to soar with the rest of the flock. There was a reason creatures like these were never returned to the wild.

A frizzy-haired older woman with pale, watery eyes waved me over to the reception desk. She wore a broken-down cardigan over a shapeless brown dress, and bifocals perched on the end of her nose. She inspected me with a practiced eye before her narrow face rearranged itself into the mandatory expression of welcome.

"Welcome to Watson Hall," she said. "I'm Mrs. Stanton, the housemistress. You must be our new senior." I must have made the right noises because she nodded. "Let me call a prefect to take you to your room." It took only a moment for her to pluck a girl out of the stream flowing past. "Sarah Jane!"

A sharp-eyed girl with delicate features and skin the color of well-steeped tea broke off and trudged over, her dark hair pulled back into such a severe knot, I wondered if her eyebrows lowered when she let it down.

Mrs. Stanton made the introductions. "This is Sarah Jane Chopra, one of the prefects. Think of her as an extension of my authority. Sarah Jane, this is Hayden Frasier's new roommate, Riley Collins."

She blinked a few times in surprise before her features settled into a blank slate. The girl would be a wicked chess opponent if she played.

"She's in 312." Mrs. Stanton held up a key attached to an ornate fob in the shape of a W.

Sarah Jane snagged the key. "This way," she said without pausing to see if I followed.

We marched past old, dark wood paneling, vintage carpets in hues of scarlet and gold, and crystal chandeliers. The place looked like it had been built in the same era as the great hall, but as the shiny elevator doors slid silently open, you could tell no expense had been spared to bring it up to date.

"Mandatory study periods are on school nights from 7:30 p.m. to 9:30 p.m., and there's no changing seats once the study bell rings," she droned in a British accent not quite as posh as those of the English diplomats I'd met through the years. More conservatively dressed than the other girls, she wore a baggy crewneck sweater and a knee-length skirt. Maybe she thought it made her look more in charge. "Curfew's at ten, and you better hope you're dead if you miss it, because otherwise I will kill you."

After my ordeal with McKenna, there was no way some little overlord of the hallways would be pushing me around. "Listen, Sarah Jane..."

"Where did you transfer from?" Behind a pair of oversized glasses, Sarah Jane didn't appear at all interested, but she'd neatly cut me off.

"Homeschooled," I said flatly.

"You've never been to a boarding school before?" She suddenly perked up, but in the same way a cat did when a mouse ran across its paws.

"Nope," I answered, now completely wary.

"Well," she said, facing forward as the elevator slid to a halt, "this should be interesting."

The doors reopened on a party. Girls mingled in the hallway, yelling over each other and the music blaring out of a nearby room. New arrivals were treated to hugs and squeals, and new clothes and tans exclaimed over. Someone's black-suited driver wheeled a cart stacked with expensive trunks and luggage down the hall while the few remaining parents looked on indulgently.

I followed in Sarah Jane's wake as she barged through it all, though nobody acknowledged her or even gave her a second glance. It appeared the prefect's high opinion of her authority wasn't shared by anyone else.

We reached room 312, and Sarah Jane zipped through the open door. I walked in a bit more slowly. Another huge disappointment might send me right over the edge.

I took two steps into the room and halted in surprise. I'd always imagined dorm rooms to be little more than prison cells with barely enough room for a narrow cot and maybe a washstand. Sort of like Jane Eyre goes to college.

This was more like Eloise at The Ritz. A bank of six-pane windows with a built-in window seat centered the elegant space, a sizable room painted moss green with splashes of fresh white trim. Pretty white bedroom sets on either side mirrored one another.

One bedroom set was completely decked-out, as if an interior design fairy had waved a magic wand over a high-end home catalog. Bedding, throw pillows, accent rugs, and wall hangings in shades complimentary to the room were perfectly arranged. The other side was naked by comparison, but at least a fresh stack of snowy bed linens and fluffy towels had been left on the bare mattress. My luggage had found its way to the room and now sat neatly stacked next to a giant armoire.

Two girls stared at us from their perch on the wide window seat. I immediately recognized Hayden, who except for a scowl looked just as fabulous in person. Thin and with legs that went on for miles, her skin glowed like she'd just spent a month at the beach, which according to her file, she had. Stephen Frasier had a collection of houses around the world, several of them in tropical locations.

The other girl wasn't nearly as striking, but neither did she look like she planned to poison my tea at the first opportunity. Her long, thick curls were a rich shade of brown, her curvy figure probably left guys panting after her in the hallways, and her skin was so clear, no freckle would dare come within fifty feet. I recognized the Prada boots she wore as a seriously expensive pair I'd tried on at Barney's.

Sarah Jane zeroed in on Hayden's displeasure. "Planned on having the place to yourself, huh, Frasier?"

"Bite me, Chopra," Hayden snapped, flipping her off.

"Meet your new roommate, Riley Collins," she said with way too much glee. "Riley, this is Hayden Frasier and Quinn Sheffield."

"Hey," Quinn said with a cheerful wave, though Hayden quickly shut her down with a glare.

Sarah Jane avidly watched the scene unfold. All she needed was a bag of popcorn to enjoy the show. I had no clue why there was so much hostility in the room, but the prefect had to go.

"Thanks a lot, Sarah Jane," I said in the dismissive tone Benson used on raw recruits. "I've got it from here."

She shot me a look mirroring Hayden's, but there wasn't much she could do about it.

When it was just the three of us, Quinn looked to Hayden. "Why don't we give Riley some space," she suggested. "I heard there's pizza in the common."

Hayden unfolded herself from the bench. She moved to the door but paused, resentment evident in her rigid stance. "You shouldn't be here," she said. "It wasn't supposed to be like this."

"Hey, this wasn't my idea," I said, completely done with this whole miserable day. I was sick of everyone acting like I'd been shoved down their throats.

Hayden stalked from the room, but Quinn followed more slowly. "Hayden was supposed to room with Rose Winters this year," she said. "They were roommates last year, and this year was supposed to be epic, being seniors and all."

"So what happened?" I asked, my clipped tone stopping Quinn at the door. "Where is this Rose?"

Her features arranged themselves into an expression of sympathy, with perhaps a touch of satisfaction as well. "You didn't hear? Rose is dead."

I spent the rest of Sunday afternoon thinking about ways to kill "Aunt" Karen and getting settled in. How dare she overlook such a crucial detail? There was a reason Harrington didn't admit seniors; they had to wait for one of them to die to make room! What else was out there waiting to ambush me?

I yanked sheets onto the bed as I fumed, dumped my beauty products into the only empty drawer remaining in the bathroom, and stowed everything else in the armoire. It had loads of hanging space as well as drawers, a shoe rack, and multi-paneled doors that became full-length mirrors when you folded them back.

The only things I took out of my disreputable duffle before jamming it under the bed were the going away presents from my dad and Benson. The custom carved chess set from Dad went right on my nightstand, but Benson's parting gift had to be stored a bit more discreetly.

Some honorary uncles might give you jewelry or a computer. Not Benson. He'd proudly presented me with a top-of-the-line Taser with a twenty-five-foot range. It was a good thing I didn't have to go through the usual airport screenings.

"Remember how to use one?" he'd asked.

It couldn't be simpler. "Point and shoot."

He'd also included several compressed gas cartridges for quick reloads. Nothing says love like giving the gift of incapacitating your enemy. It went into my new Céline handbag for quick access.

Finally winding down, hunger pangs struck. Quinn had mentioned there was pizza in the common room, so I wandered down to the end of the hall. Spacious and airy, its windows offered unobstructed views of Harrington Hall on one side, the winding Connecticut River on the other. A mixed group of students sprawled out on the two enormous curved sofas dominating the space, with low-slung game tables set at intervals along the sides. A giant flat screen commanded the entire wall in front of the area, while an open kitchen and three round dining tables were set up behind.

Best of all, there was no sign of Hayden. I didn't know how I'd react if she came at me again, but better it happen without the dozen or so people in the room to witness and spread gossip. Some were glued to a rerun of a mindless sitcom, while others read or played backgammon.

No one appeared to notice as I rummaged through the boxes of cold pizza on the kitchen counter, grabbing a few slices of pepperoni and onion before silently drifting back to my room like the resident ghost.

I checked my phone about a thousand times through the evening, waiting for the time my dad would normally be reading his morning emails. I desperately needed to see a friendly face even if it was a continent away, but I wasn't going to wake him up a second night in a row. Thankfully, I was still alone when the time arrived.

His face appeared within moments of logging onto Skype. Still unshaven, he wore a sweaty T-shirt, with a white towel carelessly tossed over one shoulder. A trip to the embassy's gym had left his face flushed but instead of chugging water, he swilled coffee.

"Hey Dad," I greeted him, determined to put a good face on it, "still no sleep last night?"

His crow's feet crinkled as he smiled. "It doesn't feel the same around here without you, but don't worry, I'll adjust. Is that your room?"

I slowly spun my new computer—maybe Karen did come with a few perks—in a 360. "Can you believe this place?"

He let out a low whistle. "How many roommates do you have?"

"Just the one," I said, keeping an ear out for her. I started to tell him about my painful meeting with Mrs. McKenna when Benson bellowed, "Are you talking to our girl?"

Dressed for the day in his usual white cotton button-down, Benson's beaming face popped up over my dad's shoulder. "Darlin' girl! Are they rolling out the red carpet for you there?"

"Well," I hemmed, knowing he would reach through the screen if he could and throttle anyone who was less than welcoming. "I just got here. I haven't had a chance to really meet anyone yet."

His eyes narrowed under bushy brows. "I see," he said darkly. "You let me know if anyone gives you any flack, and I'll be more than happy to call in an air strike."

Dad cupped his chin and sighed. He was well used to hearing Benson's outsized responses to anything that troubled me. "If you are done threatening to blow up a lovely part of the eastern seaboard, I'd like to hear more about the school."

"Well, there's a new female head of security that I'm supposed to meet with," I volunteered. "Do either of you know a Major Taylor?"

They exchanged a look that spoke volumes.

"Uh, is it Grace Taylor, by any chance?" The deceptively casual tone in Benson's voice could only mean one thing.

I rolled my eyes, thrilled to focus on something other than my misery. "Exactly how many ex-girlfriends do you have out there?"

Benson loved women, and they loved him right back. Romance in the workplace was frowned upon, but the only eligible women he met were fellow military personnel. There was little danger of forming permanent attachments because no one ever got stationed anywhere for long. It guaranteed an easy out when the relationship had run its course–at least from his point of view. He'd left a trail of broken hearts from Washington to Dubai.

"It's not like that," he protested. "Okay, maybe it is, but Grace is different." I watched in amazement as the fearless warrior fell silent and stared at his shoes. My dad, on the other hand, practically chortled.

I threw up my hands. "So, who is this Grace Taylor?"

"The only woman who ever dumped our oversized Romeo here," Dad laughed.

"Ancient history," Benson muttered, brushing it off.

I grinned. "You know what they say about history. History is *her* story, too."

We all spent a few more minutes chatting about anything other than Major Taylor before we agreed it was getting late. I wasn't tired, but if we kept talking, eventually it would slip out how cold and lonely it was here. From my dad's expression, he'd already figured it out. It's not like I expected Hayden to welcome me like a long-lost sister, but her bone-chilling reception and McKenna's outright hostility left me fighting back despair.

With curfew fast approaching, I decided to go to bed rather than face Hayden again tonight. As it turned out, I had no idea what time she returned because, surprisingly, I instantly fell asleep.

BENSON'S RULE #8

BLEND LIKE A LOCAL

Jolted awake by my alarm, it took a moment to get my bearings. My stomach curled into knots when I recognized the dorm room at Harrington. Maybe I could fake sick long enough they'd have to box me up and send me home. Or maybe I should just sit up and attempt to survive the day without hurling myself out a window.

Hayden's rumpled bed was empty, but the bathroom door was closed and probably dead bolted for good measure. I used the mirrors in the armoire to put on a bit of makeup and untangle my hair. One of my trunks had been filled with a boarding school starter kit–uniforms, the pricy laptop, a leather Mismo backpack–and I'd just buttoned up my knee-length skirt when Hayden emerged.

"Oh, no. Like, hell no," she snapped when she saw me.

I looked up, wondering what the hell I could have done wrong in the ten minutes I'd been awake to offend her ladyship. "Is there a problem?"

She stood with hands on hips. "Look at me, and then look at you. Do you see a difference here?"

One of us wore the school uniform. The other looked like she was heading out to work a stripper's pole. If her skirt were any shorter, it would qualify as a belt. Her partially opened white shirt revealed a glimpse of a shell-pink pushup bra. Her navy vest was at least two sizes too small, resembling a buttoned-up corset. White, mid-thigh stockings emerged from her black booties and showcased a racy bit of leg.

She stomped over. "If everyone knows I have a total loser for a roommate, I'll never be able to show my face again." She roughly grabbed my skirt waist and rolled it up several times. Next, she yanked open the buttons on my vest and tied the gathered ends tightly across my ribcage. Finally, she opened the top buttons on my shirt.

Despite thinking my new bras were almost too pretty to hide, I still did up the lowest button again anyway. I filled out a bra more than Hayden and didn't want to look like the stripper's trusty sidekick.

She stepped back and pointed. "Bathroom. Now."

I'd barely cleared the door before she rounded on me with a black eyeliner pen. Then she ruthlessly ran her hands through my hair, tossing my curls so I looked like I'd just rolled out of bed. When that was done, she thrust a tube of hooker red lipstick at me. "Take this. It's way too dark for me, but it should actually be kinda hot on you."

When I came out of the bathroom, she grabbed her backpack but paused to look me over with begrudging acceptance. "Just because I helped you stay off the loser list doesn't mean we're friends. Got it?"

"Yeah, no problem." I trailed her out the door, but stayed far enough behind so no one would think we were walking together. Every girl who passed Hayden in the hall checked her out, and most called out a friendly greeting. Amazingly, a few even looked me over with interest. Not a single girl wore the uniform as intended. She'd just saved me from social suicide. In Benson's rules, I now blended like a local.

Coffee, tea, fruit, and bagels were set out in the common room. I grabbed a cup of coffee and loaded it with cream and sugar. My dad never allowed me to drink it, but my eyes had been opened in more ways than one by that first wonderful pot sent up by room service in New York.

Quinn attached herself to Hayden as soon as we walked in the room. Her eyes searched me out, widening as she took in my new and improved style. She smiled and shrugged, as if to apologize for Hayden's rudeness. I didn't have the first idea how to thaw my roommate, but guessed the olive branch would have to come from me. Maybe Quinn would be an ally.

Grabbing my coffee to go, the crisp air outside immediately boosted my spirits, probably because there were only two temperatures in Karachi: hot or freaking hot. I dug out the school map and schedule and tried to pinpoint my first class. A quick rundown showed that all of the senior classes, along with the dining hall, were located in the majestic building across the commons.

"Riley!"

Von came running up, his eyes widening as he took in the new me. "Wow," he breathed. "I mean, uh, you really catch on quick. You look great."

"Thanks." I smiled.

The boys too had personalized their looks. Von wore his gray pants cuffed high with black boots and a herringbone newsboy cap, like he'd just stepped out of the last century. He peered at the schedule in my hands. "What's your first class?"

"World Geography with Bracken," I said, feeling on pretty solid ground with this one. I'd committed Hayden's schedule to memory and knew her first period was English.

He grimaced. "You won't be so thrilled if he calls on you," he warned. "The guy's a total jerk."

"How bad can he be on the first day?" Even my strictest tutors hadn't expected me to know everything on day one.

"Let's just say he's earned his nickname, Bracken the Kraken."

Great. My life just kept getting better and better.

We crossed the commons, and Von politely held the door as we entered the great hall. Benson would approve. He saw no problem with sending women into battle, but always insisted good manners opened doors guns would not.

"Can I ask you a question, Von?" No one ever said no to that question, so I delicately tacked on, "About Hayden's last roommate?"

His face fell. "Rose?" She must have been a close friend. "What do you want to know?"

"What happened to her?" I asked.

"Single car accident. Two weeks ago," he said, his voice clipped.

No wonder Hayden hated me on sight. Probably the whole campus would look at me like an interloper.

"I'm really sorry. If I'd known..." If I'd known I might have refused to come. Karen must have realized it, too, so she had purposely left that little detail out of my briefing. If she had failed in carrying out such a straight-forward assignment as delivering me to school, she could've kissed her career with the State Department goodbye.

My class was on the third floor so we climbed the stairs, stopping to toss my cardboard coffee cup into a hallway recycling bin

"Everyone liked Rose," Von said, but paused to reconsider. "Maybe everyone except Quinn Sheffield. Have you met her yet?"

I nodded. "She's Hayden's best friend?"

"She will be now that Rose..."

We'd reached my classroom, bringing an end to that depressing line of questioning. The hallways were quickly emptying, so he took a few steps back toward the stairs.

"I'll look out for you at lunch," he said before an impish grin settled on his face. "If you survive the Kraken, that is."

"Very funny," I called to his retreating back.

Rows of small tables filled the classroom, each seating two students. I found an empty spot next to one of the prettiest guys I'd ever seen. He'd blow-dried his blonde hair to perfection and had the sculpted cheekbones of an underfed model. A beautiful, salmon-colored cashmere scarf draped dramatically across his shoulders, and he wore a discreet, diamond-studded hoop in his right ear.

I must have stared at him overlong because he turned and gave me a big wink. "Admire much?"

"Oh, ah, I'm sorry..." I stumbled to apologize, but he cut me off with a huge grin.

"Are you kidding? It takes me hours to look like this. It's nice to know somebody appreciates it." He extended a hand palm down, as if he expected to have his ring kissed. "I'm Stef Corbett, at your service."

Completely charmed, I gave his hand an awkward shake. "Riley Collins. Is this seat taken?"

He leapt up and pulled out the chair with a flourish. "By all means, madam," he said, giving me an admiring once-over. "Those of us with fashion sense must stick together."

I settled in just as a prim little man wearing a tweed suit and bow tie sailed into the room. His receding hairline exposed the shiny dome of an egg-shaped head, and a bulbous nose balanced out his unusually large ears. His lip curled in a permanent state of disapproval, he looked out over the fifteen or so in attendance.

"I am Mr. Bracken," he announced imperiously. "And I don't care if your father is on the Fortune 500 list, or if your mother can trace her lineage back to the Mayflower. In this class, you will learn, or you will fail. Are we clear?"

I began to understand how this guy got his nickname.

"I don't believe in wasting time," he continued, strutting in front of the class like Napoleon addressing his troops. "At this point in your academic careers, I expect your feeble minds to have absorbed basic geographic knowledge. I will be calling on you to see if there's any hope for your futures beyond a life of shopping and alcoholism. Are you ready?"

The class hardly dared to breathe. Even my new friend slunk down low in his chair.

"Let us begin." He ran a finger down the page of an open notebook. "Is Mr. Halsey-Witter here?" A guy two rows over slowly raised his hand as if he expected it to be shot off. "Stand, please," the teacher said, and the student hesitantly obeyed.

"Now," Bracken said, leaning nonchalantly against the podium, "how many countries are there in Africa, and can you name three of them?"

The poor guy's eyes widened in fear. "Um, thirty?"

Bracken scowled in disgust. "Sit down," he ordered, consulting the roster again. "Miss Brightman-Davis?"

His next victim, a girl with caramel-colored skin and perfectly straightened hair, scrambled to her feet.

"Ms. Brightman-Davis, of the *fifty-three* nations currently recognized in Africa, please name three of them."

"Chad, Zambia, and um, um... Kenya." She sank gratefully back into her chair.

"Well, it appears we have at least one student who might become a functioning member of society." He ran his finger down the page. "Ah, here's someone with just one name. How refreshing. Mr. Corbett?"

My tablemate stood up with all the enthusiasm of a prisoner being led to the guillotine.

"Name the three major rivers of the Middle East."

"The Nile...the Euphrates..." He closed his eyes a moment as if he were racking his brains. "Um..."

"Tigris," I mumbled under my breath. We'd crossed it once while visiting Turkey.

"Tigris," he repeated brightly before diving back into his chair.

The teacher stared at me suspiciously. Maybe he'd heard me, maybe he hadn't. "What is your name?" he finally said.

I got to my feet. "Riley Collins."

"Well, Miss Collins, you seem to know so much about the Tigris," he said in a mocking tone. "Tell me what countries it flows through."

"Turkey, Syria, and Iraq," I said.

His lips thinned, even though my answer was correct.

"Define the borders of Mesopotamia."

It was a trick question. "The answer's still the same, although you could throw in Iran and Kuwait if you want to be a stickler about it."

He looked me over with renewed interest before ordering me to sit down. Perhaps I could have been a tad less cheerful about knowing the answers, but I'd never been the type to back away from a challenge. He continued to humiliate or give grudging praise as the situation warranted until the bell finally chimed. The class bolted as if escaping the spawn of Satan.

Out in the hall, my tablemate hovered. "You saved my life in there," he said. "I am forever in your debt."

"No problem. I've known Arab dictators who were warm and fuzzy compared to that guy," I joked.

"You must let me buy you lunch."

I narrowed my eyes at him. "Aren't meals included?" A laminated meal card had come with my schedule.

He waved a dismissive hand. "Details! Now let's get you to your next class, and then we'll meet for lunch." He whipped my class schedule out of my hand. "English Lit? Dear lady, follow me unto the breach!"

BENSON'S RULE #9

ALWAYS DO WHAT YOU ARE AFRAID TO DO

The day continued to be one of firsts. As promised, Von flagged me down at lunchtime as I wandered the ground floor searching for the dining hall. It sounded silly, but I kind of hoped it would look like Hogwarts. Instead, it was a ballroom-sized space of hardwood floors, wood paneling, and French doors leading to a giant patio. Round oak tables seating ten or twelve were positioned throughout, most already filling up with students. From the doors at the far end came the welcome smell of a decidedly American lunch being served, not a whiff of curry or cumin to be had. I'd been too nervous to eat breakfast.

He handed me a blue plastic tray as we walked into the kitchen area. "You can get in line for the grill or the deli, and the sushi bar is over there." No prison slop for these people. I helped myself to an organic turkey sandwich and marveled over a bottle of spring water imported from Fiji. People in Karachi counted themselves lucky if they got water by turning on the tap.

"Our table is in front by the windows," he said, as he loaded up on a burger and fries. "The window side is senior territory." It was easy to see why. The last of September's waning sunshine filtered in through the open doors. It was the most inviting spot in the room.

"Riley!" Stef waved enthusiastically from a prime table.

"I see you've already met my roommate, the mayor of Harrington," Von said, catching up with me.

"Come on, people, make room for two more!" Stef directed traffic and pulled over chairs. "Right here next to me, Lady Tigris." He patted the seat. It wasn't until I sat down that I looked across the table and right into Hayden's stony face. Quinn had claimed the seat next to her.

"Everyone," Stef announced, "this is Riley, my goddess and savior. Without her, the Kraken would have claimed another victim. Riley, this is everyone."

Before I could speak, Quinn jumped down Stef's throat. "Why do you always have to exaggerate everything?"

"Because if I didn't, my life would be as dry and dull as yours," he shot back.

"Better than being daddy's little accident," she said with a mocking smile.

Stef guffawed as if it was the wittiest remark he'd ever heard. "Coming from the school's biggest social climber, that's a great compliment."

"Knock it off, both of you," Hayden scolded.

"But she started it, Mom," Stef whined good-naturedly.

Quinn flushed at being chastised, but shrugged it off. The other seven or eight students at the table acted as if their bickering were a common occurrence.

A rail-thin guy with tight black curls and acne turned to me. "So you've never been to a regular school before?" Word traveled fast.

It was tempting to tell him there was nothing regular about Harrington. "My dad's a diplomat. This will be the first time I'll be in the States for longer than two weeks."

This started a round of stories about the longest time anyone's parents had hauled him or her off to the ends of the earth. With the focus shifted elsewhere, I started mentally mapping out our surroundings, seeking potential entry and exit points, possible threats, and promising allies. Landing at Hayden's table was what Benson called smart luck. Maybe it wouldn't be so hard to stay close to her after all.

With every table filled, the din in the place was incredible. Maybe people were just catching up after summer vacation, but it was a relief to see so much laughter and happiness filling the room. No one had brought up Rose Winters to my face, though I had overheard her name mentioned several times while passing in the halls. Maybe this would be okay after all.

I was about to rejoin the conversation when a guy strolling through a patio door caught my attention. With thick chestnut hair pushed carelessly off an expressive face, he had a Cupid's bow mouth twisted into an amicable smile. His deep blue eyes, the same shade as the Arabian Sea at sunset, flashed with humor. He'd shucked the blazer the boys were required to wear in favor of a white oxford hugging his broad shoulders and tapered waist. And he was tall, definitely over six feet.

He was perfection.

"He is dreamy, isn't he?" Stef stared, just as transfixed.

I grinned at the not-altogether unexpected comment. "What's his story?"

"His name is Sam Hudson and yes, he's currently on the market." He made a face. "And straight. And, oh my god, British. He's got that posh London accent." He let out a smitten sigh.

"I'm sure Riley could care less," Von, seated on my other side, chimed in. "I bet she's into guys with substance, not just style."

"Real subtle, dude." This came from the Chinese girl with a cute fringe of bangs sitting on his right. "I'm Jackie Song, by the way," she said to me with a smile.

"Oh, he's got substance, all right," Stef sighed. "He aces every math test, he's captain of the MMA club, and even his jokes are funny."

"There's a mixed martial arts club?" I blurted, completely astonished.

Mixed martial arts was a sport combining a host of martial art disciplines, such as jiu-jitsu, judo, and tae kwon do, along with kickboxing and wrestling. If there was a club here, it was a good bet most of these people had their butlers spar for them, but I didn't care. I'd only ever fought with men who worked security at the embassy, guys who took great care not to hit their commanding officer's favorite too hard. I didn't want the special treatment, but Benson had probably threatened death by firing squad if anyone inflicted any real damage on me.

How cool would it be to see how I measured up with girls my own age? The fact that Sam was club captain was the big, gorgeous cherry on top.

Stef misinterpreted my question. "Why people want to beat each other up like that is beyond me, but a lot of guys are into it."

Not just the guys, I smiled to myself.

Boarding school days go on forever. Just because classes are over doesn't mean there isn't something else you're supposed to be doing. How did anyone expect me to keep track of Hayden like this?

According to my afternoon schedule, I had thirty minutes from the last bell to report to the stables dressed to ride. Tromping back to the dorm, I wracked my brains for any excuse I could use to avoid riding.

I wasn't kidding when I'd told Von horses had it in for me. There'd been a few incidents of horses trying to take a bite out of me, like when I'd strayed too close during an official visit to a sheik's stables, or when we were honored guests at a military parade featuring a mounted division.

But those were nothing compared to the Sri Lanka Horse Incident.

My dad had been assigned the duty of presenting six white Arabian horses to a military academy in Sri Lanka. There was a great deal of fanfare when we arrived and despite the hot, muggy day, the enlisted men wore their heavy, olive-drab dress uniforms. The higher-ranking officers added red sashes, swooping gold braid, and chests of medals, marking it as a formal occasion. Protocol demanded everything be just so, and I'd broken down and worn a filmy lavender dress that floated about me at the slightest breeze.

My father and I were seated underneath a small, tented pavilion set up just for the occasion. White-gloved waiters served high tea, and like so many things in that part of the world, it was like we'd been sucked into a time warp. It was the 1800s all over again.

The six horses were paraded out to polite applause, each being led by a smartly dressed officer. They were then expected to line up respectfully while the usual windy speeches about friendship and cooperation were delivered. Five of the horses were with the program, but the sixth displayed a foul temper right out of the gate. He tossed his head, stamped his hooves, and squealed in frustration. About halfway through the ceremony, he'd had enough.

Seizing on a moment of his handler's inattention, he bolted loose. He galloped toward our pavilion, causing all of us tea drinkers to leap to our feet. Stopping in the center of the parade grounds, he snorted in satisfaction and surveyed his domain. A gust of wind fluttered his mane before his eyes locked on mine. And then he charged.

Tables overturned and silver teapots went flying as everyone scrambled for safety. I dashed across open ground, making for the tree line, when the drumbeat of hooves came up from behind. Without slowing to risk a glance behind me I pivoted, but the horse changed direction, too. From somewhere behind me my father yelled, "Riley! Toward the kitchens!" I instinctively obeyed.

Two or three of our waiters bravely ran toward me, silver trays in one hand and matching ladles in the other. They pounded wildly on the trays and uttered piercing war cries, but I could sense the horse bearing down. I was only a second or two from my would-be saviors when suddenly, with a horrible ripping of my dress, I lost my footing. Momentum carried me several yards before I slid face down along the grass.

Dazed and panting, I laid there wondering which body part I would have to learn to live without when my dad came rushing over.

"Riley! Are you alright?" He was frightened, but not as panicked as I would have expected with his only child bleeding out all over the freshly mowed grass. "Can you sit up?"

To my complete surprise, I easily rolled over and sat upright. The small team of waiters had captured the horse, and they were all absurdly pleased to have done so while in the company of a platoon of trained soldiers. The horse itself contentedly stood by, chewing on a piece of lavender fabric.

Looking down in horror, I was met with the sight of my lacey white panties on display for the world. Grass stains covered what little remained of my tattered dress, and blood oozed from my knees. Later my dad promised we would learn to laugh about it, but he also made it a point to say that in the future, I should remain behind whenever horses were present.

Unfortunately, that wasn't an option today. I dragged my feet the whole way but eventually arrived at the stables. There were eight other students, including Von, whose face lit up when he spotted me.

"You're late," the instructor snapped. His name was Mr. Diaz, and it was impossible to tell if he was forty or seventy. Deep lines earned from years in the sun crisscrossed his leathery skin, but his hair was that unique shade of black so dark it glinted blue in the light.

"Sorry," I sulked.

"Ah, you're the one. Mrs. McKenna said there was a girl in the senior class who did not ride," he said with an accent straight from the polo fields of South America. "We have a special horse just for you."

If that meant it was half dead and semi-comatose, bring it on.

The other students moved confidently toward numbered stalls, obviously having been assigned their mounts prior to my arrival. I scrambled out of the way as each one emerged leading a prancing horse by a rope and making their way to an area of the barn where bridles and saddles awaited.

"Your turn," Mr. Diaz said, inclining his head to the last stall in the farthest reaches of the barn. Several horses popped their heads out to see what all the fuss was about, and I would have to pass by every single one of them. It was like a dozen Hannibal Lecters all waiting to pounce as I skittered by.

"Me?" I squeaked. "I've never walked a dog on a leash, let alone a horse!"

He let out a string of invectives in Spanish. "It is a halter and lead, *not* a leash."

When you are about to meet an early and painful death at the hooves of a giant beast, proper terminology is the least of your worries.

"Hector!" At the summons, a groom emerged from one of the open stalls. "Please bring Brutus out for saddling." The groom immediately sprinted to do the boss's bidding.

I started to back away but with a glare that could peel paint, Mr. Diaz latched onto the lapel of my riding jacket, forcing me to watch as my doom emerged from the shadows.

Admittedly, Brutus didn't look any more threatening than any of the other horses. Average in size, he had a shiny chestnut coat deepening into shades of chocolate brown from knee to hoof. His mane and tail were black, and he had enormous brown eyes fringed with thick lashes. His ears perked up when he saw me, as if he couldn't believe his luck that the most reviled girl in the entire animal kingdom had stumbled into his barnyard. Once he'd killed me, his hero status in the horse world would be assured.

I screwed my eyes shut as the horse drew near, the steady clip-clop of hooves not stopping until his breath was hot on my face. Suddenly a large object hit me in the chest, and I squealed in terror, but Mr. Diaz's iron grip held me prisoner. A terrible groan rent the air, and I opened my eyes to Brutus lowering his head against my chest again, rubbing his face delightedly against the coarse wool of my jacket. The horse expelled another satisfied grunt when he shifted angles, reaching a particularly itchy spot.

Daring a peek at the long-suffering instructor, I whispered, "What is he doing?"

Mr. Diaz let go of my jacket and sighed. "He is warming up to do the tango. What does it look like he's doing?" He thrust the rope at me. "Now take his lead, and let's begin."

Mr. Diaz sent everyone else to warm up in the adjacent arena, but Von stayed behind to show me the proper way to equip a horse. He sidled up with a nod of encouragement. "Just walk toward the tack room, and he'll be right behind you, you'll see." That's what I was afraid of.

Von selected a saddle and fitted it over the horse's back. "Many horses will hold their breath while you tighten the cinch, and then you'll be in danger of having your saddle slip, but not Brutus." When it came time for the bridle, the horse complacently allowed Von to slide the bit into his tender mouth.

Then came the moment of truth.

"Up you go," he coaxed. My usual athletic ease deserted me as I gracelessly scrambled halfway over the saddle and flailed about. Gritting my teeth, I finally managed to get upright and shove my feet into the stirrups. Handing up the reins, Von informed Brutus it was time to go. I clutched at the horse's mane and held on for dear life as we strolled into the arena.

Everyone else had spaced out their mounts and was putting them through their paces. Two girls even had their horses cantering daintily around the ring.

"Please don't kill me," I quietly begged the horse, somewhat assured when his ears swiveled in my direction as if he were considering my request.

We plodded slowly around the ring for a few minutes, Brutus not altering his pace no matter how fast another rider sped by. Von soon trotted up next to me. "See? You're a natural." He was completely at ease on his gleaming black mount. His mother probably gave birth to him on horseback.

"Obviously," I ground out. My teeth were in danger of cracking under the pressure.

The rest of the session miraculously passed without any fatalities. Von stayed close at hand to help me dismount and show me how to remove the horse's tack. Then he handed me a brush. "If you really want to make friends with Brutus, here's the secret."

I cautiously approached the horse and tentatively stroked the brush across his withers. He sighed and leaned closer, so I did it again. Within minutes I was vigorously brushing him from head to tail while he moaned and groaned. By the time he'd had enough, only Von remained, perched nearby on a bale of hay. I'd been hesitant to encourage his interest, but with friendly faces in short supply I was glad he'd stuck around.

I carefully handed Brutus off to Hector before taking Von up on his offer to walk with me to the dorms. It had grown late, and the setting sun had turned the clouds into vivid slashes of color, so different from the typically cloudless skies we had back home.

"I need a shower in the worst way," I said, wrinkling my nose at the overpowering stench of horse emanating off the both of us.

He eyed my stiff-legged gait and grinned. "What you really need is a massage. I'm very good with my hands, you know."

"In your dreams," I said, snorting with amusement. "But A for effort. It's really decent of you to keep me company."

"I've only been here a year and still have painful memories of my first few days," he said ruefully. "It's got to be a big change for you, huh?"

"It's the smell," I mused.

"Yeah, I know, horses reek."

"No, I mean, that's one of the biggest changes. Everything smells so..." I breathed deeply, trying to pinpoint the scents that made Connecticut so different from Pakistan. "It smells so earthy, but not in a bad way. I can smell the river, and the wet grass, and the rotting leaves..."

He took a big sniff. "Humph, I guess you're right. I'd never really thought about it. What did it smell like where you came from?"

Karachi was not known for its cleanliness, but somebody had the bright idea to plant Arabian jasmine all over the embassy grounds. The sweet fragrance helped mask the odor of the streets. "Let me put it this way: the smell of Arabian jasmine will always remind me of home."

The path from the stables wound by Hale Hall, the upper boys' dorm. Von paused by the front doors. "You want to come over for study hall later?"

What I needed to do was find out where Hayden studied. "Where does everybody usually go?"

"The library and the common rooms are the most popular."

"Cool," I responded noncommittally before setting off for my own dorm.

If I hadn't been admiring the rapidly changing sky I would have missed it. A chill swept through me at the sight of a black drone stealthily skimming the treetops near Watson Hall. I ran the rest of the way to the dorms, cursing my stiff riding boots, but the drone zipped away at top speed at my approach.

Bolting through the front doors and past a wide-eyed Mrs. Stanton, I took the stairs two at a time, not willing to wait for the elevator. Throwing open the door, I stood panting on the threshold to find Hayden sitting on her bed, painting her toenails a stunning shade of blue.

She glanced up. "What's your problem?"

"Um, bathroom," I mumbled.

Closing the bathroom door behind me, I perched on the edge of the tub to catch my breath. Peeling off the boots, I rubbed my bruised shins while considering this new development. Was it just an accident a drone had been outside our dorm, perhaps right at window level? Had some skanky guy been using it to spy into girls' rooms, or had a hobbyist mistakenly flown it off course? Could it be part of the new security measures?

Of course, it might be none of those things. It might be someone had come looking for Hayden—and found her.

It was time to look up Major Grace Taylor.

BENSON'S RULE #10

MEET AUTHORITY WITH AUTHORITY

When reporting for duty, you present yourself to your commanding officer immediately upon arrival. I wasn't in the military, and Major Taylor wasn't my boss, but lessons instilled by Benson would never be easy to shake. I'd been slack in not seeking her out earlier, but with days more tightly scheduled than meals at Ramadan, it wasn't my fault. It was the drone sighting that reminded me I had bigger worries than just dealing with high school drama.

I managed to slip away after the last class the following day, making my way to the ground floor of the great hall. Located in the rear of the building, the security offices took up a lot of real estate. Several desks, all manned by uniformed personnel, faced the door. Three enclosed offices, each with names and titles stenciled on the door, ran along the exterior wall. I spied the Major's name on the furthest door and padded in that direction.

"May I help you?" The man stationed at what would typically be the secretary's desk might be a great typist, but he looked nothing like a deskbound assistant. The touch of gray at his temples was the only sign he wasn't in his prime. Fit and trim, his crisp blue uniform still held its creases, and his squared shoulders had that ramrod bearing twenty years in the military will give you. His silver nametag read J. Wieringa. This had to be one of the new hires.

"I'd like to see Major Taylor. My name is Riley Collins."

The spark of recognition at my name made me wonder what he'd heard about me. My true purpose at Harrington was a closely guarded secret, but perhaps he was the Major's confidante as well as assistant. He said a few words into the phone. "Go right in. She's expecting you."

I recognized the unsmiling woman from her picture, and she stood up from the desk as I entered.

"Sit down, Miss Collins." It wasn't an invitation.

I took a chair, a straight-back metal job that would be at home in an interrogation room, but she remained on her feet, towering over me.

The sleek, navy uniform she wore hugged a slender figure that appeared much younger than her forty-something years. She was quite pretty, with long, dark hair swept into a sleek bun, and suntanned skin. Her movements were spare and deliberate, as if she were in perfect command of herself and everything else around her. Her eyes flicked over me with little interest, and I sensed an impatience to be done with me as quickly as possible. I seemed to have that effect on a lot of people lately.

"I think having you here is a mistake," she announced. "You're too young, your training is spotty, and if there is a real problem you'll just get in the way."

I had watched Benson dress down rookies way too many times to react. I often stood on the sidelines and willed them to keep their mouths shut, knowing the fool who talked back would be verbally eviscerated.

The hint of a smile told me I'd passed the first test. "It's a miracle Harrington has never seen trouble before," she continued, warming up to her subject. "The safety measures in place are outdated, the lighting on campus is from fifty years ago, and McKenna fights every attempt at upgrades. As we both know, a school by its very nature is one massive soft target."

In military parlance, a target that is predictable and stuck in a routine is soft and therefore more vulnerable. It also meant if someone was truly motivated to kidnap or otherwise harm Hayden, they just might succeed.

She stalked to her desk chair and perched on it as if she expected to jump up again at any moment. The silence dragged out long enough I decided it might be safe to speak.

"I'm no cowboy, Major Taylor," I said evenly, "and I'm not looking to be a hero, but I can be useful." I had no idea if I could be remotely helpful, but I'd seen my dad look around at Cairo after the Arab Spring uprising and say, "Meh, it could be worse." Best to put a good face on it.

She cocked her head, an invitation to continue.

"Hayden Frasier seems friendly enough to everyone, and she's one of the trendsetters, though she doesn't talk much." Today several girls had come to class in knockoff versions of the way she'd worn her uniform yesterday. "Her wingman is Quinn Sheffield, who seems okay, maybe." Quinn had been friendly enough to me, but the way people scuttled out of her way when she strolled through the halls made me wonder. "Once Hayden gets used to me, we'll be fine." Yeah, right. We hadn't exchanged two words since I'd stumbled into the room yesterday.

"You're the girl's roommate, for God's sakes," Taylor huffed. "How is it you can't just ingratiate yourself?"

"Because Hayden Frasier's a total bitch, that's why," I snapped without thinking. I took a moment to regroup. "What I mean to say is..."

The Major stood and marked off a few restless paces. "You don't need to explain." For the first time she looked at me like I might be worthy of her time. "The students have only been back for a few days, and already I have a list of spoiled children I'd like to see airdropped into the Amazon with nothing but a KA-BAR knife and a granola bar."

She did paint a vivid picture.

She strode over to a metal wall cabinet and picked through a few shelves before finding what she was looking for. "Here," she said, handing me an unlabeled USB stick.

"What is it?"

"GPS tracking software. Latest thing. Using your computer, you can sync your phone with that of the subject, and you'll be able to triangulate her position using any one of twenty-eight military satellites. It has a code-breaking feature, which will get you past any password protection in sixty seconds or less." She leaned against her desk with satisfaction. "The best part is she'll never know it's there."

There was just one problem. "How am I supposed to get hold of her phone? She even sleeps with it, for some unknown reason."

She shot me a skeptical look. "Doesn't the girl ever shower?"

"I'll do it as soon as possible." The stick went into my backpack.

She tapped a fingernail against her teeth as if she were hatching an idea. "You know, if you're to blend in, it would be best if we weren't seen together. I also would rather avoid electronic communication."

I sat forward in my chair. "What do you suggest?"

"A code word to be texted whenever we need a face-to-face. Let's make it 'horses'. If it's an emergency, text 'zebras'."

Curiosity got the better of me. "Why horses and zebras?"

A faint smile crossed her lips. "Most people hear hoofbeats and think horses. If you should hear something more exotic, well then..."

"Zebras," I concluded. "Got it."

We agreed that any meetings would take place in her office right after the nightly study period. That would give me exactly thirty minutes to get back to the dorm before Sarah Jane sicced the dogs on me.

"Anything else?" She turned her attention to the papers on her desk.

"By any chance, are you using drones to patrol?"

The shocked look on her face said it all. "No. Why?"

I told her about the one seen hovering near Watson Hall the night before, and though troubled, there wasn't much she could do. We agreed I would text her immediately if I saw another one, and to hell with discretion.

"One last thing," I said. "What happened to Rose Winters?" Von had given me the Spark Notes version, but I couldn't help being morbidly curious about the girl whose place I had taken. Major Taylor was the only one I could really ask.

"There's not much to tell." She walked over to the window and stared down at the rolling landscape. "Single car accident right down the road. She'd come early, the first day students were allowed back on campus, and according to the police report she was on her way back after buying a cell phone. They found it in the wreckage unopened. Quite a loss, I understand."

Hayden had most likely been off in Saint-Tropez, or wherever it was heiresses went to perfect their summer tans. Despite their friendship, Rose had probably come early to enjoy the peace and quiet without a roommate.

Major Taylor broke into my thoughts. "How's Karl?"

I didn't think even Benson's mother called him that. "He's... good." I barely knew the woman. Volunteering that my honorary uncle turned into a heartbroken teenager at the mere mention of her name was too personal.

She turned from the window to face me, but her expression said she was miles away–6,913 to be exact.

"He talked about you, you know," she said, a smile transforming her face. "You were just a baby at the time, but he couldn't have been prouder of you if you were his own daughter."

I flushed with pride and pleasure. "Other than my dad, he's the best man I've ever known." I decided to take a chance. "I think he still misses you."

Her smile tightened as reality intruded. "But apparently he would have missed his stubborn pride a whole lot more." She crossed to the door and opened it. "Thank you for coming, Riley."

I slowly stood, feeling I couldn't leave without speaking up for Benson.

"I'm all alone here. My family has my back, but I wish there was someone standing by my side." I took the few steps to the threshold and met her flinty gaze. "What I'm trying to say is if I loved someone, I'd do almost anything to make it work."

It may have been my imagination, but her expression softened for just an instant. Finally she said, "Karl must be quite proud of you."

A few seconds later, I was out in the hall. The interview was over.

BENSON'S RULE #11

DON'T BRING ATTENTION TO YOURSELF

The first MMA club meeting was scheduled for Wednesday afternoon, and by the time my last class ended I couldn't wait to hit someone.

Other than helping me get dressed that first morning, Hayden continued to act like I didn't exist. Grief does a number on your head, and the rest of the senior class watched warily, waiting for Hayden to warm up to me. Thank God for Stef and Von, who continued to invite me to hang out with them.

I raced to the dorm and changed into a hot pink sports bra and black booty shorts. My body was tight and trim from years of working out and endless training, but I'd never worn anything so revealing. I'd told Dad it was what girls wore in MMA, but he had insisted on sweats and loose fitting T-shirts. I covered up before I left my room, slipping on a pair of navy sweats and a fitted hoodie.

I'd never sparred with a girl. I hoped there was at least one in my weight class who wouldn't cry if she broke a nail. Plus there was nothing like a good fight to break the ice.

The club met in the smallest of the school's three gyms. Like the other two, which housed the basketball and volleyball courts, the place was immaculate with spotless floors, great lighting, and top-of-the-line equipment begging to be broken in. Even the air smelled good.

Two huge mats—blue squares trimmed in red to denote sparring rings—were set side by side on the floor. Steel baskets of kick pads, mitts, gloves, and shin guards lined the wall. Across the room a large, rectangular hanging frame supported six pristine punching bags, all evenly spaced.

I stood just inside the door, relishing the familiar sight and sounds of a bunch of guys in various stages of warm up. Some worked the bags or stretched out while others held kick pads and braced for attack. It was the first time I'd truly felt at home since I'd left Karachi. Then I realized there was something else quite familiar. Once again, I was the lone female in a roomful of testosterone.

"Riley!" Von's surprised face popped up from behind the bag he'd been holding steady, and I was immediately the center of attention. "What are you doing here?"

I swallowed hard and stepped forward.

"This is the MMA club, isn't it?"

Sam broke away from the group he'd been working with and took a few swaggering strides in my direction. He wore an indigo T-shirt with the sleeves cut off, showcasing muscular arms dreamed up by a sculptor. The hue also played up the color of his beautiful eyes.

He shot me a curious smile. "Is this a joke?" He spoke in the uptown boarding school accent so many diplomats' kids acquired in the UK.

My brows drew together. "If it is, I'm not laughing."

Sam looked at his buddies, some of whom shrugged, others shaking their heads in annoyance. His smile grew. He planned to blow me off. Damn. And he was so hot. "Look, um..."

"Riley Collins," I supplied, brushing past him and heading to a nearby bench. I pulled my T-shirt over my head and tossed it down like a gauntlet being thrown. If I didn't have everyone's undivided attention before, my pink sports bra sure had it now.

"Look, Riley," he began again.

I slipped off my shoes and let my sweats fall to the ground.

A few schoolboy sniggers came from my appreciative audience. They wouldn't be laughing for long. I walked directly up to Sam. "What's your name?" It wouldn't help my cause if he knew I'd already checked him out.

He crossed his arms. "Sam Hudson, captain of the club."

"Well, captain," I said, sauntering into the center of one of the sparring mats. "If you don't want me here, why don't you make me leave?"

A chorus of delighted "oohhs" arose as the guys practically licked their lips over the challenge I'd thrown down. A few even slapped Sam on the back like he'd been promised a whole lot more than just a fight.

Von zipped over, his face tight with concern. "What are you doing?" he whispered urgently. "Sam's the best fighter in the club!"

I began to do some light stretching as if I were indifferent to the conference taking place between Sam and his buddies. "Then it'll be over in five minutes, and I'll never darken your door again."

"That's not what I'm worried about," Von muttered.

I didn't know what he meant by that, but the huddle broke apart; a decision had been made. Sam came to the edge of the mat. "Here's the deal: if you can hang on for one round without tapping out or, God forbid, crying..." That earned him a laugh. "Then we'll let you work out with us."

"A regulation round with Unified Rules?" A round lasted five minutes while the rules specified things such as no hair pulling, eye gouging, or other dirty tricks.

Sam stepped onto the mat and made a show of pulling off his shirt, much as I had done, revealing more of his perfect physique. "Tell you what. Since I way outclass you, we'll only go for three minutes." He referred to our weight class. At 115 pounds, I landed in the lightweight division. He looked to be around 170, which would make him a welterweight.

I shrugged indifferently, despite almost swallowing my tongue as he flexed the muscles on his rippling chest. I was accustomed to fighting shirtless guys, but none of them had ever looked quite like this.

"Suit yourself," I managed to sputter.

I dropped to the mat to stretch my hamstrings, and Von hunkered down next to me. "This is ludicrous," he said in a stage whisper. "If Sam kills you, you're going to die without ever realizing you're madly in love with me."

His humor lightened my mood. "Then I guess I'll have to do my best to live through this, won't I?"

Sam and I both took a few more minutes to warm up before donning fingerless padded gloves. Von velcroed me into headgear that wrapped so far around my head, it cupped my cheekbones. "School rules," he explained.

I was as ready as I'd ever be.

"Wait," Von called out, still hovering. "Who's going to ref?"

"You do it," Sam said to him, before glancing my way. "That okay with you?"

I nodded, relieved that we'd at least have a fair fight now.

"Tap gloves," Von instructed. "Let's keep it friendly."

Sam's eyes met mine as our gloves connected. Now that he no longer played captain or postured for his friends, I could read genuine concern in his expression.

"You could walk away now, and I promise no one would give you shit," he said softly. "You have my word."

I grinned, thinking about the last time a guy had tried to, in his words, let me off easy. By the time he realized he'd better shut up and fight, he sat dazed on the mat. "That's very nice of you, but I came here to spar."

We separated and claimed opposite corners. Von used a remote to set the large digital wall timer for three minutes and then announced, "Begin."

I immediately started to dance about. Sam dropped into a fighting stance.

The only way to survive the round would be to stay on my feet as long as possible and use my legs for attack. I could never match his reach or strength, and if he got me down into a wrestling match, I'd have only seconds to finish him off before he'd do the same to me.

Luckily, most guys based their strategy on fighting other guys, which usually worked in my favor.

He kept his guard up while I circled. "I'm curious," he said conversationally, over the hoots and hollers of his friends. "Why would a girl like you want to fight?"

My smile didn't quite reach my eyes. "And what kind of girl would that be?"

He still puzzled over that when, thirty seconds in, the impatient crowd called for action. He straightened slightly and said, "Are we fighting or dancing?"

The moment I waited for had come: the moment he dropped his guard. I threw myself into a side thrusting kick, a knee lift that brought to bear every ounce of my lower body strength. I aimed the heel of my foot at his solar plexus, but he turned at the last possible moment. Still, I delivered a solid blow to his ribcage before I zipped out of range.

Sam staggered a moment, and I wasted no time in delivering another kick, this time to the inside of his upper thigh. Benson had taught me there were a ton of nerves there, and a well-placed jab could make you see stars. Despite the pain I knew he suffered, he threw himself into defense. Playtime was over.

"Aren't you full of surprises?" he gasped.

I danced just out of reach. "*That's* the kind of girl I am."

I saw his muscles gather to deliver a roundhouse kick just before he let fly. If I were a guy, I'm sure he wouldn't have hesitated to aim for my head. As it was, he foolishly went for my torso, a move I quickly blocked before kicking his standing leg out from under him.

He took a face plant to the mat, and I leaped onto his back. Normally I would never take to the floor so quickly, but it was a golden opportunity. I wrapped my legs around his naked torso and locked my arms across his throat. Our audience howled in derision, egging both of us on.

"Where did you learn how to fight?" he gasped out.

"I'm home schooled. They've got tutors for everything these

days." I'd probably given away too much already, but at that moment I didn't care.

His body glistened with a light sweat as he heaved underneath me. I was still a card-carrying member of the V club, but I wouldn't be for long if I dwelled on the way his muscles bucked between my thighs. I mentally slapped myself to keep my head in the fight.

He flipped over and we both landed on our backs, though my legs were still locked tightly around his hips. "I think I'm beginning to see the advantages of sparring with girls." He ran a teasing hand up my bare leg, and the spectators roared their approval.

I increased the chokehold on his throat. There were still a few defensive moves he could use against me, but he didn't seem so inclined.

"Do you yield?" I asked.

He reached out and thumped the mat twice, drawing jeers from his friends. As we disentangled ourselves, I said in a low voice, "You let me win."

He got to his feet first and reached down to help me up. When we were face to face he said, "Let's just say that maybe we both learned something today."

He reached for a towel and left me on my own to work the bag, though I kept an eye on the other practice matches. Sam engaged in one more bout. It was a tough battle because both fighters were well matched in speed and strength. Ultimately Sam won because he had game in both standing and ground fighting. Von was right; with Sam's size, he could have totally cleaned my clock. Jogging back to the dorms to shower, I wondered why Sam had held back.

Hayden stood waiting for me when I walked in the door. "What the hell do you think you're doing?"

I regarded her blankly. "I don't know... breathing?"

She shoved her phone in my face. Pictures of Sam and me locked in steamy combat had already been posted, and our expressions said we were both enjoying it way too much. I might as well have stripped naked in front of the entire school. If my dad ever saw these, I'd be toast.

"Sam is off-limits," she snapped. "Everyone knows that." She threw her phone in her bag and began packing up her homework to go wherever it was she studied. I'd staked out the library the first night and the common room the next, but I still hadn't found out where she did homework. I needed to get that tracking software loaded sooner rather than later.

"Does Sam know that?"

She stopped for a moment and glared. "We broke up just before summer break. Maybe it's over, maybe it's not."

Damn. "I didn't know he was your ex."

"Now you do." She resumed grabbing every book from her desk and angrily shoving them into her tote bag, even for classes she didn't have the next day. When her bag was zipped, she paused. "Look, I don't give a shit that our dads were once supposedly friends. You're nothing to me. So unless you back off from Sam, I will make you sorry we ever met. Are we clear?"

I wanted to tell her I was already sorry I'd ever crossed her selfish, spoiled path, but I couldn't forget my purpose here. I shrugged. "I'm not interested in Sam." Maybe if I repeated that a thousand more times, I could believe it myself.

My phone chimed as she slammed out the door.

HORSES.

Crap.

"This is exactly what I was talking about!" Major Taylor brandished a smartphone four inches from my face, making it impossible to miss yet another picture of Sam and me.

She'd hauled me though the dark of the empty security offices until we reached her door. The only source of light inside was a single desk lamp, which lent her office a sinister air. I slumped in the same uncomfortable chair as our last interview.

"Now everyone on social media knows what you're capable of! You were supposed to blend in. This is what comes from sending a child to do a soldier's job." She slapped the phone on her desk and paced the small space like an animal in a cage.

Tears welled while I stewed, but I'd rather die than shed one in front of her. She had no clue how lonely it was here. I scrubbed the sleeve of my sweatshirt across my eyes. "Who posted those pictures anyway?"

"It doesn't matter," she fumed. "Everyone in this place watches that Instagram feed like a hawk. You better get on it if you're going to continue to put yourself on display."

I scowled at her. "How was I supposed to know?"

She stopped and took a deep breath, trying to calm down. "People like you and me don't have the luxury of screwing up," she said, her voice as unyielding as concrete. "You must think before you act and be three steps ahead of everyone else. If you don't, you will be gone. That's a promise."

I wasn't a waste of flesh, and I could prove it. "Hayden leaves the room every night for study hall."

"What?" That got her attention.

"Every night about fifteen minutes before we have to sign in for study period, Hayden leaves the dorm. I'm not sure where she goes yet, but as soon as I get my hands on her phone and get the tracking software installed, I will."

She hadn't forgiven me yet, but this had definitely given her something to chew on. "See that you do, and report back to me immediately."

BENSON'S RULE #12
FIGHT FAIR IF YOU CAN, DIRTY IF YOU MUST

My life sucked, I still hadn't been able to get my hands on Hayden's phone, but at least I'd been invited to my first party. The invite came the day following my transformation to social media star. I'd cornered Stef and begged him to show me the ways of Instagram. He'd agreed to meet me after school in the dining hall where we could score lattes and internet access. He helped me set up my account and then follow everyone in the senior class. Since most of the accounts were private, they would have to follow me back if I wanted to see their posts.

"What if no one follows me back?" Mostly I was concerned about the girls. From the way guys were checking me out in the halls, I could probably start an account dedicated to my now-infamous pink sports bra, and they'd follow it.

"Don't worry, they'll follow," Stef assured me. "It's what we do."

He then took me through the rules of the site on his own phone. "You can't post more than once a day, or it's totally pathetic," he said, scrolling through pictures and posts of our classmates. "Save your best selfies for Sundays if you want the most likes, but posting only selfies will brand you a loser."

So far we'd come across four different pictures of Sam and me locked together, and they all had a ton of likes along with several embarrassing comments. Mostly people wanted to know if Sam was tapping more than the mat. It was so humiliating.

"On Man Crush Mondays you can post the picture of your boyfriend, or," he grinned slyly, "the guy you want to be your boyfriend. Woman Crush Wednesday works the same way. I can't wait to see who posts your pic next week."

"That's a thing?" My voice rose an octave. I now had to worry about public declarations of interest? Who the hell came up with this plan?

"Relax," he ordered. "You have a whole week to check everyone out. They're certainly checking you out," he said as he came across yet another photo of me from the gym.

I put my head down on the table in misery. "I'm never leaving my room again. This is too hard. I don't want to play anymore."

He laid his head down next to mine and met my gaze. "You can't stay in your room, or you'll miss the Friday night Survival Party."

I lifted my head. "Party?" I'd been dying to go to a high school party ever since streaming my first R-rated high school movie.

He straightened up with a laugh. "Yep. We're celebrating surviving our first week back. One down, thirty-six to go."

My mind immediately flashed on my new wardrobe. Surely something in there wouldn't feel like a straightjacket. "Please say I get to wear something pretty."

"You better." With a mocking grin he ran a hand through his sculpted hair. "I can't be seen with you otherwise."

That was why I went straight to the dorm after class on Friday, hoping Hayden would spend hours in the bathroom getting ready. I didn't know how long it would take to install the tracking program but calculated her vanity would help me out.

Seated at my desk, I was deep into the weekend's homework by the time she showed up. True to form she ignored me, but it didn't take long for her to plug in her phone. A few minutes later she hit the bathroom. As soon as the shower started running, I jumped up from my chair. Just as I was about to reach for her phone the bathroom door swung open.

We both froze. "Do you have any paper clips?" I blurted, my heart pounding.

She frowned before answering. "In the desk. Top drawer."

I made a show of grabbing a handful before retreating. She snatched up a hairbrush and returned to the bathroom.

Shaking off my nerves, I counted to ten before sneaking across the room again to seize her phone. With the tracking program booted up and waiting, I quickly cabled her phone to my laptop. The slowest thirty seconds of my life crawled by, but finally it bypassed her password and began downloading the software.

Then the water shut off. The girl was part fish; she never took short showers! I jumped to my feet as if that would somehow speed the process. My computer said it needed five more minutes to download, but what if I didn't have that long?

The lock on the bathroom door clicked open, and I leapt back into my chair, covering her phone with my arm. My stomach in turmoil, she padded across the room, pulled a few things out of her armoire, and then, merciful gods, went back to the bathroom. She hadn't even noticed her phone was missing.

Expelling a pent up breath, I counted the seconds until the program finished downloading. With shaking hands I plugged her phone back into the charger and retreated to safety.

A test run revealed Hayden's phone was somewhere within Watson Hall. When I switched the app to tracking, it zeroed in on the phone's exact coordinates... our room.

When Hayden emerged again, I had dressed in a cropped white sweater with a short, black pleated skirt and a military-style jacket thrown on top. I must have done something right because she looked me over with grudging approval. She'd gone with a mash-up of a tight tweed skirt and jacket with a red flannel underneath. It was the kind of outfit only a true trendsetter could pull off.

"Who invited *you* to the party?" she asked.

"Stef." That must have been the right answer because she said, "You're coming with me."

I knew better than to think we were suddenly best friends, but it would save me the trouble of tracking her, so I grabbed my new Céline bag and dutifully followed, locking the door behind us.

It was well past sundown, and the old-fashioned lampposts dotting the walking path were no match for the darkness. Dim pools of light spilled across the trail at even intervals, offering just enough illumination to keep us from stumbling off into the void.

I rubbed the chill from my arms as we trekked right past Hale Hall and toward a giant cement pad serving as a parking lot. Two dozen cars huddled together, most of them covered with gray or beige tarps. Hayden walked up to one and started tugging off the canvas.

"A little help," she ordered. Our efforts revealed a pretty silver Mercedes coup.

"Is this yours?" Silly question, I know, but I didn't even have a driver's license. She rolled her eyes as she stuffed the cover into the compact trunk. Without a word, she got in and started the engine. Feeling awkward waiting for an invitation, I slipped into the passenger seat, though there was no way she'd be allowed to leave campus. Surely Major Taylor had taken steps to prevent that.

We arrived at the front gate and stopped next to the guard kiosk. I waited for the guard to ask her just where she thought she was going, but instead he leaned in with a friendly smile. "Good evening, Miss Frasier. Who is your passenger tonight?"

I stared at them both for a moment. "Uh, Riley Collins."

He made a note on his clipboard and flipped the switch to open the gate. "Have a good evening, ladies."

"You too, Don." We cruised on through.

I swiveled in my seat to face her. "They just let you come and go?" It didn't matter how good or bad Harrington's security was if the billionaire's daughter could leave the school anytime she pleased.

"Seniors have off-campus privileges," she said with impatience, as if

I should know all the rules by now. "Besides, my father knows if he tries to keep me prisoner here, Mom's lawyers will make his life a living hell." She turned the car toward Bridgehurst, the nearest town, and cranked up the music.

Her parents' divorce had played out in the tabloids like a tennis match. Each side had lobbed some killer shots before it was finally settled away from the glare of the spotlight, but it sounded like Mrs. Frasier had not quite finished sharpening her teeth on her ex-husband. No wonder her dad wanted an undercover bodyguard for Hayden.

We drove for a few minutes before coming to a wide spot in the road. On one side was an abandoned diner with a large "for sale" sign propped in a dirty window. On the other was a dimly lit gas station and convenience store called Stop & Shop. She pulled around the side and parked.

"What are we doing here?" I'd been silent up 'til now—who could talk over the volume she played her music at?—but I had a bad feeling about this place. There wasn't another car in sight, and it felt deserted.

"You'll see." She got out of the car, and I followed like a trained puppy.

The only person in the store was the clerk, an overweight woman in a faded T-shirt that may have once had a beer logo emblazoned across the front. Her eyes were glued to the countertop TV, and she paid us no mind as Hayden zipped to the liquor aisle with obvious familiarity.

"We may be in the sticks, but at least they have decent vodka," she said, pointing to the top shelf. "Get a couple of the big bottles of Grey Goose." She wandered a few steps further and selected a large bottle of club soda and a quart of cranberry juice.

"We can't buy this," I hissed, gesturing to the alcohol.

She stalked over with narrowed eyes. "If you want a ride back to school, grab the vodka."

I glared at her. It wouldn't bother me to walk, but Major Taylor's deeply disappointed face flashed through my mind if she learned I'd screwed up what little chance there was of befriending Hayden. I snatched two large bottles off the shelf and stomped my way to the register.

The clerk barely glanced our way, wrapped up as she was in a riveting episode of "Wheel of Fortune". She rang up the alcohol and mixers but before she finished, Hayden grabbed a package of condoms from a nearby display and tossed it on the counter.

"Smart girls always carry protection," she said with a superior air. She paid with cash, and as she stuffed the change into her bag, she nodded at me. "Get that, will you?"

Resisting the impulse to sigh, "Yes, Your Highness," I hauled the large brown bag off the counter and trudged to the door. Hayden halted me just as we stepped outside.

"See that?" She gestured to a cheap security camera mounted overhead, aimed right where we stood. "It looks like we both bought the alcohol for tonight's party, so you better keep your mouth shut."

I resolved to make sure she made it onto Major Taylor's shortlist of people to be airdropped into a snake-infested South American jungle, minus the granola bar. She flounced to the side of the building where we'd left the car but skidded to a halt at the corner. The reason became disturbingly clear when I caught up with her.

Parked next to her pretty car was a tired Ford pickup that had seen better days. Splotches of mud couldn't disguise the rust spots eating through the teal paint, and a crooked coat hanger had been jabbed into the slot where a radio antennae used to be.

The truck's owner and a buddy were running their hands over the Mercedes as if it was a hot date instead of a car. One of them, a lanky guy in his late twenties wearing a dirty T-shirt and battered cowboy hat, gave us a greasy grin. "I don't know who is prettier, you ladies or the car."

His friend straightened from where he'd been peering into the driver's side window. Wearing jeans and an open denim vest over a bare chest, he looked cut from the same cloth, but the creepy way he ran his eyes over me said he was looking for more than a bit of fun.

"Get away from my car," Hayden said in her most imperious manner. She had guts, you had to give her that.

"We don't mean no harm." The cowboy defiantly sat down on the hood of the car. "We like Harrington girls, don't we Tom? They think they're so smart."

Tom ambled to the front and claimed the other side of the hood, though they had to rub shoulders to fit. He noticed the large bag I carried. "You girls looking to party?"

"We are looking to get the hell out here," Hayden snapped as if she were reprimanding the hired help. She crossed her arms in a show of bravado, but I wasn't fooled. Her hands trembled before she balled them into fists.

Their smiles faded, and I got the feeling they were done playing nice. They too must have realized there was a complete lack of security cameras on this side of the building, the lighting was dismal, and there was no one around to help us.

"That's no way to make friends," the cowboy complained. He threw his arm around Tom's bare shoulders.

"I think you'll find my brother and me can be real good friends to you girls," Tom added in a tone promising no such thing.

Without taking my eyes off the pair, I shifted the bag to one hip and quietly slid a hand into my purse. "I haven't been at Harrington for very long," I said in a conversational tone, "but I've already learned the scientific principal of conductivity. How about you get off of the car, and I'll explain it to you?"

Hayden's eyebrows shot skyward as I spoke.

"Better yet," Tom growled, "why don't you come over here and show me?"

I shrugged. "If you insist."

I whipped out the Taser and let loose on Tom. Both barbs latched right onto his naked chest, and since the fools were shoulder to shoulder, the charge went straight through Tom and into the cowboy as well. From the way they both stiffened like they'd been starched, I estimated not a volt was lost as the charge raced through both of their bodies.

"That, gentlemen, is conductivity," I lectured in my best school teacher voice, "and the human body makes an excellent conductor. In this example, Tom has played the part of our conductor while his brother the part of the conductee. Putting an arm around each other just makes it easier to conduct the charge equally between the two of you. Any questions?" I kept up a steady flow of electricity until they slipped off the hood and slumped to the ground. "Apparently not."

"Start the car," I ordered Hayden, handing her the bag as I scampered over to retrieve the electrodes. The two jerks would be stunned, but not for long. We needed to bail.

I was barely in the car before she slammed it in reverse. We were back on the road within seconds. After a couple of minutes of driving in silence, Hayden ventured, "How did you know to do that?"

"A smart girl always carries protection," I dryly observed.

As we neared the gates of Harrington, she said, "Don't think this makes us friends."

"I wouldn't dream of it," I replied.

BENSON'S RULE #13

KNOW WHEN TO SAY WHEN

The crowd was swaying to a thudding beat when Hayden made her fashionably late entrance into Hale Hall. The upper boys' common room mirrored ours, but their sofas were covered in chocolate brown leather, and a pool table had been added to the mix—all very gentlemen's club.

Hayden carried the grocery bag before her like a conquering hero while I trudged behind like the lowly squire. She handed it off to Stef, who hovered next to a giant punchbowl filled with pink juice. It sat on a dining table cluttered with chips and dip, platters of sushi, and stacks of red plastic drinking cups.

"See the man over there with the ugly brown tie?" Hayden nodded to a teacher who must have drawn the short straw to chaperone tonight's party. In a ratty blue cardigan with leather patches on the elbows, he appeared equal parts vigilant and bored. "I know you don't want to get expelled for bringing alcohol on campus," she said with a mocking smile, "so we need to distract him for a minute. Think you can do that?"

"Do I have a choice?" I just kept digging myself in deeper.

"No. I'll block his line of sight, and you start talking. His name is Mr. Gladstone."

Having no clue what to say, I allowed her to drag me across the room.

"Hi, Mr. Gladstone," she greeted him with false enthusiasm. "Have you met my new roommate?" She angled herself as planned while I moved directly in front of him.

"Hi, I'm Riley Collins," I said, forcefully grabbing his hand and pumping it like a used camel salesman. "What subject do you teach?"

"Etymology," he answered, bemused. He craned his neck to look over my shoulder. "Would you mind moving aside? I can't see the drinks table."

"Etymology? That is so interesting!" Pretending I hadn't heard his request, I plowed forward on a subject I'd never studied but had plenty of firsthand experience with. "You must know all about those giant camel spiders we have in the Middle East, huh? Some people think they got their name from stories about how they'd leap up on camels' stomachs and rip out their guts, but that isn't true. They also don't chase people, but if you run, they like to stay in your shadow, which can be pretty funny when it happens to a rookie. The look on their faces," I laughed.

His mouth puckered like he'd sucked on a lemon. "It is *not* entomology, the study of insects. Etymology, my dear Miss Collins, is the study of language."

"Oh," I said, "*parlez vous Francais?*"

He looked heavenward. "Etymology is *linguistics*, Miss Collins. It is the origins of words."

I screwed up my face in confusion. "Doesn't come in very handy when you need to find a bathroom in Dubai, now does it?"

The guy looked ready to run away screaming. Fortunately, we were both rescued when Hayden gave the all clear. "Nice talking with you, Mr. Gladstone." She walked away without a backward glance, leaving me to awkwardly follow.

People excitedly gathered around the punch bowl, and I stood back for a minute and watched. Alcohol was frowned upon at most Middle

Eastern and many Southern Asian embassies, including Karachi, out of respect for Islamic law. I'd never so much as had a sip of champagne at a stateside Christmas party. But I'd signed on for the whole high school experience, so I grabbed a cup. It was fruity and bubbly and tasted pretty good.

The party would give me a chance to break out a little, or at least that was the plan. A few guys had already tried to catch my eye, but they wore those same knowing grins I'd come to dread. I hadn't stepped foot inside the gym since sparring with Sam.

The MMA captain was another conundrum. On one of those frequent peeks I snuck at his lunch table, I had found him looking back. I'd looked away of course, completely mortified, but he'd just grinned in the most devilish way, like we shared some sort of secret. Yeah, I knew that secret: my roommate was his ex, which made him totally off-limits. I took another gulp of punch and pretended indifference.

Across the room, Hayden had surrounded herself with the same small group she sat with at lunch, which included Quinn and Jackie Song. She was at ease as the center of attention, her popularity a natural fit for her. As she spoke, her eyes darted to me once or twice, as did those of her listeners. The story of our encounter with Cowboy and Company would be all over the school within minutes, and I groaned inwardly. I couldn't seem to live up to Benson's rule #11: *Don't bring attention to yourself.*

You can only stand alone at a party for just so long before you feel like a total loser, so I was pathetically grateful when Von swooped in to the rescue. He'd made an effort to dress up a bit and maybe it was the punch talking, but he looked pretty cute.

"Careful with that." He nodded at my drink. "It's all fun and games now, but in the morning you'll feel like your brains have been replaced with rabid squirrels."

I peered into his cup. "Coke?"

"Someone's got to make sure Stef doesn't pass out on the bathroom floor... again." He gestured to the drinks table. The rest of the vodka had been funneled into an empty water jug, and Stef poured a healthy dose over ice.

"He does that a lot?' The Stef I knew was sweet, funny, and generous; not exactly the description of a raging alcoholic.

Von shrugged. "Only on special occasions, like Fridays."

"Shouldn't we try to slow him down?"

He gave me a lopsided grin. "You'd have better luck playing the lottery, but I'm a believer in miracles." He waved his cup at Stef, who knocked the vodka back like it was the water it appeared. "Lead on."

Stef leaned against the table, his eyes momentarily closed as if savoring whatever sensations the liquor evoked. One eye peeked open as we approached. "Ah, fellow inmates," he said, raising his glass. "Shall we drink to being one week closer to parole?" He took a gulp without waiting for a response.

"I didn't realize we were prisoners," I said.

"Oh boy, here we go," groaned Von.

"Didn't you, fair Riley?" Stef said, ignoring the pained look on his roommate's face. "Look around. Everyone here is bound by expectations, by destiny, or by simple accident of birth. Even when we get off of this goddamned breeding farm, none of us will ever really be free."

I shot a sidelong glance at Von, unsure how to respond. "So what is your destiny, Stef?"

He snorted in derision. "Mine? Mine is to be invisible, to not smear the family's good name, because God forbid I embarrass anyone."

Von expelled a long-suffering sigh. "Stef, how 'bout we not go down this road for a change? You don't want to scare Riley off now, do you?"

"Why?" Stef challenged, wobbling slightly. "'Cause I might embarrass you in front of your new girlfriend?"

"Okay, that's enough," Von said firmly. He put his cup down and grabbed Stef's arm. "Come on, man. Let's go sit down for a sec while you get your sea legs." He glanced back at me with a hopeful smile. "You're sticking around, right?"

I tipped my glass in a "no promises" gesture.

Stef allowed himself to be pulled away, but that didn't stop his mouth. "I've told him it's no good, Riley," he called over his shoulder. "All love is doomed. He loves you, you love Sam, Hayden thinks she loves Sam though she has no clue what that means, and who knows who Sam loves 'cause it sure as hell ain't me..."

No one paid any attention as Von deposited him on a sofa. If anything, the determination of those nearby to have a good time ramped up higher as loud laughter rang out. Did they ignore him because they'd heard it all before? Or was it because they recognized some uncomfortable truths in his rant? In some ways, these over-privileged children were as bound by their culture as Farida was by hers.

On my own again, I sipped my drink and checked out the latest arrivals. Thanks to Stef, I knew the names and histories of quite a few. Living up to his nickname of the mayor of Harrington, he'd taken it upon himself to help me fit in as quickly as possible. Every morning before Bracken's class he dished on the school's who's who, and I took full advantage of it.

This morning he'd appeared dressed as the general of his own fabulous army. He'd pinned an array of medals and ribbons to his blazer, and his pants were bloused over the top of combat boots. A jaunty tie worn off center added a final touch of cheek.

"I really wish you'd give some fashion advice to our military," I joked.

He preened. "I know, right? I could give shock and awe a whole new meaning."

"Speaking of advice," I said, pulling a sad face, "can you help me with Hayden? Living with her is like living with a block of ice. I'm not so sure about her."

He grew serious. "You've got to give her a chance. Everyone's always coming at her all 'gimmee, gimmee'." He pretended his hands had become a grasping pair of claws. "Once she realizes you're not a leech, she'll warm up."

He surprised me. "You like her, then?"

Now he was the one surprised. "Of course," he said simply. "I love her."

"Funny, I didn't think she was your type," I said, in an effort to lighten the mood. "Does Von know?"

Stef cackled. "Von? I love him like a brother, but his fashion sense?" He crossed his arms with a cocky air. "All me. I alone have saved him from dressing like an accountant, though bless his little heart, he sure acts like one half the time. I've never met anyone so—what's the word?—precise."

Quinn chose that moment to edge up next to me, bringing me back to the here and now.

"That was some story Hayden told us," she said, punctuating her comment with a sip of punch. She looked great in a gorgeous red dress. "First you wrestle Sam, and now you're off fighting trailer trash. Whatever will you come up with next?"

Her tone wasn't admiring, but neither was it mocking, so I decided to take it at face value. "Hopefully nothing. I just want to settle in and keep my grades up."

"It must be really hard for you, though," she said, sweeping her cup to indicate the crowd of students. "We all come from one world, and you, well..." She shrugged a shoulder.

She hadn't said anything rude, but I'd just been insulted. "For the most part, I was raised in the Middle East, not by aliens," I replied tartly.

She gave me a thin smile. "Do you think that makes any difference here? Let's face it. Even if people are nice to you, you'll never really be accepted."

I stared at her a moment, wondering what she was up to. "And you're telling me this why...?"

Up 'til now we'd stood shoulder to shoulder, looking out over the crowd. Now she turned to face me. "Hayden is going through a really rough time right now. The last thing she needs is to babysit a roommate who has no idea how things work around here. Leave her alone, and I'll make sure no one gives you a hard time, okay?"

My dad once told me negotiating was nothing but a collection of lies ending with an agreement. Maybe he had Quinn in mind when he'd said it. She was right about me not knowing how things worked at Harrington, but that didn't mean I was a fool.

"Thanks, Quinn. That's really nice of you," I said ambiguously. Let her infer whatever she wanted from it.

She smiled. "I'm so glad we understand each other. Well, enjoy the party." She raised her glass in a toast and sailed off. I took a drink, hoping to wash away the bad taste she'd left behind.

I automatically scanned the room for Hayden, and was surprised to find her sitting with Stef. He'd reached the part of the evening where the high had become the low. His head rested on Hayden's shoulder, and she was comforting him. I couldn't help staring at the transformation of my roommate from evil princess to savior.

The flash of a camera caught my eye. Sarah Jane captured the two of them before aiming her phone at another couple. I worked my way across the room and got her attention.

I nodded at her cell. "Are you sure you should be doing that?" I had noticed her at the Narc table at lunch, where all the prefects gathered. They weren't a popular bunch, and I could foresee a few of the jocks getting worked up if they saw her flashing away.

"I'd like to see any of them stop me," Sarah Jane sniffed. "Besides, I'm not taking anything incriminating. Yet. And it's just for our private feed anyway."

Prefects could get away with things the rest of us couldn't. It would be the perfect cover if you wanted to take pictures interesting enough to get tabloids—or people looking to breach Harrington's security—to buy them. But how could I prove it, even if it were true? Sarah Jane openly photographed the party, but with a camera in every pocket, it could be anyone.

Hayden patiently helped Stef off the sofa, though he staggered a bit when he got to his feet. Taking her hand, he docilely allowed himself to be led him out of the party with Von bringing up the rear.

"Don't be too impressed," Sarah Jane scoffed, noticing my interest in Hayden. "Judging from the endless allowance, Daddy probably pays her to keep her brother out of trouble."

My jaw dropped. "Stef is Hayden's *brother*?" They both shared the same airbrushed beauty of a Disney princess but were miles apart in personality. It suddenly explained his affection for her.

"Half-brother on the dad's side while he was still married to

Hayden's mom. Hard to believe, huh?" She snapped a few more pictures. "She's Teflon, and he'd probably blow over in a strong wind. Maybe if you rolled them into one, you'd have a halfway normal person who could survive rehab."

I frowned, still staggered by the revelation. "That's a bit harsh, don't you think?"

She lowered her phone. "Look, Riley, I don't know about you, but I'm here on scholarship. I don't have the luxury of feeling sorry for people who have everything yet value nothing. Do you?" Her eyes flicked to my cup as I took another drink. "You seem like a decent person, but you better catch on quick. People like us don't get second chances."

She left me with my mouth hanging open once more. Did her position give her access to my files, and had she learned why I'd been sent to Harrington? Was she warning me about something specific? I took another sip of my drink, but it had lost its charm.

Why had I not been told that Stef was Stephen Frasier's son? Was the different last name supposed to buy him anonymity? Shouldn't I be watching out for him as well as Hayden? Wouldn't he be an equally valuable bargaining chip if kidnapping and ransom were your stock in trade? This made no sense to me, but a lot of things had begun to look a little fuzzy in the last few moments.

I wove my way through the ever-growing crowd to find a place to toss my almost empty cup, but smacked right into a solid wall of pale blue cotton. My eyes traveled upward into Sam's amused face. "I was looking forward to our next match, but maybe we should take it to the gym, don't you think?"

It took a moment or two to register his shirt smelled like clean laundry, and that my hand still rested on his chest where I'd braced myself when we collided. "Oh," I said, dropping my hand and taking a step back.

He pretended not to notice my pink cheeks. "So when are you coming back to the gym?"

"Oh," I repeated, my verbal skills deserting me. "I, uh, don't know if that's a good idea."

His smile wavered. "I bet we barely scratched the surface on your moves. Why would you want to stop sparring?"

I made the mistake of looking directly into those deep blue eyes but still somehow managed to murmur, "It's, uh, complicated."

"Is the complication Hayden?" He sounded disappointed. "I'm asking you to spar, not get married."

"Of course not, I mean, I know," I sputtered. Feeling like a complete fool, I took the last big gulp of my drink to mask my embarrassment. Unfortunately, I still wasn't prepared for the way the alcohol burned my throat, and I started to cough like a typhoid patient.

"Easy there, killer," he said, thumping me good-naturedly on the back. He took my cup and gave it a sniff. "What the hell are you drinking?"

"It seemed like a good idea at the time," I choked out, feeling light-headed.

He thrust his own cup at me. "Here, it's cranberry juice." He watched me take a few tentative sips. "Have you eaten anything?" When I shook my head, he sighed. "Drinking on an empty stomach is suicide. You know that, right?"

He grabbed my hand and started pulling me through the crowd. We were making progress, so obviously my feet were functioning, but it was if I sailed effortlessly across the room. The music pulsed all the way into my bones, and the faces turned to us as we drifted past registered in a dreamy haze.

A blast of cold air broke through the fog, and I realized we were outside. "Where are we going?" It occurred to me we were alone on one of the dark walking paths, though for some reason it was hard to get worked up about it.

"To Watson." He linked his arm with mine, and we strolled side by side toward my dorm. "You need to eat something, and then you need to go to bed. How much did you drink tonight?"

"Just some of that pink juice." I tried to recall if I'd ever drunk anything pink before. "What drink is pink, anyway?" I looked around at the alien landscape and suddenly longed for the familiar hallways of the Karachi embassy. "I don't belong here. I was so foolish to think I could fit in."

"Oh, I don't know. I think you're the most interesting thing that's happened around here in quite a while," he assured me.

"That's because you don't know me." I lurched to a stop and grabbed onto his shirt. "What if you found out I wasn't who you thought I was? What if I was sent here with a mission?" The words tumbled out unfiltered.

"What, like a tabloid reporter?" He wasn't taking me seriously.

"No, I'm one of the good guys," I insisted. "But I have secrets, Sam."

He seemed to think that was pretty funny. "Don't worry. They'll be safe with me."

I tipped my head back. "Everything is so different here, even the stars." Ever since I could remember, the constellation of Gemini, my birth sign, waited for me in the nighttime sky. The unfamiliar collection of stars now overhead only reinforced how alone and far from home I was. How was I supposed to survive in this alternate universe?

"It gets better," he said softly, his face also upturned to the heavens. "I left all my friends when my mom moved us to New York last year. It's the hardest thing I've ever had to do." He turned to me. "The trick is to find one thing every day you like, or at least that you don't hate. Do it long enough, and you'll finally realize it's okay. Can you think of one thing right now you don't hate?"

"I don't hate you," I said in a tone that made it clear just how much I didn't hate him.

He grinned before tugging me back into motion. "This is your stop," he said when we arrived at my dorm. "Will you be okay?"

"Sure," I said airily. "I'm always okay. Just ask anyone at the embassy, and they'll tell you I'm fine, fine, fine."

He laughed. "Yep, you're fine alright. I can't wait to hear how fine you are in the morning." He did a quick sweep of the lobby. "The warden isn't at her desk. I'd haul ass upstairs if I were you." I waved in his general direction before staggering to the elevator.

The third floor was quiet since so many of the girls were at the party.

I reached my room, but froze when I noticed the door slightly ajar. I was positive I'd locked it... at least I thought I was positive.

My Taser useless without a fresh cartridge, I silently pushed the door open and swayed at the threshold. My laptop sat on the nightstand where I'd left it. Nothing appeared to have been disturbed.

I needed to check the bathroom and open the closet doors, but I suddenly didn't feel so well. I collapsed onto my bed and blindly yanked up the comforter. Maybe if I could lie down for a few minutes, the room would stop spinning. I counted my breaths. Each time I made it to ten without running to the bathroom to hurl was a victory.

I had been wrong. This wasn't an alternate universe. This was hell.

BENSON'S RULE #14

STAY AWARE AND STAY ALIVE

I wasn't sure if the pounding came from the inside or outside of my skull. Cracking my eyes open a hair, I groaned as rays of burning light went right past the retinas and straight into my brain.

"It's about time," Hayden said from across the room. She yanked on a pair of jeans. "It's almost noon."

I glared at her. "For the love of Allah, unless you're planning to kill me and end my misery, can you stop talking? Please?"

She laughed. "It's not my fault you can't handle your liquor."

I slowly assumed a sitting position, but had to grab my head to keep it from rolling off my shoulders.

"Aspirin and water." She zipped up her pants before sitting down to pull on boots. "Some people say you should eat greasy food or drink raw eggs, but that's just bullshit."

I watched her through squinted eyelids. "Why are you being so nice to me?"

She shrugged a shoulder. "Maybe you're not such a total loser after all."

"Gee, thanks." And all it took was blowing off my moral code, risking assault charges, and braving a really massive hangover to prove it. Of course, maybe she hadn't yet heard about Sam walking me out of the party last night. I could only hope he'd had the good sense to dash right back.

Once she cleared out, I took her advice. After popping four aspirin, I chugged a bottle of water and collapsed back in bed. An hour later, I managed to shuffle down the hall to the common room. The place was a ghost town. Most likely I wasn't the only senior in a world of hurt. I scrounged up a bagel and a banana before returning to my room to hibernate.

It was dark when I woke again. Snapping on my bedside lamp, I was pissed an entire day of my life had been shot to hell. And I was alone. How much did I suck as a secret agent? My mark was nowhere to be found, and I'd nearly poisoned myself.

A quick check of the clock told me Benson would just be waking up in Karachi to hit the gym. Without getting out of bed, I grabbed my laptop for a little love and maybe a pep talk.

"Darlin' girl!" He paused to take a closer look at the image on his screen. "Why do you look like road kill?"

"Don't ask," I groaned. "I'm in an adjustment period, okay?"

He didn't look convinced. "If you say so. How was the first week?"

I sighed. "Harder than I thought it would be, but not for the reasons you'd think."

"Let's start at the beginning. Did you make friends with your target?"

I let my head plop back on the pillow. "I don't know. I think I'm making progress, but her best friend's up to something, and the guy she likes..." I trailed off, unsure of what I felt, let alone trying to explain it to Benson.

"Riley." The playfulness was gone. "You have only one task, and that is to stay close to the subject. You must do whatever is necessary to gain her confidence, as long as it doesn't go against your principles. Are we clear?"

Spoken like a lifelong soldier.

I stared at the ceiling, giving Benson a nice view of my chin. "But there's this guy..."

He muttered a four-letter under his breath. I popped back up, but regretted it instantly when my brain sloshed around inside my skull. Probably time for another shot of aspirin.

"The mission comes first," he said simply.

"It's not like he's her boyfriend. I mean, he's her ex, but I think I like him, but I don't know if he likes me…" I stopped, noticing his complete lack of sympathy. "I thought you of all people would understand."

He took a swig from his coffee cup. "It's not that I don't understand, but you can't let personal feelings interfere with your mission. You run the risk of putting both of your lives in danger."

I grumbled in frustration. "I've practically lived in a freaking convent my entire life, and when I finally meet someone worth talking to, I have to back off because Veruca Salt wouldn't like it."

He looked confused. "I thought her name was something-Frasier."

"It is!" I shifted gears. "Never mind. Let's talk about *your* love life. Your ex is quite a piece of work." I told him about my initial meeting with Major Taylor, and the installation of the tracking software. The tale of my second encounter with her—and the reason for it—could wait.

"Doesn't sound like she's mellowed much," he said fondly. "So where is your Veruca Salt now?"

I grabbed my phone and pulled up the app. My face transformed into a pout when I realized she was in the upper boys' dorm. "Probably in pursuit of Mr. Hottie as we speak."

We spoke a few more minutes. He told me how quiet it had been at the embassy, and that I should call back later tonight to check in with my dad. "You'd think you were living on the moon with the way he mopes about." That was a huge exaggeration, I was sure, but it was good to be missed.

"Oh, one more thing," I said as we were saying our goodbyes. "I'm not positive, but someone may have broken into our room last night."

He stiffened. "And you waited this long to tell me? Have you swept for cameras or bugs? What about your computer for malware?"

"No," I admitted. It was the most basic of directives.

"Do it now. Do you have a bug sweeper?"

"Sure, I packed it along with my rocket launcher."

"Sarcasm is the refuge of a simple mind," he admonished. "Use your cell phone like I showed you, but expect a package from me this week. It's time to identify your friends... and eliminate your enemies."

"You're right," I said, properly chastised.

He rang off almost immediately so I could commence my search.

Stars shot through my field of vision as I struggled to my feet. When I could move without passing out, I called the tech support line for my old brand of phone. The debugging hack required a phone call to be put on indefinite hold, and they were masters at that. When an automated voice said my call was forty-third in line for a customer representative, I put the call on speaker and slowly walked around the room, waving the phone as I went. When I neared my nightstand, the clicking noises bleeding through the dead air were unmistakable.

"Son of a bitch," I muttered. The electromagnetic field emitted by many bugs and cameras could often be pinpointed this way. Benson said it wasn't a perfect system, but it could sometimes do in a pinch. I got down on my knees and found a small listening device taped underneath the nightstand.

The phone's shrill beeping nearly stopped my heart. It was Karen on call waiting. Quickly attempting to weigh the pros and cons of answering the phone with one hand while holding a bug in the other would have been easier if my brain wasn't moving in slow motion.

"Hello?" I already regretted my choice.

"Are you alone?" No chitchat for her.

"No." For all I knew, the entire world could be listening.

"Call me back when you are," she ordered. "It's time for a report."

More homework. Great. "Okay," I sighed, switching back to the other line.

An extensive search turned up a second bug taped under Hayden's desk. Marching into the bathroom, I flushed them out of existence.

I flopped down on my bed, exhausted by the effort and freaked out by what might have been overheard, and more importantly, who was behind it. There hadn't been any cameras, but I sure wouldn't be walking around naked anytime soon. A check of my laptop revealed no activity during the time of the party, but I made a mental note to ask Benson for a debugging program.

Were the bugs planted last night, or had someone entered our room for another purpose? Who could possibly be interested in the almost nonexistent conversation between Hayden and me? Quinn? Another student? An inside man on campus?

I bolted upright, much to my chagrin, as I realized whoever planted the bugs had overheard my entire conversation with Benson. Not only had someone broken into my room, but whoever had been listening now knew the real reason I had come to Harrington.

I immediately Skyped Benson on my computer. "We've got a problem."

"Bloody hell," he swore, after hearing what I'd found. "Make sure you let Grace know."

I could happily go the rest of my life without ever crossing paths with Major Taylor again, but he was right. With a demand to call immediately if anything else weird came up, Benson signed off.

Grabbing my phone to return Karen's call, I was surprised to find a text from Sam waiting on the screen. I recognized his number from the online student directory. *Are u still fine, fine, fine?*

I pulled a pillow over my head in embarrassment. Oh God, what else did I say last night? *You can't hold a girl responsible for things she says while under the influence of stupidity,* I texted back.

Almost immediately my phone pinged with another text. *LMAO.*

I'm glad one of us was.

It wasn't until Sunday morning that I began to feel human again. Waking before Hayden, I quietly pulled on some Lycra leggings and the rest of my running gear. I braided my hair into one thick plait and pulled a knit cap over my ears. Frost hung in the air, but I was so grateful to be out of pain it was a refreshing relief.

Seeing the drone and finding the bugs meant it was time to get busy with a plan of action. Stretching into a runner's lunge, the first thing to do was to scope out the perimeter. Benson could describe every building, road, or shrub outside any given embassy within twenty-four hours of our arrival.

"Stay aware and stay alive," he would say. He not only formulated escape plans, he gauged where potential attacks would likely be staged. The river running past Harrington would be judged a weak spot. Approaches on water could be made silently, departures executed swiftly.

Tightening the laces on my trainers, I set out. The only other people on campus up this early were a few fellow joggers. I nodded to one while running past the stables, relieved there wasn't a single horse in sight.

I continued on toward the river, finding a sandy path carved into the shoreline between the water and the trees. Hitting my stride along the waterway, I noted the location of the dock and boathouse where half a dozen guys in spandex leggings and windbreakers were lowering one of the long, sleek boats into the water.

My thoughts turned to the call I'd had with my so-called Aunt Karen last night. It hadn't gone well.

"Why the hell didn't you tell me about Rose Winters?" I demanded, my *hangover stripping away all of my ingrained civility.* "I'm sleeping in a dead *girl's bed!"* It was creepier said aloud.

"Because Hayden Frasier's new roommate wouldn't have read the girl's FBI file before starting school, that's why," she shot back. *"Your reaction to the news had to be genuine."*

A childish urge had made me want to withhold news of the bugs and the drone, but I didn't. I would show them all I could be trusted with this mission.

The running path veered away from the river and curved just inside the high brick wall fronting the road to Harrington. I followed it to the main gate, where a couple of guards stood watch. Cameras were positioned to capture both incoming and outgoing traffic, but talk about a drop in the bucket. We might as well stick Hayden out in the road with a big shiny bow around her neck for all the good those few cameras would do.

When I finally came to where the wall ended, I turned my back on the road and ran along a loose boundary of trees and shrubs. As I crested the rise overlooking the lacrosse and hockey fields, I spied a herd of deer grazing complacently on the emerald green lawn. In the far distance, a thick stand of dense forest defined the back of the school's property. The river was the least of the school's worries. This place was a security nightmare.

"Riley!" Von jogged up, his mop of thick brown hair shoved under a navy blue knit cap. He wore gray sweats and a hoodie partially unzipped to reveal a sweaty T-shirt. He was such a great guy. Maybe I could forget about Sam and learn to like him instead. And maybe I could bring peace to the Middle East, and get everyone to sing kumbaya.

"Where did you go Friday night?" He fell into step just as we passed the dog kennels. Several excited yaps marked our passing. "You disappeared."

"More like dropped off the earth," I replied, not bothering to hide my disgust.

He laughed. "Not used to drinking?"

"No, and I don't plan to be." I was both desperate and terrified to fully remember what I'd said or done on the walk home with Sam. "How can anyone go through that more than once?"

"Beats me. I don't drink either." His tone said he could care less what anyone else thought of his choices.

"How do you do that?" I asked in a peeved voice. "How do you just do whatever you want, and people still think you're cool?"

He let out a short laugh. "Is that what you think? You really don't know much about high school."

"Are you kidding me? I know everything about high school. I've seen every single episode of *Gossip Girl* and *90210*... including the remake."

He laughed again. "Because those shows are so true to life."

I grinned. "Are you telling me you don't jet off to Paris or the Bahamas on every school break?"

"Nah, I don't like French food, and too much sun irritates my skin," he said.

We reached the densely wooded stretch of land running behind the school. The growth was so old and thick, an entire team of mercenaries could be lurking just a few feet inside and you'd never spot them. The trees also formed a natural barrier. It was a good bet any trouble visiting Harrington wouldn't come from that direction.

"Are trees a particular interest of yours?" Von broke into my thoughts.

"Oh... well... there just aren't many evergreens in Pakistan." I quickly switched gears. "By the way, what's the story with Hayden and Stef? Why does she get all the attention?"

The woods sloped down toward the river, and we slowed our gait to a trot.

"I'm kind of surprised she even stayed at Harrington after Rose's death," he said. "It can't be easy for her to see a total stranger take Rose's place."

I stopped as his words hit me. Von jogged a few more paces before doubling back.

"I'm a complete jerk, aren't I?" I said, not really needing an answer to know how thoughtless I'd been. I'd been so eager to prove myself, I hadn't given any thought to how my presence affected Hayden. How must she feel being saddled with a complete outsider, just days after the loss of her best friend?

"Don't be too hard on yourself," he said. "Come on, time for a cool down."

We downshifted to a walk, rounding back to the sandy path by the river.

"Hayden's a survivor—she has to be with those parents of hers," he said. "It's Stef I worry about."

"You guys are roommates, right?"

He nodded. "He's three months younger than Hayden, and his mom is not the movie star ex-wife."

I grimaced. "That can't be easy."

"Who knows?" He shrugged, obviously having little sympathy for the adults who'd put their kids into such an awkward position. "Whatever agreement Stef's mom made with Stephen Frasier, she got him to promise to give their son the same advantages as Hayden. That's why Stef's mom insisted he come to Harrington." Where he continually had to be reminded of his second-class status.

"At least he's still a member of the family," I observed.

"Barely." Von pulled up the hem of his T-shirt to swab his sweaty face, revealing surprisingly awesome abs. "Frasier hardly acknowledges his son, and I don't think Hayden knew about him until a few years ago."

"Why?" My heart ached for Stef. "Is it because he's illegitimate, or because he's gay?"

Von shrugged again. "Who knows with a guy like Frasier, but every month, Stef sinks deeper into his own personal hellhole of rejection."

Homosexuality was illegal in most Middle Eastern countries. I'd heard stories of gay men being stoned, murdered by militants, or sometimes killed by their own families in so-called honor killings. The only openly gay man I'd ever known, a tough as nails army Corporal named Mendoza, had risked his life getting my dad out of a dangerous spot in Syria. Surely Mendoza had proven his worth a dozen times over, and whatever he did in his personal life was no one's concern but his.

"Isn't there anyone here who can help? A counselor, an LGBT group, something?"

"Sure, but that's the thing about self-loathing," he observed. "You're not good enough to be in any club that would have you as a member."

"Has Hayden tried talking to their dad?"

Von shrugged. "She does the best she can, which is spending her nights doing homework with him in Hale's common."

Yes! So that's where she disappeared to every night, and I didn't even need technology to find out. Score one for secret agent girl.

"You could come, too," he said with a grin. "Calculus would be a lot more fun if we did it together."

"So says the guy with the perfect scores," I laughed. "I saw your grade on Thursday's pop quiz, you know."

"You know what they say about mathematicians," he said with a comical leer. "We must do it constantly to prove ourselves."

I rolled my eyes. "I'm afraid this mathematician only does it in theory."

He laughed as I continued my subtle interrogation—disguised as flirting, of course—about our classmates. We walked to the benches fronting the duck pond to stretch, but somewhere in the corner of my mind I had to think that if Stef ever learned I'd been sent here to protect one Frasier family member but not the other, it would confirm his darkest fears.

When I got back to my room, I tiptoed past my sleeping roommate to grab a shower before dutifully texting Major Taylor the dreaded code word. She needed to know about the listening devices. I prayed ZEBRAS would never be needed; HORSES got her plenty worked up.

I next went on Instagram and learned Stef had been right; it appeared everyone in the senior class *had* followed me back, even Hayden. With access to everyone's accounts, I laboriously scrolled back through the last several months of posts.

Rose Winters was quickly becoming more than just a name or a tragic story. She'd been a real girl who'd been friends with the people I was coming to know, a girl who'd probably wanted many of the same things I did. It was a foolish notion, this need for connection, but I wanted to see her selfies, which posts she favorited, and what pictures she thought important enough to share.

The first picture I found of her was with Hayden. It was on the last day of classes, and the roommates had their arms slung happily around each other's shoulders as they celebrated the end of finals. A little further back were more photos, sometimes in a group, sometimes alone, but almost always with Hayden. Quinn popped up often in the pictures with Hayden and Rose, but her expression was never as relaxed as those of the other two girls.

There was nothing romantic about the photos of Rose and Hayden, or the trust and comfort they displayed with each other. They were simply best friends. My momentary stab of envy was swiftly replaced with profound sadness. Poor Rose. Poor Hayden.

Then something else caught my eye. Several of the photos were familiar. I dropped to the floor and ran my hand underneath the bottom of my bed, where I'd stashed my ID card along with all the other sensitive documents Karen had handed over. The lining had already been ripped when I arrived, making it easy to use the box springs as a hiding spot.

Extracting the copies of the photos sold to the gossip rags, I compared them to ones on the class Instagram account. Sure enough, every illicitly brokered picture could be found on the site as well, posted by a number of students. They couldn't all be in on the sale of the photos.

I tossed my copies back into the envelope with disgust. This was a fool's errand. It didn't matter who took them; anyone could have pulled those photos off the feed and sold them. Besides, with drones flying over the property, anyone could be photographing the campus.

I'd rolled onto the floor again to tuck away my secrets, pushing the envelope deep into the springs, when my fingers brushed against something solid. It came out easily with a tug, and I discovered it was an expensive cell phone that was almost new except for the shattered screen. The rest of it was protected by a pretty white case decorated with a red rose.

It must have belonged to Rose, of course, which answered the question of why she had gone out to buy a new one. But why was it stashed in the bedsprings?

The pile of blankets across the room stirred as Hayden chose that moment to wake. I shoved the phone under the mattress and climbed to my feet. As intrigued as I was by the lengths Rose had gone to hide it, the phone's discovery would remain a secret for now.

If a dead girl had thought it was important enough to keep hidden, then so did I.

BENSON'S RULE #15

PARANOIA IS YOUR FRIEND

At the appointed hour that night, I reported to the security offices. As soon as Major Taylor closed her door and flipped on the desk lamp, I told her about the bugs planted in our room.

Her body stiffened. "What kind were they?"

I regarded her blankly. "I don't know... the listening kind?"

She leaned against a corner of her desk and folded her arms. "Depending on the make and model, we might be able to discern if they were just installed, of if they've been there for a while. Do you still have them?"

I shuffled my feet. "Well, no. I might have flushed them down the toilet." I mean, really, how many people were likely to get bugged around here?

She exhaled a frustrated sigh at my rookie mistake.

"At least I can tell you where Hayden's been going at night."

"Where?"

"She's been going to the upper boy's dorm to do homework with her brother. Which brings me to my next question: why didn't anyone tell me Stef was Hayden's half-brother? Isn't anyone worried about him?"

"You are an untested field agent. Until proven otherwise, you will only be given the information necessary for you to accomplish your job. As for the boy..." She shrugged.

A flush of righteous anger on Stef's behalf stained my cheeks, but expressing it would accomplish nothing.

She picked up a paper from the top of a stack. "Incidentally, we got a report from the Bridgehurst police that two men were attacked Friday night in the parking lot of the Stop & Shop by two young women driving an expensive car. Do you know anything about that?"

I steeled my expression to remain as neutral as possible but was still grateful for the long, concealing shadows thrown by the room's only source of light. "No, ma'am."

"Hmm," she murmured. "It does match up with the time you and the Frasier girl were off campus." Her voice held a trace of humor, letting me know she didn't believe a word of my denial, but she wouldn't be losing sleep over a couple of yahoos. "Very well. Is there anything else?"

"Actually, there is." I told her about my reconnaissance of the campus, and what I'd observed of the school's appalling lack of security. If that drone had been sent to check the place out, whoever controlled it now knew, too. "But what difference does it make if she can leave without a security detail anytime she wants?" The irony of those words coming from my mouth was not lost on me.

"You mean actually bring this place into the real world? That's a laugh. I should march you into McKenna's office. Maybe you'll have better luck convincing the old bat she's living in a fairytale." She tossed the police report back on her desk with disgust. "She's so concerned with her precious image that she hasn't even allowed us to install closed-circuit cameras outside the school buildings."

"I don't understand. How could that be an image problem?" Surveillance devices were so small and discreet these days, most of the time you never knew they were there.

"What if pictures of our students in an embarrassing moment were leaked to an outside source? What if the systems were hacked to track the movements of certain high profile students such as Miss Frasier? What if some bleeding-heart liberal parent, especially one who keeps the money flowing around here, thought it was a violation of privacy?" She ticked the reasons off on her fingers, growing increasingly agitated as she went. She obviously didn't find McKenna's arguments valid.

"Are you saying the only thing between Hayden and the outside world are a few rent-a-cops and me?" My body went cold. I wasn't Hayden's last line of defense. I was pretty much her only line of defense.

I gracelessly dropped into a chair, surprised to see Major Taylor eyeing me with sympathy. "Look, your only job is to act as another pair of eyes and ears for us, not put yourself in any danger. We'll keep Hayden Frasier safe."

She was trying to make me feel better, and I appreciated it, but it wasn't working. Those bugs were proof someone had their eye on us, and it was foolish to keep Hayden here. It was even more ridiculous someone with Major Taylor's supposed standing had been called in to oversee a facility where even the deer could come and go at will.

"Please don't take this the wrong way," I ventured, "but are you here because of some disciplinary action?" Benson had taken on a few troublemakers at some of our more remote outposts, so I knew how the military worked. If you screwed up, you got sent to some hellhole in the outer reaches of Mongolia, or in this case, a prep school.

"Absolutely not!" All friendliness vanished. "I have the highest commendations, a spotless record, and if all goes well here, I'll be promoted to lieutenant colonel as soon as Frasier's new software is delivered."

"That's what I was afraid of." She shot me a look of impatience, so I rushed to explain. "Think about it. If there weren't any real threats, would they have sent such a valuable asset—you, that is—to protect her? What's weirder is they've allowed Hayden to remain here and she can leave campus anytime she wants. It doesn't make sense."

Major Taylor appeared thoughtful, but she couldn't shed any light on what the powers-that-be had in mind either.

Sometimes that was just the way the military rolled.

As if wearing a uniform five days a week wasn't enough, Monday night dinners were decreed as formal dress. I would have been happy to make do with sweats and a vending machine meal, but the only way to escape these nights was to be carried out on a stretcher.

I'd managed to grab the first shower and had slipped into black, silky trousers and a soft, gray sweater, the closest thing to pajamas I could find. Hayden emerged from the bathroom just as I slapped on some lipstick and used my fingers to fluff my wilted curls.

"You look... really great," she said, pausing to give me the once-over before crossing to her own armoire. She'd wrapped her hair in a messy bun, and her shower had caused pretty little curls to spring up about her face.

"Thanks," I said, tugging at my pants. "The handbook was pretty vague. I didn't know how dressed up to be."

"Neither do the freshman," she said, her eyes twinkling with humor. "After the rumors we circulated, some of them will show up in tuxedos and ball gowns."

It wasn't exactly the hazing Benson's recruits often endured—usually involving a big spaghetti dinner followed by a ten-mile run—but we'd take our fun where we could.

She turned to dress while I slid on a pair of patent leather heels. This was the most relaxed we'd ever been around each other. I could either silently enjoy it or possibly screw it up royally by opening my mouth.

"I'm really sorry about Rose," I said softly. Her back stiffened, but that was the only indication she'd heard me. "I've never had a best friend," I confessed. "We moved too much, and it's not like there were many other kids around anyway. But I do know losing someone leaves a hole that can't be filled."

I had no memory of my mom, but I still missed the idea of her. Someone to tell me the reason my hair got brittle was I rinsed it too much after conditioning. Or that wearing pastels made me look like an Easter egg, or that underwear came in colors other than white.

The silence grew oppressive, and I'd just decided I was a complete fool when Hayden turned around. She'd pulled on a clingy navy dress with an exposed silver zipper running from neckline to hem.

"Thanks," she said, drawing on a pair of boots. "Are you ready? Let's go."

BENSON'S RULE #16

MAKE YOUR COVER WORK FOR YOU

As I strolled through the halls the next morning, people I'd never met called out a greeting. My probation, it seemed, was officially over.

It wasn't like Hayden and I were suddenly a matched set, but the truce that started in our room carried over to dinner. Glimpses of the outgoing girl I imagined existed prior to Rose's death slowly came into view as she became more talkative, and she made a point of including me in the conversation. I'd sat on one side of her, and Quinn on the other. It had been kind of fun.

There wasn't a set time period for mourning, but pain can only be endured for so long. Then it must be tucked away and revisited only in quiet moments when the wounds aren't so fresh. At least that's what my dad once told me.

"Look at you, Miss Popular." Sam fell into step, grinning all the way.

We'd given up the pretense I wasn't checking him out at meals. Now he often met my glance with one of his own, usually with a goofy smile or some other silliness.

"I cannot be seen talking to you," I said with a smile that completely contradicted my words.

He danced ahead a step, so we faced each other for a moment. "Even if it's to tell me what it is you don't hate today?" His expression said he, too, was remembering our walk under the stars.

"No," I said, laughing. "I'd like to be able to sleep at night without worrying about my roommate shaving my head or something."

"What if I talked to her? Maybe if I tell her I only want to smack you around in the gym, she might even pay to watch," he teased.

We'd reached my classroom, but neither of us was ready to end our banter. What I wouldn't have given in that moment to make everyone else disappear just long enough to pull him into a kiss.

I shook off the image. "Maybe she'll pay to see *me* smack *you* around, ever think about that, *mon capitane*?"

"All the time, Riley, all the time." With a wink he sheared off, leaving me with thoughts in my head that had no place in World Geography.

I floated into class and collapsed in my seat.

"Somebody's having a good morning." Stef's voice penetrated the fog.

"Oh, you know," I said, waving my hand airily. He'd seen the change in Hayden at dinner, but hopefully not the way Sam and I had been flirting just now.

He didn't probe any further as he scrolled through the morning's Instagram posts.

"Anything good?" I shot a meaningful glance at his phone.

"Too early in the day," he sighed. "And once again, another Man Crush Monday has come and gone, and I'm still on the shelf."

All conversation ended with the arrival of the Kraken, and the class immediately shifted gears.

An hour later, the bell finally rang, but before we could push back our chairs Mr. Bracken appeared in front of our table. "Mr. Corbett, you are excused. Miss Collins, a word." He spun around and marched back to his desk, leaving Stef and me to exchange questioning glances. Slinging my backpack over my shoulder, I begrudgingly followed my teacher to the front of the room.

He waited until the last student had filed out before looking up from grading papers. His red pencil had already slashed and burned through a small stack of last Friday's pop quiz on ancient Roman cities. He had a perpetually sour look his face, so it was hard to tell what he was thinking as he met my gaze.

"Would you like to see your quiz?" It was not the question I expected.

"Uh, yes, sir." He sorted through papers covered in red chicken scratches. One even had 'WERE YOU HIGH WHEN YOU TOOK THIS TEST?' scribbled across it. He found my paper and handed it over. It was the same as when I'd turned it in without any grading marks whatsoever.

"I don't get it," I said. "Is there something wrong?"

He leaned back in his swivel chair, the wood protesting with a loud groan. "No, there's nothing wrong. In fact, it's perfect."

We stared at each a few moments. "Um, thank you?"

He laced his fingers over his slight paunch. "No one has ever gotten that particular quiz completely correct."

A rush of heat shot through me as I put two and two together. "This is my own work! I swear I didn't cheat! In fact..." I halted abruptly when he calmly raised a hand, calling for silence.

"It was a pop quiz, for Pete's sake, it's not like you knew it was coming."

My anger cooled, but not completely. The guy was toying with me. "I'm going to be late for my next class, so if that's all..."

"I need a teacher's aide."

I took half a step back in surprise. "What does that mean, exactly?"

He waved a hand over the papers on his desk. "Grading tests, logging in scores, some light filing..." He glanced at his empty coffee cup. "And black with two sugars."

"And you want me?"

He cut me the thousand mile stare he usually reserved for people who asked abusrd questions. "Unless you're now the head of Human Resources, and I clear my personnel needs through you, yes."

I shifted my backpack, a delaying tactic while I wrapped my head around his offer. "Would that mean I ace the class?" That wasn't a real concern, but less homework would free me up to focus more on my mission.

He scoffed. "Hardly. You would still be expected to know that the Balkans are *not* an alien race on *Star Trek*."

Extra work and more time spent with a teacher who had the grating personality of an overworked camel? No thanks.

"It's really nice of you to ask, but I'm just getting the hang of things around here."

The chair squeaked again as he sat upright. "I gave you more credit, Miss Collins. I would have at least expected you to ask what's in it for you."

I felt like smacking my head over such a rookie move. My dad always said to never walk away from a one-sided negotiation without finding some leverage, even if you had to beat it out of them with a crowbar. "You're right. I guess you caught me off-guard here. Please tell me why I should accept the position."

His eyes gleamed like a marketplace vendor who was about to close a sale. "First, a letter of recommendation from a highly-regarded instructor at Harrington will carry a lot of weight on your college application." I had no clue what kind of reputation he had with college administrators, but his tone conveyed I should take this seriously. "And secondly, I wouldn't be so quick to dismiss a valuable ally, if I were you. From what I hear, you might need one."

My shoulders stiffened. "What have you heard, sir?" Had the local police gone over Major Taylor's head to report the scuffle at the Stop & Shop to McKenna?

"Let me put it this way," he said, with a Cheshire cat grin. "Something is making people nervous around here, and the only thing I've been able to learn is it somehow involves you."

Everyone had their phones in hand as classes let out for lunch. A lot of people posted just prior to the midday break because it was one of the few times of day everyone checked the school feed at the same time. Racking up "likes" was very important around here.

I didn't think much of it until entering the dining hall. Several people turned to look at me—too many. My stomach curled. Couldn't I get through an entire day in this place without falling flat on my face? I hurried toward the food stations and then kept going, bolting right through one of the kitchen doors.

The lunch ladies bustled about the stove and prep area, but paid me no mind as I found a patch of white-tiled wall to lean up against. Embassy kitchens were always warm and hospitable places, and I grew up knowing there were always treats and a sympathetic ear to be found there. Not so at Harrington. The first time I'd said "thank you" to a white-aproned woman handing me a plate of lasagna I thought she'd faint. There was an unspoken divide between the students and the staff.

It didn't take long to figure out what had everyone's attention. A photo of Sam and me talking this morning had made the school feed. The picture had captured my body as it leaned toward his. There wasn't a caption, but my expression betrayed exactly what was on my mind. And Quinn had posted it.

First I wanted to strangle my phone, then Quinn, and then myself. How could I have been so careless? Benson had accused me of ignoring inconvenient truths, and he was right. Quinn had fired a few warning shots, and I'd been too naïve to take them seriously. No wonder she hadn't mourned the loss of Rose; Quinn was too busy trying to take her place.

Petty rivalry had no place in my mission. Neither did throwing myself at the totally wrong guy, but I'd think about that later. All that mattered now was Hayden, and it was time to do damage control. I straightened up and tugged my skirt into place. Quinn had no right to choose Hayden's friends, and I bet Hayden felt the same way.

The lunch line had dwindled, so it took no time to grab a sandwich— not that I was the least bit hungry now. I brushed off the stares that followed me to our table where Stef and Von had loyally saved my usual spot. I sent them both grateful nods as I claimed my seat.

Across the table Quinn coolly met my glare, her mouth twisted into a mocking smile. Hayden didn't look happy, but her friend's satisfaction wasn't lost on her. The subdued conversation around the table reminded me of the hushed chatter you hear just before the curtain rises on a play. Everyone waited for the show to start.

I caught Hayden's eye. "Sam and I are just friends. Why anyone would post something just to create drama is beyond me." I stared at Quinn, who flushed in anger.

"Yeah, right." Quinn snorted with indignation. "I sure don't look at my *friends* the way you do."

"Probably because you don't have any," Stef quipped.

"Shut up, you little stain," she retorted.

"God, would you two just stop it?" Hayden glared at her brother and supposed friend. Silence reigned for a few moments before she turned to me. "You're not full of shit, are you?"

"No, I'm not," I said simply.

"Fine," Hayden said, closing the door on the subject. "Anyone want to split a brownie?"

As dessert got passed around, Quinn's eyes were on me. The hardness in her gaze told me the bad blood between us was just heating up.

"Collins!"

Entering the lobby of Watson Hall a few days later, Sarah Jane motioned me over to the housemother's desk, where she hovered like a vulture protecting road kill. "This came for you."

She pointed to a small black footlocker on the floor behind her. A combination padlock secured it along with three layers of tamper-evident tape stamped with the words DIPLOMATIC BAG. My heart leapt. Benson's care package had arrived.

"It doesn't look like a bag to me," she said. "What is it?"

I gritted my teeth, annoyed by her challenging tone. "Books. They were too heavy to carry on the plane."

She continued to block my access to the box. "Have you read the section in the student handbook about contraband?"

As a matter of fact, I had. There wouldn't be any drugs or alcohol in the shipment, but everything else would definitely be on the list of forbidden items.

"It's from my dad," I assured her. "What do you think's in there, a surface to air missile?" Knowing Benson, it would be the only thing he hadn't sent.

She begrudgingly stepped aside while I hoisted the box into my arms with a grunt.

"I'll be stopping by to check out those books," she called as I made my way to the elevator.

Once in my room I ripped off the tape and checked the back of the lock for the combination. It wasn't written there, of course, but the clue needed to open it was. In this case, it was MY HOMETOWN.

Going to my computer, I pulled up the longitude and latitude for Benson's birthplace of Sydney, Australia: 33 52 S/151 12 E. The first three sets of numbers popped the lock. Benson would be proud.

A grin stole across my face as I pawed through the contents. Somewhere in Karachi, a CIA agent was going to get a nasty shock when he found his storage locker cleaned out.

There were cameras disguised as everything from phone chargers to smoke alarms, from books to a bedside clock. I found the promised bug sweeper, along with recovery sticks for digging up deleted phone data, software for hacking just about anything, and a transmitter in the shape of a computer mouse.

On the exotic side, there was invisible UV spray you could apply directly to an object, such as a doorknob, that would later reveal if someone had tampered with it. A UV light could also be used to target a suspect since the residue was a bear to wash off.

There was nail polish that changed colors if you dipped your finger into a drink laced with drugs, night visions goggles, a set of lock picks, a telescopic baton, and Japanese throwing stars, which I'd only recently learned how to use. There were even two smoke grenades, though God only knew what scenario had popped into Benson's head to make him think they were an appropriate addition to my arsenal.

The first order of business was to safeguard our room from any future eavesdroppers. Using the handheld detector labeled Bug Killer, I performed a thorough sweep, and thankfully the room was still free of both cameras and listening devices.

Then, pulling over a chair, I unscrewed the existing smoke alarm from its ceiling bracket and replaced it with a motion-activated one that, in addition to alerting us to a potential fire, would digitally capture and retain all activity within the room for a seventy-two-hour period.

The camera clock went on my nightstand, its lens aimed squarely at the door. It would provide a live feed on my phone 24/7.

I synced the mouse transmitter with my own computer. Not only would it record every sound made within the room, it would transcribe every word to a file buried deep within my hard drive.

Lastly, a small case of USB sticks containing various hacking applications were fished out before I secured the cache with an electronic thumbprint lock. With few places to conceal it, I had to settle with stashing it under a pile of sweaters in my wardrobe.

Sorting through the software, I deliberated on what to do about Quinn. I could care less if she used Hayden as a stepping stone to social glory, but I couldn't let her interfere with my orders to win my roommate's trust. How could I get her to back off?

I read the pamphlet on the benign-sounding Pathways, a program promising to divulge every text, outgoing call, and email from any given phone. I weighed the stick in my hand. Benson wouldn't hesitate to seek out every advantage he could to ensure a mission's success, so why did I?

I thought of what a cagey tribal warlord had once told my dad. It was right after a band of radical extremists had retreated from the nearby area, much to the relief of the military and locals alike. As glasses were being raised in a toast, the man whispered in my father's ear, "Until the snake is dead, do not drop the stick." Sure enough, the enemy struck again within weeks.

There was no room for delicate sensibilities. I fitted the Pathways stick into my computer. Once it downloaded, I pulled Quinn's phone number from the student directory and plugged it in.

My phone chimed with a text from Von. *Meet me for dinner in 5? The dining hall ran out of gorgeous.*

I snorted with laughter before returning fire. *But apparently it's fully stocked with bullshit. See you in 5...*

The program needed time to initiate a digital pathway anyway, so I set the computer aside, happy in the knowledge that all of Quinn's electronic secrets would soon spill right onto my screen.

BENSON'S RULE #17

SYMPATHY IS A LUXURY YOU CAN ILL-AFFORD

Is this seat taken?"

I spun around to inform Von he was late but instead found Sam standing behind the next chair with a food tray in hand. It was a ridiculous question because I sat alone at a table meant for twelve. Dinner service had just begun, and it would be another half hour before the place filled up.

Before I could tell him it would be a really bad idea, he plopped down an overloaded tray. It would totally set me back if Hayden walked in right now, but Benson hadn't covered this scenario in my training.

"Sorry about what happened today," he said. He'd sent me an apologetic shrug at lunch, but that was our only communication since the picture had posted.

"Um, it's okay," I said, stirring my lentil soup and praying my roommate had decided to get dinner out of the vending machines. "I told Hayden you and I were just friends, and she was cool with it."

"I knew she would be. I'm not *that* hard to get over," he said with a laugh.

I shoveled in a spoonful of soup. It was the only way to prevent inappropriate questions about his relationship with Hayden from popping out... and then I grimaced. The soup tasted like hot, bland mush.

Sam slid over a few packets of saltines. "No one orders that soup more than once, but these will help." He picked up a bottle of gross-looking green juice and gave it a shake. "So how did you end up at Harrington in your senior year?"

"It was for health reasons, mostly." At his questioning look, I rolled out the approved backstory, leaving out any mention of the State Department or a certain software billionaire. His eyes danced at the description of the brawl in the marketplace. "My dad felt staying in Pakistan might interfere with my plans to continue breathing," I concluded dryly.

"And he thought high school would be safer?" He shuddered in mock horror.

"At least it's not evil goat herders who want to kill me here..." I trailed off.

He twisted opened the cap, his expression subdued. "You know about Rose Winters, right?" At my nod, he continued, "Man, I still can't believe she's gone. Anyway, Quinn was always the extra man there, you know? And now that she's not, she'll do whatever it takes to never go back there again, including posting pictures she shouldn't."

I tried the wretched soup again—which now tasted like warm, salty mush–and tried to resist feeling pity for Quinn. *Sympathy is a luxury you can ill-afford*, Benson would say, *if you plan to survive in battle*. We weren't at war, or at least I hoped we weren't.

I cut my eyes to the dining hall entrance for the tenth time, praying for Von to appear. So much for being irresistible.

"By the way," I said, changing the subject, "I didn't thank you for walking me home the other night." I dropped my spoon, giving up on the soup. "I didn't say anything really embarrassing, did I?"

His eyes shimmered with humor. "Oh, that reminds me. You owe me a secret."

I gave him a wide-eyed look. "Say what?

"You told me you had secrets, so I told you one of mine." He gulped down his juice. "I've never told anyone how much I hated coming here, not even my mom."

"You didn't want to go to boarding school?"

He unfurled his napkin, gently spilling silverware across his tray. "It's not that. I was in a boarding school just outside of London, the one my dad went to. I liked it there, but my mom was never happy about it. She's American." He got busy attacking a giant slab of meatloaf. "When my dad died of a heart attack, he was barely in the ground before she dragged me to New York." His voice grew melancholy when he mentioned his dad, as if his father's death still left him adrift.

"I lost my mom," I said. "But I was so young, I don't remember her."

He nodded in solidarity. "I went to this miserable day school on the Upper East Side and got into so many fights, I wasn't invited back."

"I bet you won them all though, huh?" I picked at the peanut butter cookie I'd scored for dessert.

He cracked a smile. "MMA was pretty big at my old school."

"So your mom sent you here as punishment?"

He shrugged. "I wanted to go back to my old school in England, but she wouldn't let me leave the East Coast. Harrington was a compromise."

I'd never suffered from the loss of my mother. My childhood had been filled with love, joy, adventure, and tolerance. I even had a distinct memory of Benson in a princess crown and fairy wings as we sat down for a tea party. But what if he hadn't been there to help my father pick up the pieces? I'd never really thought about it like that before.

"It must have been hard for both of you," I sympathized.

"You mean it's not all about me?" His mouth twisted in a deprecating smile. "That took me a whole year in family counseling to figure out."

I waved a hand in a grand gesture. "Zat is me, Fraulein Doktor Riley," I said in a thick German accent.

He laughed as he polished off his meal. Silence stretched for a few moments before he blurted, "Hayden and I aren't getting back together, if that's what you're wondering."

"Why not?" He arched a brow at the question, and my cheeks

reddened. "I mean, not that I was wondering or anything, but she's beautiful and rich, and she still seems to have a thing for you. Why wouldn't you want her back?" Part of me was watching my mouth run on in utter horror. I practically delivered a commercial on his fabulous ex.

"Have you ever been lonely?" he asked.

It wasn't the answer I expected. "I'm an only child. I've been alone my entire life."

He shook his head. "It's not the same thing. You can be lonely in a crowd... or at a boarding school. The problem was I didn't know Hayden any better after six months than I knew her after six days."

"You're the one who ended it?"

He nodded. "She's a good person, despite her ridiculous parents, but those walls of hers are getting higher by the day."

What must it be like to be the daughter of parents so rich and famous, everything you did was examined and judged? How would you ever be sure that friendships and relationships were genuine, or conversations would be kept private? Could you ever let your guard down, even with your boyfriend, and learn to trust? I couldn't believe I felt sorry for the Frasier heiress, but I did.

"Sorry I'm late!" Von's laden tray clattered down on the other side of me, and I sagged with relief. His lip curled as he noticed my highly questionable dinner choice. "You ordered the lentil soup?"

"What can I say, it was there when I wanted it," I said pointedly.

"I'll share my meatloaf with you," he gallantly offered, completely missing the subtext. He leaned forward to catch Sam's eye. "Thanks for keeping Riley company."

"Glad you could join us," Sam retorted. "So Riley, when are you coming back to the gym?"

"That's not a good idea," Von said before I had a chance to reply.

"I wasn't asking you," Sam said tightly.

"And you shouldn't be asking her either," Von said. "Has she mentioned to you what her father will say if any more of those pictures surface?"

"No, because she doesn't think about her father when she's with me," Sam said with a certain satisfaction before turning to me. "What if I guaranteed no pictures?"

I barged into the conversation before Von could voice more objections. "You can do that?" An excited thrill shot through me. I was dying to spar again and also moved that he'd go to such lengths for me.

Von scoffed. "What are you going to do? Take away everyone's phones?"

"Who's taking away phones?" Stef slid into the vacant chair next to Von. He, too, had ordered the meatloaf.

"Nobody's taking away phones," Von said impatiently.

"Well, that's good," he said brightly. "Hey, Riley, didn't anyone warn you about the soup?"

Not wanting to be sidetracked, I asked Sam, "Do you think I can come back to the gym tomorrow night?" It would be Friday night, which meant no study period.

"Not tomorrow night," interjected Von. "It's the boathouse party."

"Oh, yeah, you have to come," Stef agreed.

"After last week I'm afraid to ask, but what's the boathouse party?" I'd had enough celebrating to last the entire year.

"Much smaller than the Survival Party, and no chaperone, only prefects, but we can go to the gym instead," Sam offered.

I had no interest in another party, and going to the gym with Sam sounded heavenly, but my mission came first. If Hayden was going to the party, then so would I.

"Are parties allowed anywhere on campus?" I wondered. Would I have to track her movements every weekend?

"Not in theory, but first they have to find us," Von said. "And then as long as we're back in our dorms by eleven and not caught with contraband, it's cool." He turned to me. "So I'll meet you in Watson's common tomorrow at eight?"

Sam didn't look pleased about being scooped by Von, and my heart did a happy dance.

The rest of the chairs filled up quickly after that. Only one seat remained vacant—the one next to Sam—when Hayden and Quinn approached with their dinner trays. Hayden's assessing gaze took in my proximity to her ex, no doubt wondering if I'd played her the other day. Sam jumped to his feet.

"Join us, Hayden," he said, pulling out the empty seat.

Whether he did it to help smooth things over between Hayden and me, or to reach out to a friend still recovering from an unimaginable loss, I didn't know, but he'd also delivered a very public snub to Quinn. From the way Sam struggled to keep a straight face, he realized it, too.

Hayden paused for a moment, her eyes darting between Sam and Quinn. "Do you mind, Quinn?" she asked.

Quinn flushed. "Not at all," she said, though it was obvious nothing could be farther from the truth. Just like my blunder in the marketplace, this moment would certainly come back to haunt me.

Quinn stalked away as Hayden settled in, and talk turned to the usual chatter about homework assignments and who might be hooking up. The stilted conversation between the exes soon relaxed, and they even shared a laugh. At one point, Hayden's eyes met mine, and I read in them a measure of gratitude. She'd already lost one friend, and even if she and Sam weren't a couple, my presence here had perhaps helped prevent her from losing another.

BENSON'S RULE #18

TAKE DOWN THE BIGGEST FOOL, AND THE REST WILL FOLLOW

A **giant stack of graded papers hit the table with a thud.** Mr. Bracken had ordered me to report for work as soon as classes were over on Friday.

"Tests," he said, pointing out the obvious before moving on to the big, sleek desktop computer opened to a spreadsheet. "Computer. Grades go from one to the other. Got it?"

In answer I grabbed the top paper marked with a B and the words, "There may be hope for you yet," and entered the grade under the student's name. He retreated to his desk and we worked in near-silence, broken only by my snorts of amusement as I read the endlessly creative ways the crusty teacher had for berating ("Catherine the Great died of a stroke—get your mind out of the gutter") or damning with faint praise ("Congratulations for staying awake in class this week").

Thirty minutes later I dumped the stack back on his desk. Without looking up, he thrust his empty coffee cup at me. It took several minutes to locate the teachers' lounge and when I did, the last person on earth I wanted to see had beaten me to the coffeepot.

"Riley," Mrs. McKenna greeted me with a chilly smile. "Why am I not surprised to see you in the staff lounge, which is off limits to students?"

I hoisted the cup like a cross before a vampire. "I'm Mr. Bracken's TA now. He sent me for coffee." I glanced at the mug and inwardly groaned at what was printed on it: THIS MIGHT BE SCOTCH.

"I see," she said, still blocking access to the pot. "Was this before or after your half-naked pictures appeared, or perhaps the report from the Bridgehurst police came in about an assault at a convenience store?"

I swallowed the claims of innocence burning in my throat. It was so tempting to defend myself, especially in the face of this woman's attitude, but she held all the cards. "I couldn't say, ma'am."

A mask of superiority settled on her features. "Ah, well, let's hope you continue to be such a model student, especially in the next twenty-four hours."

"Ma'am?"

She strolled away from the coffee machine and toward the door. "It'll all be clear quite soon."

I puzzled her words all the way back to Bracken's class and wondered if he might shed some light. I waited until he took a satisfying gulp—it was fresh-brewed with two sugars—before daring to open my mouth. "Mrs. McKenna said something's going down in the next twenty-four hours."

He smirked at me over the top of his mug. "Is there a question there, or are we talking about your popularity with the head of school?"

"My question is," I ground out as politely as possible, "is there something going on that would be to my advantage to know?"

He scratched his chin as he regarded me. "I want to know something first. Why is our esteemed leader in such a twist over you?"

Everyone has an angle, my dad liked to say. Every time he went in to pave the way for a new trade agreement or to notch back tensions between regional factions, there were always a dozen people involved with a dozen different agendas. The sooner you discovered and satisfied each one, the faster you got your deal done. What did Bracken want? Was it simple curiosity? Or did he use information like soldiers used sandbags to secure a position on shaky ground?

"She was forced to admit me." That seemed safe enough to offer up.

His ears perked up like a dog at a bone factory. "How on earth did you manage that?"

I gave him a tight smile. "Quid pro quo." That was another diplomatic rule: a favor for a favor.

He let out a sharp bark of laughter. "Alright. If no one's warned you yet, Gretchen is very fond of surprise inspections. It's supposed to be students chosen at random, but I'm betting there'll be nothing random about this one."

My mind flashed on the box in my closet filled with smoke grenades, throwing stars, and everything else guaranteed to get me tossed out of school if McKenna got her hands on it. I nodded my thanks before gesturing to the room at large. "Is there anything else you need me to do?"

He grinned. "I'm thinking I should send you on your way. I wouldn't want to lose the most entertaining TA I've had in years."

I turned to go when his voice stopped me. "And Riley? Rumor has it Gretchen may be in the mood for a sail tonight, just so you know." My lips twitched as I realized what he was hinting at. The boathouse party wasn't as big a secret as everyone hoped.

When I entered my room ten minutes later, the green light on the bedside clock had turned red. Unless Hayden had come and gone, someone else had been in our dorm. It took one press of a button to determine the time the sensor had detected movement. Flipping open my laptop, I pulled up recent footage from the smoke alarm camera, which offered a panoramic view of the room.

"Son of a camel trader," I swore when the culprit appeared. It was Quinn, big surprise. She hadn't shown up for lunch today. I watched as she let herself into our room, most likely by lifting Hayden's key, and marched directly to my wardrobe. Pawing through my clothes, she settled on the beautiful navy pea coat it hadn't been cold enough yet to wear. Glancing around first as if she thought she was being observed, she slipped something out of her pocket and into the coat. Within moments she escaped back out the door.

Running to the wardrobe, I pulled out the coat and quickly

discovered what had been left for McKenna to find: a baggie of what I assumed to be weed. I'd never seen it or smelled it, but it looked like something from Nadira's exotic spice rack. It would have gotten me kicked out of Harrington for sure. Fuming, I flushed it down the toilet before cutting the baggie into strips and flushing that down as well.

Between homework and working for Mr. Bracken, I hadn't had a moment to check out what the Pathways program might have discovered, but I resolved to do so at the first opportunity.

My personal contraband, including the Taser that would tie me to the assault at the minimart, went into a large Prada tote. I grabbed Hayden's car keys off her dresser, and ten minutes later, it was safely stowed in the trunk of her Mercedes. It was a safe bet she would never fall under scrutiny, and even if she did her dad could just add another wing or something onto the library to get her out of trouble.

For the five minutes it took to put on my makeup, Hayden hovered. Turning from the mirror, I learned why.

"Would you make a Stop & Shop run with me?" Last week she'd tersely informed me of my duty, but every day she unbent a bit more.

"Sure. Give me a sec." I texted Von my apologies for not being able to meet him before the party as planned. I also warned him McKenna had gotten wind of tonight's party, and we should change locations.

Done, Von texted back. *I'll spread the word to meet at the barn.*

Shouldn't we also plan some evasive maneuvers if she finds us there? I texted.

LOL, G.I. Jane, he texted. *Like what?*

I quickly rattled off a list of ideas and hit send.

Maybe it was the memory of what went down last time we went to the convenience store, but as we drove out the gates of Harrington, Hayden seemed especially glad of my company.

"Stef really likes you, you know," she said.

"He's the sweetest guy I've ever met." Sarah Jane had been right when she'd described him as fragile. There was something almost childlike about his enthusiasm and vulnerability. "He's lucky to have you."

"I'm lucky to have him," she reflected. "Sometimes I think he should have been the one to grow up in the highest room in the tallest tower, you know?"

Or at least granted more than the barest of acknowledgements by his father, but I kept that opinion to myself.

We pulled into the convenience store parking lot, and Hayden hit the brakes. The crusty Ford pickup was in the same spot as last week. Cowboy and Tom probably came by the same time every Friday night, and it was our bad luck to be on matching schedules. The look of apprehension on her face mirrored my own.

"How badly do we need vodka?" Since I never planned to touch the stuff again, it was no skin off my nose if we turned the car around.

She grimaced. "Stef would kill me if we came back empty-handed. He says the Friday night parties are what makes life bearable for him."

"Fabulous," I muttered, knowing that despite our budding friendship, she would be expecting *me* to risk life and limb to enable a guy who needed a twelve-step program, not another cocktail.

"Pull into the parking lot and flip a U." She did as instructed so the Mercedes was ready to tear out of the lot at a moment's notice. "Pop the trunk, would you?" She shot me a confused look but pulled the latch.

I removed the telescoping baton from the tote stowed there just hours before and slid it up the sleeve of my jacket. "Keep the motor running." I sighed and squared my shoulders.

A bell jingled as I pushed open the door of the Stop & Shop. Behind the counter hunched the same clerk, and like an instant replay from last week, she had her eyeballs glued to a game show. The Inbred Twins were nowhere in sight, but I proceeded with extreme caution, reaching the liquor aisle without a problem.

"Keep your gun hand free at all times," Benson admonished every new recruit, and it was excellent advice to take now. With my right hand cupping the baton, I hauled a half-gallon of Grey Goose off the shelf with my left. If anyone wanted any mixers, they could get it their own damn selves.

I saw them before they saw me. The brothers were at the cash register paying for a six-pack of rotgut beer and a couple of packs of smokes, looking just as greasy and unhygienic as before. I circled around behind them. Cowboy spied me over his shoulder and flinched. Tom followed suit and though his eyes widened, he didn't look quite as freaked out.

Take down the biggest fool, and the rest will follow was another Benson tactic. I didn't take my eyes off Tom.

They finished paying, and Cowboy hurriedly scooped up the beer. His brother moved more slowly, obviously debating whether they had a shot at revenge, but my complete lack of fear had to unsettle him. His kind would like the ones who didn't fight back.

"Hello there, boys," I said in a conversational tone. "Are you here for your weekly science lesson?"

Cowboy practically leapt out of his boots. "Come on, let's get out of here," he urged, as if he couldn't wait to flee the zip code.

In an unhurried movement, Tom scooped up the cigarettes before turning to face me. He tapped the pack against his palm in deliberate strokes.

Thump-thump.

His wintry eyes ran over me with equal parts hatred and lust.

Thump-thump.

"You're mighty brave for a little girl on all on her own," he said at last.

Thump-thump.

"Oh, I'm not alone," I answered pleasantly. I flicked my arm and the baton shot out of my sleeve with a satisfying click.

Cowboy cannonballed out the door. It took a moment longer for common sense to penetrate Tom's thick skull, but then he, too, decided he was out of his league. He pocketed his cigarettes and followed his brother.

"Do make sure you give your kindest regards to my friend on the way out," I called to his retreating figure. "I'll be watching."

They both paused as they neared the Mercedes, with Cowboy removing his hat and bowing low to the bewildered Hayden. Tom was less biddable, but a glance back at me and my baton caused him to reconsider. He dipped his head in a stiff greeting before escaping to their dilapidated ride.

I set the bottle on the counter and for once, the clerk tore her eyes from the television screen. She stared at me in astonishment as she wordlessly rang up my purchase. A moment later I was on the sidewalk watching the rusty truck squeal past Hayden's car. I retracted the baton before slipping into the car.

She looked at me in amazement. "What did you do?"

"Just asked that they show you some respect." I buckled my seatbelt before meeting her gaze with a grin. "But don't think this makes us friends."

The gathering was smaller than last Friday's, but bodies still managed to fill up the tack room and the adjacent space stacked with dozens of hay bales. Someone had thrown blankets across a few of them, and now two people with acoustic guitars and a girl with a flute perched there, jamming on a pop song. A few couples sucked face and swayed to the music.

Someone had hauled the trusty punch bowl down from the upper boys' dorm along with a stack of red Solo cups and set them on a hay bale. I handed the liquor off to Stef, who got busy mixing it with two giant plastic bottles of Mountain Dew. I found a can of 7-Up in a cooler and popped the top.

"Make it two." Sam smiled from the other side of the ice chest. He plunged a hand into the icy water and came up with a root beer. Pulling the tab, he held up the can. "To smarter choices and happier Saturdays." We touched cans with a dull thunk and each took a sip. "Speaking of smarter choices," he said, "what are we doing here?"

At my confused look he added, "Why are we taking such risks to come drink sodas in a smelly barn? Aren't you worried about being caught with that?" He gestured toward the punch bowl. "I wasn't even going to come tonight... until you said you'd be here."

It was wrong to encourage him, but at that moment it was hard to remember why. I opened my mouth without a clue what to say when Von barged in.

"I don't know what you did, but Hayden is sure impressed," he said, nodding to where Hayden mimed Cowboy bowing to an appreciative audience. She was more animated than I'd ever seen her, and people laughed with amusement. Von wore an expression of innocence as he glanced between Sam and me. "Did I interrupt anything?"

"No," I rushed to say, preventing Sam from disagreeing. "Did you make the arrangements?"

He saluted. "Everything is ready for a possible invasion, ma'am."

Sam frowned at both of us. "Invasion?"

Just then Sarah Jane, the last person I would ever expect to see at an underground party, popped up with her phone. "Smile, everyone!" The shutter clicked and she moved on to the next group.

"What is she doing here?" I gasped in horror. "We are so dead!" The contingency plan Von and I put in place would be useless if she opened her mouth.

"Nah," Von said. "I know she's a pain, but Luke is sick. I didn't have a lot of other prefects to choose from."

"And you trust her not to throw us under the bus if a teacher or McKenna shows up?" Sam asked.

Von smiled smugly. "I trust her to look the other way for the summer internship at my mom's law firm."

I wasn't sure how to feel about that. Sarah Jane was annoying and no one liked her, but you had to admire the way she fearlessly bulldozed her way through the halls with a clear sense of purpose. If she was willing to compromise her position for a job, though, maybe she wasn't as principled as I thought.

Von's phone chimed with a text, his face tensing up when he read it. "You nailed it, Riley," he said before yelling to the crowd, "Code Red! Code Red!"

Like a choreographed dance, two girls swooped in and whisked the punch bowl away. A broad-shouldered guy I recognized from the MMA club dashed around with a big bucket, and everyone tossed in their cups. Jackie Song produced an identical bowl that Stef filled with more Mountain Dew, and people lined up for refills. The whole process took less than sixty seconds.

When McKenna marched in a minute later, there was a group of well-behaved students quietly enjoying a classical piece of music, maybe Mozart, being played on guitars. The music died away as Sarah Jane stepped forward. "Good evening, Mrs. McKenna."

"Sarah Jane," the head of school said, as startled as I had been to see the prefect—or at least she pretended to be. Someone had to have informed on us, and in my mind the prefect was the prime suspect. "What are you doing here?"

"We wanted to play some music, but didn't want to disturb anyone if they were trying to get some studying done," she said earnestly. "Would you like some punch?"

"As a matter of fact, I would." She crossed the room to Stef. "May I try yours?" The woman definitely had someone on the inside.

He quickly handed over his cup while McKenna pulled a wrapped plastic stick out of her pocket. She uncovered it and dipped it into the cup. After checking the reading, she thrust the cup back at him. She repeated the test with a few other students until she arrived in front of me.

"You seem to have acclimated to our school quite well," she observed, noting Von on one side of me and Sam on the other. She unwrapped another test stick and dipped it into my 7-Up.

"Yes, ma'am," I said, realizing there was some truth to that statement. I'd been so worried about keeping tabs on Hayden that I'd barely contemplated having fun.

Unable to find fault with the situation, she gave us all a look clearly conveying she had her eye on us before sweeping out the door. The music resumed, but we all held our positions until Von's phone chimed again and he announced, "All clear!"

There was a smattering of applause, but he held his hands up calling for silence. "Tonight's near miss was brought to you by Riley Collins. She's the one who set this up, and I must say, I think this playbook should be standard operating procedure from now on."

The applause swelled again, and I smiled with some embarrassment. Hayden hoisted a glass in my direction, a move that didn't go unnoticed by Quinn. The party resumed, but before Sam and Von could start their verbal sparring, I escaped to the side of the tack room where Sarah Jane stood alone.

"What do you want?" She glowered.

I shrugged. "I'm just surprised, that's all."

"You've been here for what, two weeks? And look at you. You've got Sam Hudson following you around, and Hayden Frasier bringing you to parties." She made no attempt to mask her resentment. "I've been here three years, doing everything like I'm supposed to do, and the only reason I got invited tonight was because you people needed me. What's it all been for?"

I shook my head, not quite following her reasoning.

"I'm *not* going to spend my life being an afterthought. If I have to break a few rules to get a prime internship, who are you to judge me?"

She was right. It obviously infuriated her to sell a bit of her soul to fulfill her dream.

"I'm not judging you, Sarah Jane," I said, thinking of the compromises I'd recently made for my future. "In fact, I know exactly how you feel."

BENSON'S RULE #19

OVERCONFIDENCE IS THE MOST DANGEROUS FORM OF CARELESSNESS

So are you into Von?" After last night, Hayden probably wasn't the only one wondering what was going on between Von and me.

The entire third floor was enjoying a relaxed Saturday afternoon. Most doors along the corridor were thrown open, ours included, so people dropped in randomly to gossip or ask questions about a given assignment. Several girls I shared classes with had come and gone, the friendly atmosphere a nice change from the pressure cooker we all lived in during the rest of the week. Quinn had yet to spoil things by showing up, which was both a relief and unnerving. At least if she was around, I knew what she was up to.

"I like him, but I don't know if I *like* him like him," I answered.

The truth was a lot more complicated. Putting duty before desire, I'd avoided Sam for the rest of the party, though his eyes had followed me as I moved about.

Von hadn't questioned his good fortune at finding me unattached and remained glued to my side the rest of the night. It was easy hanging out with him; he was funny, cute, self-deprecating, an outrageous flirt, but most of all, he was safe. There wasn't this constant magnetic pull like I felt with Sam, which was all the more reason to stay as far away from Hayden's ex as possible. But Von also felt solid, like he'd have your back if you ever needed to ditch a body, no questions asked. Kissing him might even be fun.

Shaking off the unexpected flush of heat, I tried to refocus on the chemistry textbook propped up front of me, but it was no good. My mind turned to the Pathways program, and what the electronic mole might have dug up on Quinn. I didn't dare access the program where Hayden could so easily catch a glimpse of my screen, but my stomach churned with the possibilities. Part of me hoped there were no secrets or embarrassing confessions, so I wouldn't have to decide what to do with the information. Protecting Hayden from foreign threats and ensuring our country's security was a noble cause. Blackmailing some girl on a power trip was a bit sketchy.

"McKenna's on the floor!" Quinn ducked through the door, barely glancing at Hayden before zeroing in on me.

"Hmmm," Hayden murmured from the depths of a novel, completely unconcerned.

I realized immediately why Quinn had waited until this moment to drop in. She wanted a ringside seat for the room search we both knew was on its way. McKenna didn't disappoint, sailing though the door less than a minute later. With her was Officer Wieringa, the buttoned-up security guard who'd been stationed outside Major Taylor's office.

"Room check," McKenna announced.

Imitating Hayden, I lounged on my bed, pretending to be engrossed in the details of molecular collisions.

"Would you ladies please stand up?" The guard was as cordial as if he were asking for a dance.

We made to rise, but McKenna waved us off. "Oh, that's not necessary," she assured the officer. "Let's just do a closet sweep. I'm sure there will be nothing to find, right girls?" Her glance encompassed Quinn, who looked a little too pleased with the situation.

Alarm bells went off. McKenna's quick arrival at the barn last night was suspicious, and now she and Quinn had exchanged a blink-and-you'd-miss-it moment. Had McKenna directed Quinn to plant the weed in my closet? Was Quinn her informant? Come to think of it, the administrator hadn't checked Hayden's cup last night; was that part of Quinn's deal?

I continued to act fascinated by my science homework as the search of my wardrobe commenced. A few minutes later, Wieringa closed the closet doors and shook his head. "All clear."

Quinn's reaction was exactly as I expected—momentary disbelief quickly followed by a flash of anger—but McKenna was more understated in her displeasure. She'd most likely expected to reclaim authority over Harrington by booting me out, but other than a burning glance directed at Quinn, she stalked from the room with the officer tagging at her heels. They hadn't bothered searching Hayden's armoire even for show.

Quinn stood awkwardly in the center of the room.

"You look disappointed," I observed.

Hayden's eyes appeared over the top of her novel, taking us in.

Quinn's face shut down, all uncertainty erased. "Don't get too comfortable here. You won't be staying long."

I let the textbook drop in my lap. "Really? Is that what McKenna told you when you ratted us out last night?"

Her stunned expression told me I'd hit the mark, and it took her a few moments to come up with a feeble response. "Piss off," she snapped, before flouncing out the door.

"Should I ask?" Hayden said.

"Probably not," I said, my tone conveying it wasn't worth the bother. I'd already decided it would be best to keep my mouth shut about Quinn because if Hayden was forced to choose sides, I wasn't all that sure I would win.

I tossed my homework aside. "Want to hit the gym?" The question wasn't simply a diversionary tactic. The lack of regular exercise was making me feel claustrophobic in my own skin.

She shook her head, settling back into the romance novel that wasn't required reading. "I'm good."

I threw on workout clothes and went in search of the equipment room. The school's map showed it was in the cluster of buildings dedicated to athletics, which would take me near the MMA gym.

Autumn leaves crackled underfoot as I trotted down the path. Approaching from the other direction came one of the dog patrols occasionally spotted on the outer reaches of campus. I often heard an occasional "woof" at night as they did their nocturnal duty. Like the others, this was a beautiful German Shepherd. She was a poor excuse for a guard dog though, wiggling from head to tail as I neared.

"Now, Scout," the handler admonished as the dog eagerly tugged at the leash. She lunged at my legs, sniffing delightedly at all the new smells presented for her olfactory pleasure. Her joy was infectious, and I laughed.

Her handler, a stout woman with brown hair haphazardly gathered into a ponytail, gently scolded her. "You are hopeless, dog."

I leaned down and rewarded Scout with a blissful scratch behind her ears. "She says work is boring, especially when there're so many other fun things to see and smell, huh, pretty girl?"

The woman sighed in frustration. "I've never met a dog less interested in work. She'd better get it together, or I'll make sure she's given to a family of vegetarians. How would you like tofu for the rest of your life, Scout?"

Scout's tail said that was fine with her. With a final pat, I continued down the path, hoping the other dogs were better trained and wouldn't confront intruders by licking them to death.

Arriving at the door marked SPORTS CLUB, I yanked on it several times in disbelief. How could it be locked during one of the few times students could actually get over to use it? Frustrated, I scanned the fading sky, but a cold breeze made running less than appealing.

The crunch of footsteps caught my attention. A guy in workout clothes let himself into the MMA gym. Of course that door was unlocked.

"Thanks a lot, universe," I growled, stomping toward the door he'd just disappeared through. Maybe Sam wouldn't be there. And I sure as hell wouldn't be sparring with anyone unless I was dressed like a nun.

Guys packed the place but were too busy sparring, punching bags, or running on treadmills to notice when I slipped in with head down. Trying to blend into the scenery, I grabbed a pair of gloves and warmed up by taking out my frustrations on a solitary bag hanging in the corner. I didn't want to think about Quinn and what her next move would be in her bid to take me down. I wiped Sam from my mind, and the dangerous potential he had for complicating my life. One by one I let all my worries and desires fade away, letting the blaring music eclipse the noise in my head, and allowing my body to take control.

Hit. Kick. Jab.

Sweat drenched my T-shirt, so I yanked it off and kept going. The rhythm of the music filled me, pushing, driving, releasing.

Hit. Kick. Jab.

"Bend your knee a bit more before you strike. You'll get more power that way."

I drew up with a start, the trance broken. Mirrors covered the walls, revealing Sam standing directly behind me with arms crossed, as if he'd been observing for a while. "Go on, try it again."

Shaken from my daze, I angled my knee as he suggested and kicked the bag.

"That's right. Did you feel it? Here, face me."

The next few minutes were more like a charged dance than a training session, though if he felt it, he didn't let it show. He kept up a running dialogue of encouragement and instruction as our bodies met and parted. A blocked hit turned into an embrace; a spinning kick delivered in slow motion became a caress as his hand turned it aside; a corrected stance ended with his fingers sliding over my glistening skin.

We were both facing the mirror, his hands on my hips, when he fell silent. Our eyes locked in the reflection, and slowly, deliberately, he splayed his fingers across my naked torso and pulled me against his body. To any casual observer it looked like merely another correction of my form, but then his cheek brushed my hair like a cat marking his turf, and a shiver ran through me.

"You feel it, too," he whispered in my ear.

He left me breathless, and it had nothing to do with the workout, but what did it matter? I only needed to keep it together for one short year, and then I'd be free. Ivy League colleges that wouldn't have looked at me twice would now consider my application because I'd be a Harrington graduate. I'd no longer be a friendless desert rat, but an equal. Doors would open, opportunities presented, friends made. And all I had to do was resist a gorgeous, smart, and interesting guy because hooking up with him would royally piss off my reason for being here and endanger my objective.

I broke out of Sam's embrace. "I can't." I had the gloves stripped off and my jacket zipped up within seconds. I only had so much resolve, and it would be best to be long gone before it died. Slamming out the gym door into the crisp twilight, I fled in the direction of Watson Hall.

He caught up to me before I'd cleared the sports complex. "Riley!"

I halted and reluctantly turned to face him. He'd grabbed a sweatshirt before dashing out after me, but neither of us was dressed for the weather. I shivered, this time from the cold, and he stepped closer. The light was quickly dying, but I could read the uncertainty in his expression.

"You still owe me a secret."

I pulled my jacket closer and fiddled with the zipper. How tempting it was to let it all spill out, to unburden my fears and concerns, my reason for being there. But what would I say? That the State Department had foolishly chosen me to watch over the daughter of their resident genius, but had neglected to tell me she might be in real danger? That it was odd her former roommate had stashed a broken phone where it should never have been found on the same day she died? That Quinn had most likely teamed up with McKenna and might even now be planning ways to get me tossed out of school? Even if he didn't think I was a total head case, it wouldn't be fair to unload on him.

I settled for a version of the truth. "Hayden is the reason I got into Harrington. I owe her."

His face fell. "So that's it? We pretend there's nothing going on between us because a girl I broke up with three months ago won't like it?"

"There is nothing going on between us," I said. If this didn't end here and now, I would end up doing something *I'd live to regret.*

"Really?" He slowly wrapped his hands around my waist, and my heart thudded. We'd touched each other a dozen times in the gym, but the darkness lent new intimacy to our conversation. "You feel nothing when I do this?"

"No," I said breathlessly.

I didn't resist when he gently tugged until our bodies touched in too many places to count. "How about now?"

I shook my head, not trusting myself to speak.

His eyes locked on mine. He lowered his face until our lips were a mere inch apart. He paused, giving me time to say the word that would stop him from going any further, but my thoughts deserted me.

"Liar," he murmured before he pressed his mouth to mine.

Dinner would have to come out of the vending machines because there was no way I could face anyone tonight. My face burned every time I thought of the kiss, my first kiss, and I alternated between complete giddiness and berating myself for being a fool. Who knew what Sam thought because when our lips finally parted, I'd run back to the dorm like my hair was on fire.

After I refused a second invitation to go to the dining hall, Hayden finally left the room. First I grabbed a quick shower, and then my laptop. Flopping across the bed, it was time to see if there might be anything useful in Quinn's phone. I no longer had any qualms about blackmailing her if it would get her off my back.

"You've got to be freaking kidding me," I breathed a few minutes later.

Overconfidence is the most dangerous form of carelessness, Benson would say, though I was pretty sure he'd stolen that from a *Star Wars* movie. Still, Quinn obviously thought she was above suspicion. She'd recklessly left an electronic trail proving she'd been the one to sell the private pictures of Hayden to the tabloids. The texts detailing the transactions went back for over a year. The prices negotiated weren't pennies, but neither was it the kind of cash that would impress a girl who wore Hermès and Gucci in excess. Selling the pictures was an offense worthy of expulsion; why would she take such an awful risk?

It took several minutes to capture screen shots of the evidence, and all the while I debated how best to use what I knew. It would earn me brownie points with Karen, but she wouldn't jeopardize my cover to nail a money-grubbing classmate unless they discovered there was more to Quinn than greed.

Sending it to McKenna would get me tossed out on hacking charges. Even emailing it to her anonymously wouldn't do any good if Quinn was her snitch. McKenna would most likely delete the evidence before going on a hunt for the perpetrator. If I confronted Quinn privately, how could I be sure she would back off? It might simply motivate her to get rid of me even more quickly. No, however I used the information, there couldn't be any room for error.

My dad would probably be appalled at what I was considering, but Benson would cheer me on from the sidelines. Before reaching out to him, I did a quick scan for bugs, but the room was clean.

"Darlin' girl!" Benson's face appeared on my computer screen, his cheeks pink from his morning shave. "Did you get the box of goodies I sent?"

"Yes, but smoke bombs? Really?" I teased.

"You never know when they might come in handy. Did I ever tell you about the time I was trapped in a blind alley in Bagdad during the Iraq War?"

As much as I enjoyed his colorful stories, Hayden could walk in at any time, so I needed to cut to the chase. "No, but I've got a problem." With each new charge I leveled against Quinn, his jaw clamped tighter until his face looked like it was made of cement.

"It seems pretty cut and dried," he said when I'd finished. "End them before they end you, remember?"

It was rule #20. "I know, but how?"

He smiled in the way that usually sent the rookies running for cover. "I've got just the thing."

BENSON'S RULE #20

END THEM BEFORE THEY END YOU

Sleep was impossible.

It had taken a few days to design a plan of attack as fitting as it was final, and as I lay staring at the ceiling, I knew it was ready. Admittedly, halfway through keying in the senior class' cell numbers I started having doubts. The plan was rock solid, and exposing Quinn's sideline business could never be traced back to me, but where did taking defensive action end and becoming a mean girl begin? She threatened my mission and deserved what was coming, but what did it say about me that I was reveling in the anticipation?

Even the dogs were restless that night, with the occasional bark echoing across the grounds from the kennels. Sometimes another dog on patrol answered with a concerned "woof," but it had the reassuring feeling of a town crier announcing, "Three o'clock and all's well!"

Then there was the encounter with Sam. I kept replaying the moment like a song that spoke to the most secret part of me, shivering with quiet excitement each time. He had to know I'd purposely dodged him at Friday night's party, and my urgent getaway after our kiss wasn't exactly subtle, so why didn't he take the hint? Oh, yeah, maybe it was the way I'd kissed him back like he was going off to war.

I bit my pillow as a jumble of conflicting emotions rushed through me, both dreading and welcoming the first streaks of dawn outside my window. By the time the alarm went off, it was a relief to face the day.

Morning classes were a blur. Though I sat there and dutifully took notes, my mind unerringly strayed to the cell phone tucked inside my boot. Call me paranoid, but I didn't want to let it out of my sight. It felt dangerous and explosive. It would take only two keystrokes to activate the macro that would send all of Quinn's texts to the entire senior class and McKenna as well. Every phone would chime, buzz, or vibrate with the news Quinn had cashed in on her best friend.

It had to be done, right?

The midday bell chimed. I'd intended to put the plan into action when the class gathered for lunch, but now it felt incredibly heartless. I knew next to nothing about Quinn or what drove her. If I hit those buttons, there'd be no going back for either of us.

Dragging my feet with indecision, I was one of the last to arrive in the dining hall. Making a production out of selecting a tuna sandwich and a bottle of water didn't change things. The lunch hour was still at its peak, and Von waved to indicate my chair was waiting... right across from Quinn. At the next table over Sam smiled in invitation, but now was not the moment to add more drama to my life. I ducked my head and bee-lined to my usual spot.

The chatter went on around me. A new softball bat with a four-figure price tag had been delivered to Jackie Song from a Division I school dying to recruit her. Stef planned to organize a game of chardonnay pong for the weekend because beer, he said, was just too low-rent. And Von ran down a list of hookup spots to avoid between dinner and study period unless you had company. I started to relax, thinking maybe there was another way to handle Quinn... but then she opened her mouth.

"So, Riley," she said.

My shoulders tensed as if to absorb a blow, and I willed myself to relax. "Yes, Quinn?"

"I noticed you haven't posted your man crush yet," she drawled.

"You're right, I haven't." I took a bite of my sandwich, wondering where her vaguely rude and intrusive observations were headed this time. She could care less about my responses, and only needled me for sport, like she did every time we were together for more than five minutes.

"So who's it going to be?" Her eyes flicked between Von to my left, who followed the conversation avidly, and Sam at the next table over. Then she assumed an expression of mock embarrassment. "Oh, maybe you're waiting for tomorrow to post your woman crush? There's no shame in that, you know."

"All you need to know, Quinn, is that it's certainly not you. The gift you left in my coat pocket made sure of that. I'm going to grab a cookie," I said to the table at large, though I'd barely touched my sandwich. "Anyone want anything?"

Shouts of "chocolate chip!" and "peanut butter!" followed me into the kitchen, nearly empty except for the lunch lady wearing an immaculate white apron around her thick middle as she worked.

I grabbed a large plate and got busy filling orders, though I was in no hurry to get back to the table. Since I hadn't been able to resist mentioning the weed Quinn had planted, she was probably formulating her next plan of attack. I'd faced down much scarier people than she and held my ground, so why did I let her get under my skin? What was her end game? To provoke me into a rash action that would get me suspended or expelled?

The click of high-heeled boots came up behind me. "You can't prove anything," Quinn hissed.

I casually grabbed another chocolate chip cookie. "It doesn't matter. I know it was you." I didn't bother to mention the video because I, too, would get busted if my surveillance tactics were revealed.

"Oh yeah?" she challenged. "What are you going to do about it?"

I turned to face her. "How about nothing, Quinn? I don't know what I did to you, but I'm sorry, okay? Let's call a truce and get on with our lives." I wasn't a diplomat's daughter for nothing.

She stared at me as if I were speaking in tongues. "Get on with our lives? You don't get to decide that." She took a step closer, purposely invading my personal space. "I've been watching you, and this innocent act you've got going doesn't fool me. I've seen the way you look at Sam, and I'm going to make sure Hayden does, too. You're a nobody from nowhere. And you know what else? You... are... in... my... way." She bit off each word before slamming her hand down on the plate I held, sending cookies skittering across the floor. "Oops, you dropped something."

She stalked back out to the dining hall. I glanced over at the lunch lady, who was doing her best to be invisible. She'd probably seen far worse but valued her job too much to comment. As long as girls like Quinn thought they could get away with treating people like dirt, there'd be people who'd shrink into themselves to avoid being noticed.

I reached for my phone and powered it on. My finger hovered for a second, maybe two, before I keyed in the brief sequence and pressed "send".

A cacophony of beeps and ringtones accompanied Quinn back to the table. I hovered in the kitchen doorway as people reached into backpacks, purses, and pockets. A hush descended on the senior tables, punctuated here and there by a gasp or a giggle. The only one not thumbing through evidence of Quinn selling out her friendship with Hayden was Quinn herself since I'd excluded her from the program.

Mostly I watched Hayden. Her face lost all its color. Heads came together and the low hum of gossip kicked in. Slowly, one by one, people stared at Quinn, who had been checking her own phone and was oblivious to the wildfire soon to engulf her.

The moment I'd been waiting for came soon enough. Quinn glanced up to see dozens of people glaring, and she visibly flinched. "What?" She looked at Hayden for enlightenment. "What's going on?"

The fortitude that must sustain Hayden through countless media events, photo ops, and public scrutiny surfaced. She calmly turned to Stef. "It's on your phone, too?"

He nodded, his eyes full of compassion for his sister.

Hayden handed Quinn her phone, and all conversation stopped. Nothing was more interesting than the drama playing out here. When Quinn finally looked up from the screen, her chin trembled.

"What happened to you, Quinn?" Hayden was near tears, but she clenched her jaw as if defying them to fall. "How did you get so broken?"

Quinn started to weep. "You don't understand. I didn't mean to hurt you... I just needed the money. You have no idea what it's like to have nothing... to be nothing! I'd never worn anything that hadn't first been worn by somebody else until my grandmother died. Even then, the money wasn't enough. I *needed* it, don't you understand?"

Those fabulous Prada boots of hers had come at a very steep cost.

"You have to believe me," she sobbed. "I'm so, so sorry."

"Me, too." Hayden snatched her phone back and stood.

Quinn scrambled to her feet. "Hayden, please, we have to talk about this."

"No, we don't. In fact, we don't ever have to talk again." She glanced around the room at all the eager faces. To her credit, she strode out the door like her famous mother walked the red carpet, with head held high above the fray. She might be crumbling inside, but no one would have the satisfaction of seeing it.

Quinn dropped back into her chair like a lifeless doll. The crowd quietly gathered up their things and shuffled off to class. I was one of the last to leave, stopping by the table to retrieve my backpack.

"You did this, didn't you?" Quinn's voice was detached, as if she were reciting lines in a play she didn't understand.

"I don't know what you're talking about." I put the plate of cookies in front of her. "I got you chocolate chip. Sorry yours fell on the floor." I dug out a pack of tissues and slid them across the table before leaving her to absorb her lonely new reality.

McKenna brushed by me as I walked out the door. She gripped her phone like a weapon, and her lips were pressed together in outrage. I'd momentarily forgotten she was included on the phone chain.

The rest of the day, I pretended to be as shocked as my classmates. Theories about how the information had appeared on everyone's phones got tossed about. Some were pretty ridiculous, like a power surge, while others were more insightful, like a hacker seeking revenge. Everyone regarded the computer science nerds with a suspicious eye, and a number of students raced to delete texts from their own phones.

Hayden was absent from Chemistry that afternoon, the only class we shared. After the final bell, I made my way to our dorm to find her slumped on her bed, combing through the entire chain of stolen texts. Despite eyes red and swollen from crying, her mouth was a narrow line of fury. She must have come to the text from a certain tabloid editor who had offered a bigger payday for pictures of Hayden drunk, partially clothed, or in an embarrassing situation, to which Quinn had texted back: *I'll try.*

I kicked off my shoes and took a seat on my own bed. Quinn had forced my hand, and I regretted Hayden would have to pay for it. I'd just added another brick to her wall, the wall Sam had found too chilly to scale, all in the name of keeping her safe. There was no reliable intel indicating the heiress was in danger, and neither the drone nor the listening devices were imminent threats. Had I done the right thing? Benson would say, "Fight fair if you can, dirty if you must," so why did I feel so shitty?

"My mom will laugh her ass off when she hears about this," Hayden said, in a voice almost too low to be heard.

"What makes you say that?"

She looked up from her phone. "She told me not to come here. She knew stuff like this would happen." She let out a humorless laugh. "Who knows? If Rose were here, she might have sold me out, too."

What could I say? I'd thrown her to the wolves as well, in my own way. "I'm sorry."

She threw the phone down. "For what? You didn't have anything to do with it. In fact, I'd think you'd be glad."

I stared at her. "Why would you think that?"

"Don't play me. We both know Quinn hates your guts."

"She doesn't hate me," I countered. "She doesn't even know me. I think she hates herself."

A spark of understanding shone in her eyes. "That makes a weird kind of sense. She never thought she was good enough. If she did, she wouldn't have cared so much about being my friend." She caught my look of surprise. "I'm not a complete waste of space, you know."

"Then why were you friends with her?" I genuinely wanted to know what Hayden got out of it in return.

"You wouldn't understand," she said, more regretful than smug.

"You're right," I confessed, crossing the room and perching on the edge of her bed. "I probably wouldn't. I don't know what it's like have my every move watched and picked apart, or to make the front page of a magazine because I cut my hair. But I do know what it means to be kind."

She scooted back against the headboard and pulled a pillow across her lap in an unconscious bid for protection. "I'm glad somebody around here does."

"Look, Hayden, I'm not your enemy, and I don't want anything from you," I assured her. "Mostly I'm hoping we can get through the year with all our body parts still attached."

She laughed as if I were kidding.

With fingers steepled in contemplation, Bracken regarded me over a stack of quizzes still to be graded.

"How did you do it?"

"What?" The stapler fumbled right out of my hand. For the past twenty-four hours, the Fin de Quinn, as the French club dubbed it, had been all anyone talked about.

"I want to know how you got into Harrington. It's obvious you're smart, but no one gets in unless Gretchen wants you in. What do you have on her?"

I retrieved the stapler and hoped he didn't notice my trembling fingers. The guy had practically given me a heart attack. His wasn't an idle question though; Mr. Bracken didn't engage in small talk. He had something to tell me, but there wouldn't be any free rides.

"Quid pro quo?" I asked.

He inclined his head like a king granting favors.

"A request from Harrington's board of directors." I couldn't reveal exactly what that request was, but Bracken's intel had proven quite valuable already, and I needed to know what he'd heard.

"If that's all kids needed to get in here, they'd be lined up six deep at the gate." He leaned forward in his chair. "No, there's something more."

We stared at each other a few moments as I tried to discern why he was so interested. "If you're looking for something you can use against Mrs. McKenna, you're asking the wrong person."

He drew back in offense. "I would never stoop so low."

"Then why?" I demanded. "What are you looking for?"

He rose stiffly from his chair and paced a few steps before returning to his desk. "I've been a teacher here for twenty-two years, and during that time Gretchen has stuck her neck out again and again for this faculty." He angrily tugged his tweed vest back into place. "If she's in trouble, I want to know about it."

Could there actually be a sentimental streak in the crusty old man? It suddenly occurred to me that with their flinty personalities, he and McKenna would be well suited for one another romantically, but I shut down that train of thought immediately. If that particular image got stuck in my head, I'd gag.

"She's not in any trouble that I know of, but I can't say any more. You see, the reason I'm here is, well, it's classified." It felt silly to say, like I was playing at some spy game, but I couldn't compromise the mission.

He stared at me a beat before throwing back his head with laughter. He braced himself against his desk as he howled, slowing down only when he was in tears. Wiping his eyes, he finally caught a breath. "That," he chortled, "is the funniest thing I've heard in a very long time." Not finding it all that funny myself, I frowned. That, of course, only set him off again.

I stood up and tossed my backpack over one shoulder. If I wanted to be laughed at, I'd head down to the stables. A trot around the arena on Brutus would be sure to get everyone rolling in the aisles.

"Wait." He took a deep breath, attempting to ward off the last of the giggles. "As I've said, Miss Collins, I've been here twenty-two years. I know how things work. Right now, Gretchen is trying to figure out how you crucified Miss Sheffield because she's afraid of what you might do next."

I started to protest my innocence, but he held up a hand. "Save it. Your only chance is to admit nothing, but make sure she knows there won't be any more public humiliations. Do you think you can do that?"

McKenna was a formidable opponent with decades of experience in the political arena. If she forced a confrontation, how was I supposed to tell her she had nothing more to fear from me without her badgering a confession out of me? And confession, Benson would say, "is only good for the soul if you're a priest."

I nodded, though it was more in gratitude for the warning than in answer to his question.

"Good luck then, Secret Agent Collins," he said with a straight face, before completely losing it again.

BENSON'S RULE #21

NEVER OVERLOOK A POTENTIAL ASSET

'd barely had a minute to absorb Bracken's warning before Sarah Jane intercepted me as I trotted down the main staircase.

"McKenna's looking for you," she said. Her tone lacked its usual belligerence, and it made me even more apprehensive.

"Do you know why?"

She shrugged. "My guess is she's going to interrogate the entire senior class over those texts, and she's starting with you. Just deny knowing anything, and you'll be fine."

"Thanks," I said, bemused she'd offer me advice. "I appreciate the heads up."

We lingered on the staircase landing, sunlight filtering through a giant stained glass window depicting the Harrington coat of arms. The prefect seemed in no hurry to send me on my way.

"You're not like them," she observed. "You don't act like you're better than anyone else."

"Thanks," I said again, not sure how else to respond. "I hope this means we can be friends." *Never overlook a potential asset*, Benson would say. Having a prefect on my side could be useful, and if she would lose the resentment she wore like armor, she might even be fun.

Her curt nod said she'd take it under consideration, making me rethink using "fun" and "Sarah Jane" in the same sentence. We then parted ways as I trudged back up to the second floor. Ms. Portman wasn't at her desk, but the door to McKenna's lair stood ajar. Muttering "quid pro quo," like a talisman, I knocked.

"Come in," she ordered.

Her eyes narrowed at the sight of me, and my stomach clenched. *Always do what you are afraid to do* was another Benson rule. When I told him he'd plagiarized a Ralph Waldo Emerson quote, he'd smiled smugly and replied, "It doesn't make it any less true, now does it?"

McKenna sat at her desk. Forcing my feet across her beautiful antique rug, I met her stare without flinching–outwardly at least. "You sent for me?"

She tossed down her pen and leaned back in her chair. "What do you know about the dissemination of Quinn Sheffield's texts?" She didn't bother to invite me to sit.

"Nothing," I said, not bothering to feign surprise. "But I sincerely hope neither you nor the school suffers because of it."

"Pretty words," she said. "I will be conducting a thorough investigation. Despite Quinn's wrongdoing, we don't condone the gross violation of privacy that occurred here. We will find the perpetrator, and he or *she* will be punished."

"Mr. Bracken speaks very highly of you," I said, changing tactics. "He said you always have his back, just like you do for the rest of the staff here. I know Harrington means everything to you."

"Is there a point here?" Despite the fact she was seated and I stood, she still somehow managed to stare haughtily down her nose at me. I could imagine lesser souls turning into puddles at her feet.

I soldiered on. "I'm not saying I had anything to do with what happened to Quinn Sheffield, but I would certainly never wish anything like that to happen again." It was as far as I could go to promise no further embarrassments without admitting guilt. "While you're investigating, you may want to check out the rest of your security protocols."

She paused for a moment, as if turning over my words to see if they contained a veiled threat, but then deciding I was simply a nuisance to be flicked aside. "Despite this breach, I have complete confidence that Harrington remains the safest and most secure school in Connecticut."

There was a definite rhythm to sparring. You entered the ring, took your opponent's measure, and then moved into serious combat. With a start, I realized we were following the playbook in our verbal match. It was time to engage.

"Yes, let's hope you're right," I said, with a faint smile.

Her hard stare told me I had her attention. "What are you implying?"

"Nothing, ma'am," I said, with wide-eyed innocence. "But in the few weeks I've been here, I've seen a lot of things that may lead other people to think the school isn't as secure as you believe." The outdated lighting, the lack of security cameras, the open campus that invited trespassers all sprang to mind. "I would hate to see something else happen that would call your leadership into question." There it was, the full frontal attack.

She pushed out of her chair and slapped her palms on the desk. "I have the full support of the board and the alumni association. They would never let some little troublemaker who doesn't belong here threaten to push me out." It was a good defensive move on her part, but I wasn't finished.

"But surely it's occurred to you," I said pleasantly. "If I'm not qualified to be a Harrington girl, then what *am* I doing here?"

Her nostrils flared as she recognized the echo of her own words. Slowly she sat back down and picked up her pen, resuming the pose of a busy executive.

"Thank you for stopping by, Riley. I am delighted to hear you will do your utmost to prevent any further intrusions into our students' privacy." She looked me over with grudging respect. "Perhaps you're a Harrington girl after all."

"Thank you, ma'am."

We had tapped out and retreated to our respective corners.

A low-budget rental car squatted in front of the upper girls' dorm when I returned from class the next afternoon to change for another pointless equestrian lesson. I would never learn to ride; what I did would more aptly be described as clinging.

Dozens of students, mostly seniors, lined the walkway in front of Watson Hall stretching from door to road. Overhead, a few girls leaned expectantly out their windows. A low level of chatter hummed through the somber crowd as if gathered at the scene of an accident.

I sidled up to Von and Stef. "What's going on?"

"Walk of shame," Stef said in a hushed voice.

At my confused expression, Von said, "Quinn's leaving."

That came as no surprise. She hadn't been seen since the incident, and the rumor mill claimed she'd been expelled the following day.

Everyone fell silent as the front doors of Watson Hall were thrown open. Two of the school's security guards emerged wheeling trunks and suitcases. A hugely overweight woman, an older and frumpier version of Quinn, followed. She stared straight ahead as she marched to the car and wedged herself in behind the wheel, leaving the bemused guards to play valet.

The car's trunk packed and closed, Quinn trudged down the front steps with Major Taylor leading the way. Quinn was like a deflated balloon. Her shoulders sagged, her hair hung limply around a face blotchy from crying, and it even appeared as if she'd lost weight. She huddled inside a heavy cardigan, though the mild afternoon breeze didn't warrant such a defense.

At the door to the car, Quinn stopped and scanned the crowd. Any remaining hope she harbored that Hayden might forgive her vanished with the realization her former friend couldn't even be bothered to come witness her final humiliation. When her eyes fell on me, she noticeably stiffened and raised her chin. I imagined she'd rather die than allow me to see her defeated.

The passenger window slid down with an electronic hum. "Quinn! Get in the G.D. car!"

With her head held high, she climbed in and slammed the door behind her. Within moments the car sped away, flagrantly disregarding the ten miles an hour speed limit on campus. Most of the onlookers, including Von and Stef, faded back to their dorms or set course for the practice fields, but I remained to watch the little car zoom down to the school's front gates.

"Congratulations." I didn't have to turn around to know Major Taylor had quietly moved in behind me.

"I've done nothing to celebrate," I said, still facing the road so it appeared as if we just happened to be standing near one another.

"No? The impediment to the Frasier girl is gone, and the kill shot has Karl's fingerprints all over it. 'Identify your friends... eliminate your enemies'," she said, quoting one of Benson's rules.

I bristled at the notion I should be dancing on Quinn's grave. "It's done. I'd rather put it behind me."

"You feel sorry for the Sheffield girl?" Her voice held a note of surprise.

"Not exactly. She did the wrong thing for the wrong reason, but is it that much better if you do the wrong thing for the right reason?" My dad called it moral flexibility, but I'd never quite understood the term until now.

When no response came, I glanced behind me to see if she'd slipped away as stealthily as she'd arrived, but Major Taylor remained, her eyes downcast.

At last she said, "You'd be surprised what you will do with the right motivation. Keep me in the loop next time. We're in this together, remember?"

And then she was gone.

Hayden put on a good front. She tossed her hair with indifference as she walked by clusters of people chewing over her every move. Was Hayden secretly glad, as the rumors claimed, to be rid of Quinn? Now that her buffer was gone, would she go back to being the same outgoing girl she'd been before Rose's death? And who would claim the coveted position of her BFF? Everyone knew the job came with an automatic invitation to spend the winter holidays on the Frasier's private island in the Caribbean, so there were plenty of girls eager to apply.

Whether it was due to Quinn's absence or time lessening the pain of her grief over Rose, Hayden showed signs of lightening up. She had a quick wit and sly sense of humor, especially when it came to her own surreal life.

At dinner that night, Von teased her about how she'd used the vocabulary words *forfeiture* and *domestic* in English class. "My parents' divorce resulted in the forfeiture of one of my dad's jets, but since its range was limited to domestic travel, he got over it quickly," he quoted with glee.

Hayden laughed good-naturedly.

Later in the common room, Jane Song flipped on one of Tory Palmer's romantic comedies. "Is this cool?" Jane asked. "I love this movie."

"No worries," Hayden assured her. "I get along with my mom just fine when she's on Netflix."

I also joined her for the first time in the guys' common room for study period, though on the walk back to our dorm I was disconcerted by the mist settling on the ground, making it feel like we were trudging through a spooky, B-movie graveyard. Add that to the almost nonexistent lighting, and I suddenly longed for my footlocker full of weapons and gadgets. I would retrieve it at the first opportunity and vowed that from then on, I'd always carry my Taser and baton when we walked at night, ready to ward off intruders or the possible vampire attack.

"Have you done your chem labs yet?" I asked the following night as we walked out of Hale Hall after study period. We both had a ridiculous amount of homework for Chemistry, and part of me hoped we could collaborate.

"No. I'm behind on everything," she admitted. Left unspoken was the sympathy pass she'd undoubtedly get from our teachers for at least a week. "God, I'm sick of this place."

I surreptitiously monitored our surroundings as we started to cross the grounds. "Where are you applying to college?"

She snorted with disdain. "I don't get to apply for college. I have early acceptance at Stanford."

"That's fantastic," I exclaimed, curious as to how that could be a bad thing.

"Not if you'd rather go someplace else. It's my dad's alma mater and he gives them buckets of money, so once again I'll be Miss Stephen Frasier's Daughter."

It was obvious the last thing she wanted to hear was how lucky she was, or how much I envied her easy entrance to a university at the top of my list. "Have you told him how you feel?"

"No," she sighed. "He's so excited that I'll follow in his footsteps. I know I should be grateful, but sometimes I wish I could move to the middle of nowhere and, I don't know, hang out at a mall or something."

"Is that what typical American teenagers do?" I'd seen a few horror movies depicting that particular pastime, though it never seemed to end well for them.

"I don't know. If we ever meet one, we'll ask," she joked.

"I think you should apply to the colleges you want to go to," I said.

"Just like that?" She gazed at me as if I'd proposed a radical idea, like wearing designer knockoffs. "Blow off Stanford, and my dad's expectations, and jump ship?"

"Why not?" Her family had more money than the gross national product of several small countries I could name. Hayden could surely get her hands on cash for tuition if her dad balked at a change in plan.

We made it to Watson Hall without any ghouls rising up from the fog and raced up the stairs, too impatient to wait for the elevator. Somewhere a pair of fleecy sweats called my name.

Hayden had changed into her PJs and had a toothbrush in her mouth when she popped out of the bathroom. "What are you doing this weekend?"

I squinted at her, wondering if this was a trick question. "Anything that doesn't involve vodka."

"I'm going to New York. You should come with me." Her eyes danced as if this was the most brilliant idea in the history of brilliant ideas. She dashed back into the bathroom to rinse.

"Can you do that?" What would Major Taylor say? What would her dad say?

She stepped back out and shrugged as if it were no big deal. "Weekend pass, Dad's penthouse at the Four Seasons, a little shopping, and I'll take the Mercedes."

"Shouldn't you have, I don't know, a bodyguard or something? You're not exactly inconspicuous." I had to discourage her from taking such a risk without professional security, though the invitation was tempting.

"Every time my dad makes me have a bodyguard, they always report back on every single detail of my life," she complained. "If I ask them to cut me some slack, they always say my dad's paying them, so they need to follow orders. I'm over it."

I flopped across my bed, waiting my turn in the bathroom. "Are you planning to do something your dad wouldn't approve of?"

She grinned. "Most definitely."

My mind raced at the security implications, but maybe there weren't all that many. After all, nothing had come from the wayward drone, and who was to say Quinn hadn't planted the bugs to monitor any conversation between Hayden and me? You could buy anything online, and it would have been like her to do something like that. The more I thought about it, the more likely it seemed.

The money Karen had forked over remained hidden under my bed, begging to be spent at some overpriced boutique, and there was a pile of clothes in my closet waiting to be shown off. Hayden would go whether I went or not, and I had a duty to protect her.

"Let's do it," I said.

"Yes! We'll go Saturday morning. Have your people email school with permission for a weekend pass."

"My people?" I laughed. "You know most of us don't have people, right?"

Her smile dimmed just a bit. "Not all of us can be so lucky, you know."

As I took my turn in the bathroom, I wondered which one of us she was talking about.

BENSON'S RULE #22

KNOW YOUR STRENGTHS... AND WEAKNESSES

The hallways of Watson Hall thinned as girls headed out to the weekly underground party, but I couldn't be bothered to get off the couch. Our classmates would surround Hayden, so her safety for the next few hours wasn't a big concern. She'd dropped by the common room on the way out the door to find me sprawled lazily across one of the sofas watching an old movie.

"You're not going to the party?" she asked.

She wore a long-sleeved minidress in a geometric pattern paired with over-the-knee boots and tights. Glancing down at my grubby sweats and cozy Henley, I decided she might look awesome, but I was more comfortable, which was all that mattered at the moment.

I shook my head. "Nah, I need to chill tonight."

A few minutes later I'd raided the vending machines and had an assortment of junk food covering all the four basic food groups: sugary, fried, chocolate, and unidentifiable. Just when I thought the night couldn't get any better, Sam texted. *Going to the party?*

I texted back, *Nope. Watching TV & eating crappy food. Bliss.*

My phone quickly chimed again, but this time it was Von. *Where r u?*

Before I could respond, Sam texted again: *Want company?*

I texted *Watson common* to Von, and to Sam I texted *Sure*. I debated slapping on a fresh coat of makeup and running a brush through my hair, but that required effort. I could already tell if I ever had a boyfriend, he'd better like his girls low maintenance.

A muttered argument announced their arrival. From the sound of things, neither guy much appreciated running into the other on the way up. I stifled a grin as they shuffled into the room, plopping down on the sofa on either side of me.

"Oreo?" I offered up the snack pack, knowing you can't stay grumpy when you're eating one. A surprising amount of American junk food found its way into military shipments overseas, and Benson's guys always got the best stuff first, including anything chocolate. By the time I got to it, the Oreos were always gone.

Begrudgingly they helped themselves and before long, we were all scarfing down enough processed foods to petrify our innards.

"So, Sam, you look like you're dressed for the party," Von pointed out, as he went for the bag of chocolate-covered pretzels. "Don't let us keep you."

Truthfully, they'd both cleaned up and looked great in their respective ways. Sam's clothes were classics: black jeans that hugged his long legs, and a gorgeous blue cashmere pullover. Von tended to go more funky and creative, and tonight he wore skinny jeans in a bright shade of sapphire with a retro print button down.

"No problem, dude," Sam shot back, resting his arm on the sofa behind me. "The party's right here with me and Riley. And you know what they say about three's a crowd."

Before they decided to arm wrestle for me, I jumped in with a challenge of my own. "Do either of you play chess?"

Sam let his hand fall on my shoulder. "I used to play with my dad."

Von didn't miss the subtle move, and he wasn't pleased. "I was the president of the chess club in high school... I mean, the one I went to before I came here."

"Ohhh, I'm so intimidated," Sam goaded.

"You will be when I'm finished with you," Von snapped.

Sitting there on my hands while the two of them battled it out wasn't what I had in mind. "How about I play you both?"

"I'm going first," Von announced, getting up to drag over one of the nearby game tables.

"No, I mean, why don't I play you both," I offered with an innocent smile, "at the same time?" There was a program on my computer that allowed me to play up to four games simultaneously. Competing against two players wouldn't be a struggle.

"Aren't you full of surprises?" Von grinned. "What say we make it even more interesting?"

Sam dragged a second game table over. "You mean like if I win, you'll call it a night?"

"Don't get your hopes up, pretty boy." Von turned to me. "I'm thinking more along the lines of if I win, you'll let me take you on a ride. There are some really great trails not too far from campus, and there's a full moon tonight."

"You mean like on a horse?" No words could have upped my game more. "What are your stakes, Sam?"

He'd pulled a chair over to sit opposite and set up the board. His face lit up as an idea popped into his head. "A rematch. You come back to the gym, and I promise: no cameras."

"Alright, guys," I said, settling in. "You're on."

"Wait," Von protested, "What about you? What if you win?"

I waved him off. "Don't worry about me. If I win, I'll have the satisfaction of having beaten both of you."

Sam shot Von a troubled glance. "Dude, do you get the feeling we've just been played?"

Von leaned over the board with a supreme air of confidence. "It's not too late to bail. I'll let you know how it ends."

Sam pushed up his sleeves and hunched over his game. "Not a chance."

Von made an opening move, which I immediately countered. Sam's mouth dropped at the speed of my play. He put a few more minutes into devising his opening gambit, but I countered his move just as quickly. Neither of them laughed now.

Three moves later I captured one of Von's pawns, and Sam snickered. A minute later one of Sam's rooks fell to me, and Von sneered. They were so busy watching what the other did they weren't noticing how they were each being lured to their doom.

A visiting British diplomat by the name of James Digby once pompously bragged of his chess skills while we were seated at a boring state dinner. Twelve at the time, I volunteered that I often played with my dad. Mr. Digby thought it adorable. After dessert was served, my father arranged a match for us in the sitting room. After a few minutes, Digby lost the opinion I was adorable.

He was a good player, but I was better. As the snare around his king tightened, his comments about my strategy became mocking. He acted as if I were a fool falling into a trap of his design. Of course, that only spurred me on to make my win more decisive. As I delivered the final death blow to his king, the man flipped the board before I could call checkmate. Pieces scattered everywhere as he stomped from the room.

Later, when Dad came to my room to say goodnight, I apologized.

"What are you sorry for?" he asked. "Being a better player? Not throwing a game to an arrogant opponent?"

"But that man was really upset." *I climbed into bed and adjusted the pillows.* "Shouldn't I have been more polite?" *Protocol dictated every move in the diplomatic corps, and my main directive was to be polite.*

"Manners have nothing to do with it." He sat down on the side of my bed. "Never be less than you are because it's what people want or expect of you. Rise to every challenge, and be gracious when you win. The true test of character, which Mr. Digby utterly failed this evening, is to also be gracious when you lose."

Since that night, I'd played every game as if my life depended on it and discovered the truth in my father's words. Chess was a game where the screws slowly tightened, and a person's nature would often be revealed by how they dealt with the pressure. Drawing Sam and Von into games was the perfect opportunity to peel back a layer of social veneer to what lay beneath.

As I collected an increasing number of chess pieces from each of their boards, it was telling. Von became completely absorbed, analyzing my offensive and spending long minutes calculating his defense. Sam wasn't as serious about it. He was giving it his best shot, but a smile played across his lips as he watched me, as if the journey was more important than the destination.

My phone played the short tune announcing a Skype call. "Hi, Dad," I said, moving my knight to check Sam. "Can I call you back? I'm in the middle of a few games." I countered Von's move. If he reacted the way I predicted, check was two moves away.

"Oh? Who are you playing?" I turned the phone and made the introductions. Both Sam and Von politely said hello. Turning the phone back, my dad grinned mischievously. "Do they know you're a chess champion?"

"Oh, come on!" Von jumped from his chair while Sam started to laugh.

I pretended to scowl at my dad. "Thanks a lot. I'll deal with you later." I hung up the phone, cutting him off mid-chuckle.

Turning back to my opponents, I did my best to appear apologetic. "Shall we call it a draw?" I didn't want them to feel like they'd been suckered.

"No way," Sam protested. "This is actually kind of cool."

Von resettled himself and leaned over the board. "There will be no draw," he said with a sparkle in his eye. "I will learn your moves, and next time I will win."

We'd see about that.

It was later that night when I called my dad back. He wasn't going to be thrilled with the idea of letting me loose on the streets of New York, but he had to understand I didn't have a choice.

It was Saturday morning there, and he was already dressed for the day and in his office. His hair, usually so effortlessly groomed, looked like it had been styled in a wind tunnel. That's when I realized he must be wearing yesterday's clothes and had never made it to bed.

"Hey, kiddo, did you win?" he asked cheerfully, his tired eyes searching my face for clues to my wellbeing.

"Dad, what's wrong?" Only the threat of imminent violence would keep my father at his post all night. "Is that why you called earlier?"

He swiped a hand through his hair, and the results were no better than before. "Nothing you haven't seen or heard a hundred times before."

I stared him down. He loved to talk about his work and approached each new challenge as a learning experience for me. It was unlike him to be evasive. "What is it? Does it have anything to do with what happened before I left?"

He broke eye contact and glanced away, a dead giveaway I'd guessed right. "You're safe, and the girl you rescued is safe. That's all that matters."

Not if my interference had resulted in more people getting hurt. New York was suddenly trivial, and the problems consuming me meaningless.

He changed course. "So how's school?"

I shrugged. "It's okay." I'd debated all day whether to tell him what had gone down between Quinn and me. Dad, especially in his exhausted state, might not understand that I'd been forced to take such drastic measures.

"Hayden Frasier is going to New York this weekend," I volunteered.

That woke him up. "What about security?"

"She refuses to have a bodyguard, but it's not like I can stop her from going."

He nodded. "Do you have reason to believe she's in any danger?"

"I don't know," I hedged. "Probably not, but she invited me, and I think I should go with her. Her dad's got a suite at the Four Seasons, and it would be cool to shop in a real store for a change." Online shopping was my favorite thing in life, but I longed to stand in the middle of Barney's shoe department once again and revel in the smell of fine leather.

"You want to go?" he asked.

"You'd let me?" I couldn't believe how easy he was making this.

"I trust you to make smart choices. It's not like we're talking about a weekend in Baghdad here." Maybe not, but this was a big step for him.

"Would you email school and tell them I can go?"

He nodded, pleased to see my face light up with excitement. Benson popped up over my dad's shoulder. "Darlin' girl! Did your friend like the treat?"

Dad sent him a curious glance. "What did you send?"

"Ah, you know, mate, stuff she's been homesick for," he answered vaguely. "A pound of Turkish delight, some of Nadira's walnut baklava, you know, that kind of thing."

"Yeah, it was great. One of the girls I shared the baklava with was completely knocked out by it." I could tell Benson got the message by his wolfish grin.

My dad rubbed his chin, sure he'd just missed something of significance but not certain what to make of it. The three of us chatted easily for a few more minutes, but then my father's phone rang, and he switched into work mode. With a final reminder to be safe, he ended the call.

I composed quick emails to Major Taylor and Karen, alerting them both that Hayden was spending the weekend in the city, and my dad had given his permission for me to accompany her.

With all my duties fulfilled, I ran to my closet to decide what to pack. In less than twelve hours, my American Express card and I would take New York by storm.

BENSON'S RULE #23

THERE'S NO SUCH THING AS A COINCIDENCE

The star treatment began the moment Hayden's little Mercedes pulled up to the limestone fortress known as the Four Seasons Hotel in Manhattan's Midtown. Uniformed bellmen and parking valets descended as Hayden swung her long legs out of the driver's seat and accepted the proffered hand of an attractive doorman.

I'd dressed for shopping in fitted black jeans, a cropped pullover, and red Chuck Taylors. Hayden had tossed comfort out the window in plastered-on skinny jeans, tan Givenchy pumps, and a khaki varsity jacket. She looked ready for a photo shoot.

"Good to see you again, Miss Frasier," the doorman murmured deferentially.

Throwing her shoulders back, she accepted the greeting as her due. "Thank you, David. The bags are in the trunk." She strutted into the foyer, ignoring a couple of tourists who pulled up short at her entrance. Perhaps they didn't recognize her, but they knew she was Somebody.

The girl who strode through the hotel's elegant lobby bore only a passing resemblance to the girl who walked the halls of Harrington. This version of Hayden had the confidence of a runway model, aware of turning heads but accustomed to the attention. She was in her element, slipping into an atmosphere of money and privilege with the same comfort I felt in my oldest pair of trainers.

"Miss Frasier." The obsequious man at the front desk practically bowed. "It's always a pleasure to welcome a member of your illustrious family. Why, your mother stayed with us for the Tony's just a few months back. I'm terribly sorry she didn't win this time."

Hayden shrugged it off as of no importance. There was always next year.

The clerk waved over an eager bellman. "Please see the Frasier party to their suite."

In moments we were on an express elevator shooting up fifty floors, our ears popping as we soared into the clouds. If the moonfaced bellman accompanying us was tempted to make small talk, the impulse was stifled by Hayden's supreme air of boredom when he opened his mouth. I felt sorry for the guy, but we were in her world now and would play by her rules. I schooled myself to appear unimpressed by our opulent surroundings.

Breaking my vow immediately, I gasped when our escort swung open the door of the Frasier suite. I am not ignorant of the world, or the extravagant habitats of the rich and famous. I have visited royal palaces and presidential estates, but this place was something special.

"I know," the bellman winked conspiratorially. "This place gets me every time."

It was a crisp fall day in New York. Muted sunshine illuminated the city skyline sprawled at our feet. Giant windows and glass balconies offered spectacular views from one end of Manhattan to the other. The interiors were equally stunning. Crystal chandeliers, hand-lacquered walls, exquisite artwork, and designer fabrics blended artfully into a rich tableau, clearly conveying no expense had been spared or detail overlooked.

"Would you like to me to show you around?" The bellman, whose nameplate identified him as Gordon, was delighted to prolong his visit.

"Thank you, that will be all," Hayden sniffed.

Our bags arrived moments later. I'd brought along the Prada tote filled with gadgets, so it along with an overnight bag were stowed in a cavernous bedroom that could probably sleep six. The adjacent bathroom was done in wall-to-wall marble and was large enough to host a handball match.

"C'mon," Hayden urged. "You can unpack later. There's a new boutique in Soho everyone's talking about. Maybe we can find something new for tonight."

On the drive in, she'd called some exclusive midtown restaurant on the car's speakerphone and been immediately connected to the owner.

"Darling! It's Hayden," she'd gushed. Apparently there was only one Hayden in all of Manhattan that mattered.

"Angel! I've missed you dreadfully!" His Italian accent was so thick, I only caught every other word.

After professing their undying love for one another, she informed him we'd be coming in for dinner that evening. From his outsized response, the news was more exciting than if life had been found on other planets. For all I knew, we were on another planet. When she finally hung up, she seemed amused by my faintly nauseated expression.

"Welcome to my world," she'd said knowingly.

With a fresh coat of lipstick and a toss of my curls, I met Hayden back at the elevator. She dug an oversized pair of dark sunglasses out of her bag as we zoomed back down to the lobby. It was a pleasant day outside, but hardly glaring beach weather.

"Seriously?" I asked.

She slipped on the sunglasses and allowed just the faintest of smiles. "You'll see."

As soon as we stepped out onto the pavement, I did see. Word had gone out among the city's paparazzi that Hayden Frasier was in town. Two or three guys who all looked like they'd slept in their clothes and had gone days without shaving loitered on the sidewalk. With multiple cameras slung around their necks, they called to Hayden and began flashing away.

"Hey, gorgeous," one of them called to me. "Are you famous?"

"Not even if you paid me," I muttered, stepping into a cab that had immediately pulled over. Nothing like the flash of celebrity to open doors and stop jaded taxi drivers.

The shopping trip went pretty much the same way. Photographers followed us, adolescent girls asked for selfies with Hayden and even me, and sales clerks fell over themselves to be of service. We spent about fifteen minutes trying on sunglasses to add to Hayden's collection, and the paparazzi ate it up. From a security standpoint it was a nightmare, but at least if she was kidnapped it would be photographed from about a hundred different angles.

We staggered back into the suite just as the sun started to set, and ribbons of orange-colored clouds streaked across the sky. Loaded down with beautiful shopping bags almost as gorgeous as the clothes they contained, I admired one made of fabric with silken handles and another of creamy, textured paper with flowers pressed into the weave. This never happened with online shopping.

"Be ready at eight," Hayden called out, as she and her multiple bags disappeared into a separate wing.

"No problem. That'll give me plenty of time to swim laps in the bath." I'd seen backyard Jacuzzis smaller than the tub in my bathroom.

The time flew by as I enjoyed every amenity the room offered. The array of bath soaps arranged on an onyx tray filled the air with scents of green tea and lavender, and a thick loofa polished my skin until it glowed. On a silver hook a snowy white robe waited to wrap me in luxury. I could get used to this.

The two women who later stepped into a town car were worlds away from the high school girls we'd been just hours before. I'd shimmied into a midnight blue silk cocktail dress with a matching coat and a sky-high pair of Jimmy Choos. A dramatic sweep of eyeliner and a lush red lipstick aged me a few years, and Hayden nodded in approval. She'd gone the polar opposite in head to toe white, pulling off the image of icy blonde to perfection.

"Whatever happens tonight, just go with it," she said. "If you don't know what to say, say nothing. Got it?"

"I have been off the farm once or twice in my life," I said dryly, having attended state dinners since the age of ten.

"Not like this," she promised.

The driver's friendly dark eyes met mine in the rearview mirror. "Good evening, ladies. My name is Steve. Where may I drive you this evening?"

His accent told me his name was probably Tariq or Malik, but it certainly wasn't Steve. Hayden gave him the name of the restaurant, and we were on our way.

Dimitri, the Italian restaurateur, swooped in as soon as Hayden made her entrance. We were whisked to a large table in the center of the room where we were put on display like cattle on an auction block. No I.D. was required for the vodka tonics she sipped in a steady stream, though I stuck to club soda.

Dinner, such as it was, involved tiny bits of food artfully arranged on huge plates the size of hubcaps. I didn't know whether to eat it or hang it on a wall. Dimitri checked back so often, it was like a threesome. His personality was bigger than the portions.

The rest of dinner passed in a blur of smiling faces, air kisses, camera flashes, and ready laughter. Our party swelled with the addition of four or five of Hayden's society friends who latched on somewhere between the restaurant and our arrival at a trendy nightclub. Their collective attitude straddled the line between excess and boredom, dressed up in the most expensive designer clothing with apparently nowhere of interest to go.

As we crammed into the town car, a guy wearing a shiny suit and way too much hair product gave me such a thorough once-over, I wanted to punch him.

"Who are you, sweetmeat?" he asked.

Hayden shot me look that caused me to bite back the nasty retort waiting to fly. "Er, Riley Collins, and you are...?" Not that I cared.

"Ty Overstreet." Despite his weary expression, he keenly observed whether I recognized the name of one of New York's oldest and richest families. It was a curious test, making me wonder which reaction would get him to back off. I feigned ignorance, glancing out the window as Steve drove us south to the trendy Meatpacking District.

It was the wrong choice. Ty grabbed my hand as we jumped from the car. I shot a desperate glance at Hayden, but photographers were already surrounding her. Dozens of people watched sulkily as we immediately bypassed the long line waiting behind a velvet rope. A leggy hostess in black leather shorts led us past the dance floor where sweaty bodies writhed and strobe lights flashed in time to the pumping music. Once we'd all jammed into a tiny booth, Ty flicked a credit card at the hostess and barked an order for champagne.

The blaring music limited conversation to screaming into each other's ears, so I retreated into the role of observer. The more my companions drank, the more desperate they seemed in their quest for fun. Ty draped his arm around my shoulders. I stiffened, but since we were all packed together there was no way to gracefully extract myself.

This wasn't what I expected and, frankly, it was boring. I had been Hayden's plus one only until she hooked up with the group of rich kids she called friends. It was a rude reminder I had a job to do.

From our vantage point on an elevated platform we had a panoramic view of the entire crowd, so like a good secret agent I checked out the little dramas happening all around. The girls on the dance floor losing themselves in the music, and the high-fiving boys anticipating an easy score; the steady stream of people to and from the DJ's booth—a sure sign the guy was dealing in more than music—and the two stiff, unsmiling men who were obviously club security. They lurked at the end of the bar like they were on a stakeout. One, wearing a cheap navy suit, had a broom-like mustache that concealed his entire upper lip; the other sported horn-rimmed glasses and khaki pants more fitting for a computer store salesman.

Benson often lamented the biggest hindrance to his team assimilating into native populations was the rigid posture instilled into all military personnel. These guys had bigger problems than that, but hopefully their mark, most likely the DJ, wouldn't be as observant.

Ty decided that would be a good moment to stick his hand up my skirt. Years of being trained to instantly act upon a threat kicked in without thought.

"What the hell?" If the table hadn't been bolted to the floor, it would have overturned when he hurdled out of the booth, clutching his nearly dislocated thumb. The music drowned out the rest of his rant against my virtue and parentage, but the meaning was clear as he hopped about in pain, though I knew it wasn't that bad. The same thing happened to me when I was learning how to use a crossbow. With a bit of ice and some Tylenol, he'd be perfectly fine in a day or two.

I turned back to my tablemates to find Hayden calmly studying me. She was more clear-eyed than I would have expected after all those vodka tonics, making me wonder if she'd switched them out for plain soda water long ago. I glanced at her in query, and she responded with a head jerk to indicate we should bail.

I tried to brush past Ty, but his mouth twisted into an angry sneer as he roughly grabbed my arm. The boy was obviously a slow learner, but this time I took a moment to consider that inflicting visible damage on the scion of an important family would probably come back to bite me. The fist that should have hammered his nose sunk into his fleshy middle instead, and all color drained from his face as he sank to his knees.

This time it was Hayden grabbing my arm as she tugged me through the steamy crowd and into the brisk night air. Steve had illegally parked the car across the street and leapt into action when he saw us coming. He yanked open the back door and peeled out as soon as we dove inside.

Hayden burst into peals of laughter. "Did you see the look on Ty's face?" She cracked up again. "He didn't see that one coming."

I impatiently brushed the hair out of my eyes. "You don't mind that I handed your friend his ass on a platter?"

"Oh, puleeze," she drawled. "We're not friends. He just wants to make the tabloids, and I'm his best shot at getting anyone to notice. Ty The Upskirter's had it coming for a long time."

The driver butted in. "Where to ladies?"

Much to my relief, Hayden said, "Four Seasons."

I slumped back on the seat. "God, I'm starving."

Hayden perked up. "Me too." She hit a few digits on her phone. "This is Hayden Frasier. I'd like to order room service."

Steve's eyes darted to the rear view mirror, but he wasn't checking us out. He did it again, and then again, his brow furrowing deeper each time.

I leaned forward. "What is it?" I asked quietly in Arabic so as not to alert Hayden.

His eyes widened. "I've made three turns in the last eight blocks, and a black SUV has stayed with us," he said, answering me in the same language. "Maybe it's just paparazzi, but they were parked outside the club, too."

Every tabloid editor in town knew where we were staying, so it probably didn't matter, but my training insisted otherwise.

"Can you lose them?"

His eyes crinkled in amusement. "Buckle up."

I did as instructed and gestured for Hayden to do the same, mouthing "paparazzi" at her. She nodded absently as she continued her phone call and reached for her seatbelt.

I'd downloaded a traffic app before we'd left Harrington and pulled it up now. "7th Avenue is jammed at 34th," I informed Steve, nervous about being boxed in even if it was just by overzealous photographers.

He took a screeching left through a yellow light and found a parallel route, but two minutes later the SUV was back. Steve muttered a word I'd only heard once during an argument over a parking spot in Karachi, and though I didn't know the translation, its meaning was clear.

"Sorry," he apologized, catching my eye.

"No problem." I consulted my phone again. "Turn right! Turn right!" The street directly ahead was stalled with bumper-to-bumper traffic. He hit the gas and veered into the right lane, cutting off a taxi as we made the turn. The yellow cab laid on the horn and slammed on its brakes, forcing the SUV behind it to do the same.

"Great driving!" I exclaimed, feeling sure we'd be safely delivered to the hotel long before they could catch up.

"What language is that?" Hayden had finished her phone call and regarded me with bemusement.

"The holy language of Islam," Steve cheerfully volunteered from the front seat. "Your friend speaks it quite well."

Hayden stared at me another moment. "Aren't you full of surprises?"

Twenty minutes later we were back in the suite, sitting barefoot around a giant tablecloth spread on the carpet in front of a picture window. I probably should have alerted Karen and Major Taylor about the suspicious SUV, but a very accommodating waiter had laid out what appeared to be everything on the hotel menu, and now Hayden and I were happily passing plates back and forth. This was my idea of dinner.

"You handled yourself really well tonight. My friends can be a total pain in the ass," Hayden said, grabbing a toasted wedge of grilled gruyere cheese with bacon and tomatoes before passing it over. "You've got to have one of these."

I took the plate, confused by her compliment. "I don't get it. Why did we hang out with people like that douchebag Overstreet if you don't like them?" There was something about sitting cross-legged on the floor and picking at food with your fingers that invited honesty.

"You wouldn't understand." It was the same evasive answer she gave when I'd asked why she allowed Quinn to use her as a stepladder.

"Maybe if you talk slowly and use short words, I can keep up."

She took another bite of her sandwich and eyed me like I was one of those sleeping vipers you find in the more exotic marketplaces of Pakistan. Mostly they were sluggish and slow to attack, but that didn't mean they weren't dangerous.

"You remind me a lot of Rose," she said. "That's a compliment, by the way."

"I'm sorry I'll never get the chance to meet her." I suddenly realized that with all the other drama going on, the phone stashed under my mattress had completely fallen through the cracks. I resolved to dig it out as soon as we returned.

Hayden reached for the fries. "Rose was the first person I'd met in a long time who didn't treat friendship like a transaction."

"That's kind of gross," I blurted.

She scowled. "I told you, you wouldn't understand."

"Actually, I think I do." My dad had dated several eligible women in the years since my mother's death, but like Benson, he always ended it before it got too serious. He joked the romances didn't last because he could never find a girl as special as me, but as I grew up it was more likely he was afraid to open himself up again. Benson once told me my father was a different man after the death of my mom.

"I get why people want to be your friend," I said, swiping the fries before she could eat them all. "I also understand why you'd keep your distance from people like that. What I don't get is why you'd hang out with people like Overstreet to begin with."

"You mean why don't I stay home and read a book or watch a movie?" She described my usual Saturday night with derision.

"Well, yeah." I took a bite of lobster ravioli and practically swooned. "Oh, my God, you have to try this."

We'd polished off the pasta when she said, "There are certain expectations that come with being the daughter of people like my parents."

Starting to fill up, I dropped my fork and reached for the covered tray we'd been saving for last. I lifted the lid to reveal a tasting assortment of artfully arranged desserts.

"You're right," I said with mock severity. "From now on, I will expect you to always order enough desserts to put us both into diabetic comas."

She snorted with laughter. "I'm serious. If I'm not seen in the right places with the right people, I'll become Tory Palmer's loser daughter or Stephen Frasier's socially inept child. That stuff can follow you around for life."

"Okay, so you want to polish your public image, I get that." I dragged a spoon through the most amazing brownie sundae known to mankind. "But why Quinn?"

Hayden attacked a caramel cheesecake with single-minded determination, and I wondered if I'd pushed too far. After a few bites she said, "After Rose... it was easier not to fight it, you know?" She glanced up, and I could read the sadness on her face.

I didn't know, but there were a lot of things in Hayden's life I hoped I'd never have to experience.

I gazed out the window at the carpet of lights Manhattan became when viewed from fifty stories up. It was seductive, as was the wealth and power making our every wish a reality from the moment we'd arrived, but I wouldn't want to trade places with her. All the money in the world could never make up for parents who left their kids to navigate such a treacherous world all on their own.

"Maybe you should give yourself time to figure out what you want, not what other people want or need you to be. You might actually like staying in and watching a movie on a Friday night." I shrugged with a self-deprecating smile. "I do."

She groaned. "Wouldn't you know I get the only roommate at Harrington whose idea of a hot date is a remote control." She followed her words with a warm smile. I had a feeling I might have more company on the sofa next Friday.

I scooped up a bite of pumpkin crème brulee topped with whipped cream and chocolate shavings. "Oh, my God...." I moaned in ecstasy.

She grinned. "I know, right?" She started in on the other end. "My dad and I order this every time we're here."

"It can't be that often," I said, pointedly gazing at her perfect figure.

"It'll be a lot more soon, at least for my dad. His assistant said we couldn't use the suite for the next few weeks because he'll be in town. Apparently his new software program has been fast-tracked."

The spoon froze halfway to my mouth. Had the announced deadline been a ruse to throw off competitors, or had the delivery date truly been moved up? What, if anything, did Karen know about this? My mind raced at the implications.

"C'mon," she urged, oblivious to my sudden shift in mood. "Don't make me eat this all by myself."

I'd instantly lost interest in dessert but took another bite to be social. "Has your dad told you what he's working on?" Hopefully he'd shared some of his project details with her.

"Yeah," she said, growing thoughtful. "It's supposed to be the ultimate code-breaking software, but I don't know if that's a good idea. He's says if everyone knows each other's secrets, it'll end wars before they can even start. The thing is, though, I think it might be dangerous."

"What makes you say that?"

"Our house in Silicon Valley is guarded like a prison these days with, like, triple the usual number of security. I wish he'd either stop the project or give it away to everyone." She was smart and observant. Surely she'd seen the possibility of being used as a pawn in the high-stakes game her father waged.

"Have you ever thought you might be in danger, too?" I asked.

She tossed her head, glossing over any fears. "It's not like I have anything to do with it."

Now I knew she hadn't been drinking vodka all night as she'd appeared. My dad called alcohol the great truth serum, and if ever there was an occasion to admit there might be trouble ahead, it was now.

BENSON'S RULE #24

IF ALL ELSE FAILS, GO WITH YOUR GUT

Sleeping until noon was a rare luxury unless I was sick, or more recently, nursing a hangover. Both Dad and Benson rose with the chickens, and they insisted everyone else did the same. When I stumbled into the suite's dining room at midday, Hayden was drinking coffee and watching some reality show about buying wedding dresses. I poured a cup and sat down in front of the big screen.

When a Southern bride-to-be burst into tears because her mom called her choice of dress tasteless and tacky, Hayden asked, "Brunch and shopping before we drive back?"

"Game on," I replied. "Let me grab a shower."

Going shopping, I texted Karen from the bathroom.

Again??? Karen must have seen the charges already.

SF may have moved up the timeline for delivery. That should take her mind off my spending.

She fired back, *Is HF the source?*

Yes. BTW, we got followed by a black SUV last night. Probably nothing... I texted just as my battery died. I'd forgotten to pack my charger, but maybe Hayden had one in the car.

I turned on the shower and slipped out of my PJs. Stepping into the hot water, the anticipation of hitting up Barney's shoe department for the second time in a month filled me with excitement. If Karen texted me again, I didn't know or care.

It was late afternoon when we finally revved up the Mercedes and drove out of the city. It had been one of the best weekends of my life, a fantasy made all the better for knowing it had an expiration date. Admittedly, there had been a moment at Barney's that was pretty cool.

We were strolling through the store on the way to the shoe department when one of the salesgirls who'd helped outfit me weeks earlier crossed my path. "Good to see you again, Miss Collins." She smiled as she passed, not even noticing the celebutante beside me. The stunned look on Hayden's face was priceless.

We'd left New York behind and were sailing along the multi-lane highway cutting through Connecticut. I envied Hayden her confidence behind the wheel. I hadn't gotten my license yet because driving in Karachi was practically a death sentence. Between non-existent lanes, craters laughingly called potholes, and no discernable speed limit, it was easier to get in a taxi and close your eyes. Odds were you would get where you were going in one piece.

The music blasted, and while my phone charged, I idly admired the passing scenery as it became more rural. I hadn't yet tired of the concept of trees. At some point I became aware Hayden had sped up and began changing lanes abruptly.

I straightened up and looked around. "What's going on?"

"Damn paparazzi have been following us for miles," she complained. "I've tried to put some distance between us, but they're getting closer."

I checked out the side mirror. My body went cold when I saw the black SUV. If Stephen Frasier had fast-tracked Rosetta, maybe threats against his family had been fast-tracked, too. Hayden had given the local photographers so many photo ops, she was bound to be on the cover of every magazine next week. There was no reason for them to follow us out of state.

I picked up my phone, the only weapon I had. "I'm calling 911." I'd been smart enough to bring my Prada tote, but foolish enough to toss it in the trunk.

"I can lose these fools," she said. "My mom sent me to stunt driving school for exactly this reason." She stepped on the gas, and the Mercedes shot forward.

The SUV did the same, cutting off another car in a dangerous maneuver. I had a very bad feeling about this.

"9-1-1, what is your emergency?" The operator's calm voice was in complete opposition to my growing fear. While Hayden whipped the car around drivers who honked at us in irritation, I quickly explained our situation.

"Paparazzi are following you?" Her tone held a faint note of dismissal.

"Would you please send help?" I was sure by now the people behind us weren't photographers, but I also didn't want to blow my cover.

The SUV gained on us. Hayden drove like she spent weekends competing in NASCAR races, but our pursuers were taking huge risks. Several other drivers had been forced to slam on their brakes, and the SUV only narrowly avoided a major collision. It was a miracle nobody had been killed yet. What would they do if they caught up to us? Surely they didn't want to run us off the road. A live Hayden was much more valuable than a dead one, or at least I hoped.

The operator's voice cut into my racing thoughts. "We have units in the area. They are converging on your location."

Our pursuers pulled up along the driver's side, and I fumbled the phone. Two very familiar men were in the black SUV: the driver wore a distinctive mustache in place of an upper lip, and his passenger peered at us through horn-rimmed glasses. They hadn't been checking out the drug dealing DJ at the nightclub last night after all.

"Watch out!" I yelled, as the driver yanked the wheel in our direction. Despite my ambiguous warning, Hayden smartly jerked the wheel and sent the car flying into the far right lane.

"They're trying to kill us!" Hayden sounded more affronted than frightened, as if she still believed the assailants were crazed fans.

"Get off, get off!" An exit was fast approaching and with any luck, the SUV wouldn't be able to whip over in time. We shot down the curving off-ramp at a speed that might have doomed the larger vehicle if they'd been able to negotiate the last second maneuver. The Mercedes barely held onto the ramp as it was, the tires squealing in protest as we ricocheted onto the road below. I unconsciously braced for impact.

Hayden sped through a stop sign without pause. "Now what?"

"Just go! They will probably get off at the next exit and backtrack, so put as much distance as you can between us and the highway!"

Taking a perpendicular tact away from the highway, we whipped through a small town's commercial district—thankfully quiet at this time on a Sunday—before zipping through a tree-lined neighborhood of pretty little homes. Several anxious glimpses behind us revealed we were alone, but Hayden wasn't slowing down, which was fine by me. We had just ripped down the area's main street at a high rate of speed when the sirens sounded. Thank God.

I picked up the phone from where it had been sliding across the floor. "Are you still there?"

"Yes, ma'am," answered the operator. "Did you lose your paparazzi?"

"Yes," I said, letting out a sigh of relief, "and the police are here."

Hayden pulled over, with the squad car tucking in right behind.

"Not state police if you're off the Interstate," she warned. "The units I sent are still searching the ninety-one."

An insistent tap on my window alerted me there was a rather displeased police officer demanding my attention. He was most likely a local of whatever small town we'd just blown through, unaware of our brush with two predators whose agenda was still unclear to me. I rolled down the window and smiled.

"Hello, Officer."

"Turn off the car, and hang up the phone," he promptly ordered. Every button on his uniform sparkled, the creases on his pants sharp enough to cut, and he wore his hair at regulation length and not a centimeter more. This guy meant business.

I held up the phone. "But…"

He plucked it from my hand, punched "end", and set it on the dash. I shot a look of trepidation at Hayden, who immediately shut off the ignition and unleashed her famous smile. "I'm so glad to see you, Officer. The most dreadful thing just happened…"

Her words dried up at his unrelenting stare. "License and registration."

While she was digging through her cluttered Birkin bag, another officer appeared at her window. It must be a slow day. She thrust the requested items at the new arrival, an older and less polished version of his partner.

He looked them over a moment before asking incredulously, "This is your car?"

Hayden's mouth tightened in indignation. We were both shaken by what just happened, but losing it with these guys wouldn't help.

Don't do it, don't do it… I silently chanted. Law enforcement officers, from military MPs to the armed henchman who stood loyally by the side of the village chieftain, were all generally cast from the same mold. They were expected to be invisible until beckoned, mete out justice with the wisdom of Solomon, and check their egos at the door. The only thing they asked for in return was respect. I had a horrible feeling Hayden hadn't learned this particular life lesson.

"Of course it's my car," she snapped. "Who else would it belong to? Don't you even want to know why we were running for our lives?"

As expected, the officer didn't take kindly to her attitude. "Step out of the car please, Miss."

She angrily climbed out of her seat while I slumped lower in mine. I could just hear the painful phone call between Major Taylor and me when I called to tell her we were in jail somewhere in rural Connecticut. To top it off, I'd probably get my arsenal confiscated. Wait!

"Officer," I said to the man still standing sentry at my window. "May I reach into my bag for a document you might be interested in seeing?"

Benson had lectured me several times to never making sudden movements if you found yourself under the gun.

At the officer's curt nod I extracted my State Department card, which I'd grabbed when packing the cash and American Express card, and handed it over. He leaned closer, skeptically comparing me with the picture on the card. "Is this for real?"

Things were not going well on Hayden's side of the car, as evidenced by her voice pitching ever-higher.

"The girl with me is Hayden Frasier, the daughter of Stephen Frasier," I said in a confidential whisper. His startled reaction told me we were on the same page. "I've been assigned by the State Department to make sure she gets back to school safely, but if you take us in my cover will be blown. Please, we've invested a lot of time and taxpayers' money into planting me at her school. Can you help a girl out here?"

He stared at me for a few moments without any indication he'd heard a word I said. Then he straightened. "Hey, Bill," he called to his partner, retreating to his patrol car. With a warning to Hayden not to move a muscle, Officer Bill ambled back to the squad car as well. I watched in the side mirror as my card was passed to the older man whose mouth puckered in derision. We were doomed.

Hayden leaned in through the open window, practically vibrating with anger. "He doesn't believe a word I say. He won't even check to see that we were being chased down the highway. I've never been treated like this!"

I didn't want to appear unsympathetic, but playing the princess card was pretty weak. "Calm down, Hayden," I sighed, reaching again for my phone. "They're just doing their jobs. The harder we make it for them, the longer we'll be here."

With a huff she withdrew and presented me with her back.

I needed to text Karen with our whereabouts while I still had access to my phone. Waiting to call her from jail would spike her blood pressure like a triple espresso. Looking at my phone, I was surprised to discover several messages from her that had gone unnoticed until now.

Confirmed HF's info is correct. Get out of the city NOW.

What is EST time of departure?

Riley, where are you?

RILEY???

Oops. I immediately texted: *We're out of NY and safe, but something happened. More later…*

I glanced into the side mirror to see both cops headed our way. The younger one split off as they approached, and he stopped at my window. He handed over my ID card. "All I can say is I hope you're older than you look if our government is putting the fate of the nation into your hands."

I perked up. "We can go?"

"It looks that way." He didn't appear convinced this was in the best interests of the American people, but the paperwork was in order.

Moments later Hayden opened the car door and dropped back into her seat, her face smug. "It's about time they realized who I am."

We'd lost our pursuers, but they had to know where we were going. They were probably waiting for us somewhere up ahead on the way to school. I'd instructed Hayden to take back roads as far as we could, but eventually we'd come to the only route leading to Harrington. This was a ZEBRA moment if ever there was one.

Within moments of stealthily texting the word to Major Taylor, my phone rang.

"Hello?" I pretended not to recognize the number on the screen. "Oh, hello, Major Taylor. Yes, I'm with Hayden Frasier, and we've run into some trouble on the way back to school. I'm glad you were monitoring the police scanners and recognized the description of Hayden's car," I said, making it up on the spot. I went on to explain the incident in further detail along with my fear that the mysterious men were waiting to pick up our trail again.

"Where are you now?" Her voice was tight and strained as befit an officer who'd have her hat handed to her on the way out the door if anything to should happen to her charge. "I'll text you the route I want you to take," she said after I'd told her our location. "A marked car will intercept you, and escort you back to campus."

One lone rent-a-cop against two dangerous attackers felt like tossing a kitten into a ring of bulldogs. "Maybe you could send more? Like all of them?"

"Let me assure you, Miss Collins, the people I'm sending will be sufficient for the job," she said crisply. "One of them is my first lieutenant, whom I trust implicitly." Office Wieringa came to mind. She was right; that guy was no mall cop. "Have you contacted anyone else about this?"

"No," I said, not wanting to mention Karen in front of Hayden.

A few moments later, my phone chimed with directions so detailed, the woman could go work for Google Maps if she ever tired of the military. Following her instructions, we picked up the Harrington patrol car along with an escort from the Bridgehurst police precisely where we were told to expect them. With that much backup, I was almost disappointed when we reached the school's front gates without spotting the black SUV.

Hayden had retreated into thoughtful silence the whole way back to school. The girl with trust issues bigger than the Sahara might be reconsidering the events of the last few weeks, from the highly unusual break with school policy that launched me into her orbit, to the mysterious unmasking of Quinn, who just happened to be my nemesis. How would she react if she found out I was there under false pretenses? Could she see past the circumstances that brought us together to the genuine affinity growing between us? The idea of damaging our budding friendship upset me more than I would have thought possible not too long ago.

She broke her silence after zipping into a parking spot. "How did you get the head of security on the phone so fast? I saw you texting her."

"My dad's in the government," I explained, having come up with a fast excuse in case she called me on it. "I wouldn't be surprised to find that he'd programmed the number for National Air Defense into my phone."

She shook her head as if she wasn't buying it. "Those men tried to kill us, but I'm beginning to think I wasn't the one they were after." She pinned me with a stare.

"Who are you, Riley Collins?"

BENSON'S RULE #25

DISTRACTIONS ARE FOR OTHER PEOPLE

We barely made it back in time for study period, so I was able to duck Hayden's question. Leaving our bags in the car, I ran to the dorm to find Sarah Jane counting down the seconds on her phone. I was glad to see she hadn't completely lost her power trip mojo.

Afterward, I didn't wait for a summons to make the trek to meet Major Taylor. She would want every detail of our highway encounter starting with descriptions of our pursuers and ending with my distress call. I lamented not taking a picture when they pulled up alongside us, but near-death experiences have a way of affecting one's picture-taking abilities.

"What could they have been thinking?" I asked when she'd heard the whole story. "If Hayden wasn't practically a stunt driver, I don't know that we'd have made if off that highway alive. But what value does she have to them dead?"

Major Taylor was grim. "My guess is that her death, had they succeeded, was intended to be a message to Stephen Frasier: he better reconsider his plan, or he'll be next."

"Do you think the new delivery date is freaking everyone out?" Since

Karen had been able to confirm the truth to that rumor, chances were the entire spy world knew it, too.

Before she could respond, my phone announced an incoming Skype call. Once we were safely inside the gates of Harrington, I'd texted Benson with a brief summary of our encounter on the road, and that I needed to speak to him right away before Dad heard about it. My dad made a living knowing everyone else's business, but I wanted someone on my side before this particular report made its way to his desk.

"It's Benson," I told her. "I can't leave him hanging." He'd probably just woken up and seen my message.

"Are you alright?" he said urgently as soon as his pale and unshaven face popped up on the tiny screen.

"I'm fine, but I guess I won't be leaving campus again until this is all over." It felt like shades of Karachi all over again, a prisoner in an elegant cage.

"That's right you won't. I may even contact Grace Taylor to make sure of it," he threatened, still frightened for me.

"Don't bother, she's right here." I turned the phone to capture Major Taylor standing at my shoulder, catching them both off guard.

"Karl," she murmured, running a hand self-consciously across her hair as she smoothed back any strays escaping from her ponytail.

"Uh, hiya, Grace," he greeted her, rubbing a hand over the stubble on his chin. "I guess this phone call should have waited until I'd showered and shaved."

She laughed softly. "Nonsense. You were concerned about Riley, and making sure she was safe was your first priority." Her smile transformed her entire face, making her look years younger.

"You look wonderful, Grace. You haven't changed a bit. What's it been... fifteen years?"

"Seventeen." She said it quickly, as if she'd been keeping track.

"And a Major now," he said proudly. "I always knew you were destined for great things."

Sadness flickered in her eyes, but vanished as quickly as it had come. "It was you who went looking for great things. I would have been happy with something else."

Whoa, this was getting way too personal for my taste. "Here," I interrupted, thrusting my phone into Major Taylor's hands. "How about you just have somebody drop this by my room when you guys are done?"

Recalled to her senses, she said in a businesslike tone, "That's not necessary. I'm sure Karl wants to hear what happened today. Maybe he'll have some insight."

So once again I recalled the relevant details of the past twenty-four hours, ending with, "Don't you think someone should let Stephen Frasier know? I mean it's obvious Hayden's on the game board now. She and her brother should both be taken somewhere much safer than this place. No offense, Major Taylor."

I told Benson about Stef and his father's apparent disdain for him, warning, "Just because Stephen Frasier is a douchebag about his kid doesn't mean Stef is safe, you know."

"Ah, geez," he lamented. "This was just supposed to be a walk in the park for you, Riley, but I don't like where this is headed. Grace, is there any chance these kids can be stashed somewhere safe until all this blows over?"

"I can make the recommendation, but..." She paused as if deliberating whether to reveal something that perhaps she shouldn't. "Here's the deal, Karl. I don't know that Stephen Frasier even knows what is really happening in the world outside his lab, or wherever it is he's working. My impression is he's in genius mode, and his handlers will do anything to keep him focused on his work. Everyone not directly linked to the project is, uh..."

"Expendable. Grace, I need a favor," Benson said, an odd undercurrent of anxiety in his words. "I need you to promise me that if anything goes down there, you will put Riley first."

She and I both blanched, but Major Taylor found her voice first. "I can't believe you're asking me to neglect my sworn duty! The Karl Benson I knew would never—"

"Grace!" He cut her off. She still held my phone, but now she brought it closer to her face. There was no chance he'd miss the chill in her eyes.

"Remember Dubai?" he gently asked. "If you and I had... what I'm trying to say is, if the child had lived..."

"Stop," she whispered.

"I can't. Riley is like a daughter to me, the one you and I should have had. Please, promise me you'll protect her."

The suffering on Major Taylor's face was unmistakable, and I wanted to be anywhere but in this tiny office watching my proxy uncle rip scabs off old wounds. I couldn't believe he'd asked her to put my needs, his needs, before the success of the mission. It went against everything I thought I knew about him and his sense of honor and duty. I also realized, though, his request hadn't truly shocked me. What made Benson such an effective leader, teacher, uncle, and friend was his great capacity to love.

"I promise to protect Riley as if she were my own," she finally said, her voice filled with suppressed emotion. "But I also have a job to do."

He bowed his head in acknowledgment. "Understood."

"You would have made a great father, Karl," she said softly.

They were silent for a few moments. "Is Riley still there?" he asked. She handed me the phone and turned away.

"You need to call your dad, kiddo," he said to me.

I cleared the thickness in my throat. "He's going to want me to come home."

Back to being a virtual prisoner within the embassy, back to endless days of boring tutors, and back to a life without Hayden, Sam, Von, and Stef, people I had come to care about. "Can't it wait a few days? Please?"

His stern visage softened. "You can talk to him tomorrow, but no later."

Curled up in bed with her face buried in a book, Hayden ignored me when I walked in. It was like we were back at square one with a noticeable chill in the room. I sighed, wanting to tell her everything, but knowing if she refused to keep my secret, she could do irreparable damage to my mission. Today's close call brought home once again the seriousness of our situation. It also made it imperative to pay attention to anything out of the ordinary, and a hidden phone certainly qualified as suspect.

A moment later she tossed her book down and padded into the bathroom. Taking advantage of her absence, I quickly plucked the dead phone out from under my mattress and cabled it to my computer. Even if it wouldn't power on, the memory might still be intact.

After a few long minutes, my patience was rewarded when the phone's display flashed on to reveal a screensaver. It was a photo of four people squeezed together in classic selfie pose. Rose, with her friendly smile, held the camera slightly elevated while Von, Stef, and Hayden grinned up at the lens. Their faces were slightly distorted by a spider web of cracks, the biggest one slashing Rose's face directly in half. Knowing what her future held, it weirded me out to see it now.

I ran my thumb across the screen, tapped at icons, and played with the power button, but it was completely non-responsive. Retrieving data from a broken phone was pretty routine if you had the right software. Or if the phone was too badly damaged, you could extract the chip with a blast of super-heated air and insert it into a working model. I had a general idea of how to do this from watching a forensics team recover photos from a charred cell phone found at the scene of a suspected terrorist bombing in Egypt.

Since I didn't have the right equipment to heat the chip—not even Hayden's ridiculously expensive ionic, tourmaline-boosted ceramic blow dryer was up to the job—hopefully one of Benson's software programs would do the trick.

I pulled out the case of USB sticks. Sorting through them as quickly as possible, I found one tagged, *Forensic Software for Mobile Device Analysis*, which seemed an overblown way to say, "Get Junk Out of Your Phone." Booting up the program, the software went to work.

My thoughts turned to the unexplained events beginning to pile up. *There's no such thing as a coincidence* was one of Benson's favorite sayings. It was just the word people used when they couldn't see the other people who pulled the strings.

Rose had been killed while driving one of the quiet back roads to school. It was possible she was dodging a deer, but what if she, too, had met with a certain black SUV? Her death should have left Hayden alone in her room every night from curfew to breakfast because the school didn't admit seniors. Had my arrival thrown a wrench into somebody's plans?

Then there was the mystery of the concealed phone I was now positive had belonged to the dead girl. If it were my phone, I would have either taken it with me in hopes the people at the phone store would know how to transfer the data or left it on my desk. Rose had arrived before Hayden and was alone in the dorm. Had she been hiding it from someone in particular?

My computer chirped, telling me the info dump was complete. I disconnected the broken phone and stashed it in my desk drawer. If the phone's chip had survived undamaged, all of Rose's photos and data history was now on my hard drive. With Hayden still locked in the bathroom, I could search Rose's pictures unobserved.

There were plenty of the usual selfies and pictures of prettily foamed lattes, but I also came across dozens of shots of the school grounds. For some reason, she'd been interested in the exterior of Watson Hall, and the roads surrounding and leading up to campus.

Pulling up her texts, I gasped when the name Aunt Karen appeared at the top. With shaking hands I pulled up a group chat between Rose, Aunt Karen, and someone named Devin. Rose's last text to them had a photo attached of a man dressed in the dark green coveralls of a Harrington groundskeeper, distractedly pushing an empty wheelbarrow across the commons. The hair on the back of my neck stood up as I recognized him as Mr. Mustache, the driver of the SUV. The accompanying text read, *New to staff today, but not doing much work.* The photo was time stamped the date before her accident.

Racing to dig up Rose's contacts, my worst fears were confirmed. The phone number for Aunt Karen on Rose's phone matched the number for Aunt Karen on mine. Rose had been reporting to my handler.

Why hadn't Karen told me Rose was an agent? Had she been the one to report our whereabouts in New York to our would-be killers? Had she seen this photo and told Mr. Mustache his cover was blown, but he could buy some time if Rose didn't live to show it to anyone else? And who the hell was Devin? I slumped in my chair, trying to make sense of it all.

By the time Hayden emerged from the bathroom trailing scents of citrus and peppermint, a part of me was ready to climb under the covers and wait for my dad to come get me. The last girl who'd roomed with Hayden, one who presumably had been enlisted to keep an eye on her, was dead. Was I next?

BENSON'S RULE #26

HIT 'EM WHERE IT HURTS

The steady breathing coming from the other side of the room told me I was alone in my wakefulness. Tense and worried, I lay there mulling over every interaction with Karen, and wondering why she hadn't made her move against Hayden during the time between Rose's death and my arrival. Maybe using Hayden was just a fallback plan, one that had been triggered with the accelerated delivery date for Rosetta.

An explosion of barking from the distant kennels carried over the silent grounds, and almost sent me flying from the bed. I waited for answering barks to come from the rest of the pack out patrolling the grounds, but realized after a minute none were coming. Clambering upright, my heart raced when I couldn't come up with any logical reason why the foot patrols would be suspended, especially after the traumatic events of yesterday.

I slipped out of bed to retrieve my Taser. Too late I remembered the Prada tote containing that weapon along with everything else Benson had sent was still in Hayden's trunk. *Preparation is everything*, he always said. How could I have been so careless? What would I do if someone came bursting through our door? Throw my pillow at him?

It was the middle of the night and getting caught out of the room could mean serious consequences, but feeling like a sitting duck was even worse. Quietly pulling on jeans and a hoodie, I crept over to Hayden's desk to fish around for her car keys. Her bedside lamp suddenly flicked on and I stiffened, caught in the act.

"What are you doing?" She propped herself up on an elbow, her face pinched in mistrust.

We stared at each other a moment. If I was truthful, I might well be on the next flight out to Karachi, but if I wasn't, any chance we had of being friends would die an early death.

"I'm an agent with the State Department," I confessed in a rush. "I'm afraid your life might be in danger."

"I knew there was something weird going on, but seriously?" Her voice was heavy with skepticism.

Dashing back to my bed, I dropped on all fours to extract my ID. "I can prove it."

As I rooted around in the mattress, Hayden called out, "You're not doing much to boost my confidence level."

"Here," I said, presenting my State Department card.

She quickly sobered. "When were you planning to tell me this?"

"Um, now?" I shoved a stray lock of hair behind my ear and smiled weakly.

Another burst of howls erupted from the kennels, and Hayden jumped out of bed. She grabbed a pair of sweats from the floor and slipped them on.

"What's the plan?" She sounded eager rather than angry.

Taken aback, I said, "You're not going to kill me?"

She thought about it for a moment. "It's irritating that people thought I was too delicate or whatever to hear the truth, but that's not your fault. I can also say I'm not all that surprised." She shot me a knowing glance. "You did get kind of sloppy here and there."

I bristled for a moment before remembering we didn't have time to discuss my tactics. "I need your keys. I might have, uh, stashed a few things in your car."

She retrieved them from her purse. "Okay, let's go."

"You can't go," I protested. "We don't know who or what might be out there. Lock up as soon as I leave, and don't open it for anyone. I promise you, I'll be right back."

The lockset was sufficient for keeping out the casual visitor, but if someone really wanted to get in, a swift kick would probably do it. There was no time to waste.

"You have five minutes," Hayden warned. "And then I'm coming after you."

The halls were deserted. Dim wall sconces provided the only source of light, tapering off into total darkness when I reached the stairwell. Fortunately, long, narrow windows on the landing captured just enough moonlight so I didn't kill myself on the steps. I made it down one flight and turned sharply to descend the next when I suddenly plowed into something instantly recognizable as a person. Hands clutched at me, and I reacted with an elbow strike–hard.

A cry of pain was followed by a familiar voice. "Are you trying to kill me?"

"Von?" I ventured, taken aback.

He flipped on a flashlight and placed it under his chin. The effect was a creepy Halloween mask, but one definitely recognizable as Von. He rubbed his midsection where the point of my elbow had connected.

"What the hell are you doing here?" I said in a harsh whisper. "You'll get expelled if anyone finds you creeping around."

"Is Hayden in your room?" he whispered.

I sent him an odd look. "Really? Since when have you been into her?"

"Riley, listen to me," he said. "Perimeter alarms have been tripped, and Hayden could be in danger. I detected at least four, maybe five intruders entering the grounds by the northwest boundary."

I reared back in astonishment. "What are you talking about?"

"I don't have time to explain everything, but I'm with the State Department, and I think something is going down."

"*You're* with the State Department?" I sputtered in outrage. "When were you going to tell me?"

"Uh, now?" He pulled a slim leather wallet from his back pocket. Flipping it open, he shone the light on a card identical to the one I'd been issued, but the name next to his picture read "Devin Sanderson".

"*You're* Devin?" That confirmed Karen was his handler, too.

"I'm assigned to Stef, and you're here to protect Hayden, just like Rose was," he explained. "I wanted to tell you, but after Rose died we put everything on lockdown."

"Who's *we*?" I demanded to know. "Because if you're talking about Karen, she's no friend of mine." I explained what I'd found on Rose's phone, and my suspicions.

Von swore. "I just texted her. If she's betrayed us, whoever's on the grounds now knows we're coming." He shifted on his feet, thinking fast. "Keep your weapon handy, and go stay with Hayden. I'll see if I can delay them." He whipped out his phone.

"Who are you texting?"

"Major Taylor," he said, as his fingers flew across the keyboard. "If I text the word "scorpion", she knows I mean business."

"Scorpion? You got *scorpion*?" I huffed with indignation. I was surprised she hadn't assigned me "kittens" and "puppies".

"Now go," he ordered, turning to leave.

"Uh, Von? My, uh, Taser? It's kind of in Hayden's trunk." I felt like a complete fool. "I was just going out to get it."

He heaved a sigh and pulled a .9mm pistol out of his jacket pocket. "Let's go."

"Wait, I have a Taser, and you've got a gun?" I asked, forgetting my embarrassment.

"Riley!" he snapped through gritted teeth. I think I liked the flirty Von better. At the bottom of the stairs he started toward a side door, one that usually triggered an alarm that would wake the whole place up. I started to protest, but he cut me off. "Don't worry, I disabled it."

We ran out the door— and smacked right into Sam.

"What's going on?" Sam gasped, taking a step back.

"Get back inside," Von ordered. "It's not safe out here."

"Well, it's not safe inside either," he protested. "Stef is hiding in my room because you told him they were coming for him, whoever they are. It doesn't help that the dogs are barking their heads off." Sam caught sight of Von's weapon. "Whoa, dude, what's with the gun?"

"Intruders are on campus, and my guess is they're coming for either Hayden or Stef, or both," he told him. "We're agents with the State Department." He thrust his ID at Sam.

Sam stood speechless for a moment before turning to me. "Both of you?"

I nodded.

"Then let me help," Sam said. "Stef and Hayden are my friends, too." Then he met my gaze. "I don't want to see anyone get hurt."

Von paused for a moment, most likely calculating the low odds of survival if he took on a team of armed intruders alone. He nodded curtly. "Stay close."

We dashed in the direction of the parking lot, keeping to the shadows, which wasn't difficult. As we passed by Hale Hall, I waited for ninjas to burst out from the nearby trees, but nothing moved. Even the barking from the kennels had stopped.

"What happened to the dogs?" I whispered.

"Good question," Von whispered back. "My guess is they've been neutralized."

The thought of anyone laying a finger on sweet little Scout royally pissed me off. As soon as I had my Taser and a few other choice accessories, I was going to go all ASPCA on them.

We made it to the car park without any alarms being raised. The three of us crouched down low as I led the way to where we'd left the Mercedes. There was no getting around the short honk of greeting the car gave when I disabled the alarm, and we all froze.

"What are we doing?" Sam hissed.

"Riley needs a weapon," Von answered.

Easing the tote out of the trunk, I unzipped it and pocketed my Taser. I also grabbed the set of throwing stars and a smoke grenade for good measure, shoving them into the kangaroo pocket on my sweatshirt.

"What else you got in there?" Sam asked with the enthusiasm of a kid let loose in a toy store.

"Here, take the other smoke grenade," I offered, digging it out. "And I think you'll like my baton."

"I think there's a dirty joke in there somewhere," Sam said with wry amusement.

"Are we done here?" Von asked. "Riley, go back through the side door and keep watch over Hayden. Sam, come with me. I know where they entered the grounds, and I bet we can intercept them on the back side of Watson."

Sam reached up and cupped my cheek. "Be careful, Agent Riley."

I grinned, excitement and fear heightening my senses. "You, too."

Sam flicked open the baton. "Let's roll."

We split off, the guys sprinting toward the tree line while I went back the way we came, zipping from tree to tree until reaching Hale Hall. There I hugged the outside wall, taking the route around the back of the building.

Gunfire echoed from the direction the guys had taken, and I stiffened. A few lights flicked on overhead, thinning my cover.

What if something had happened to them? As the trained agent, Von would take the lead on any action, but who knew what waited for them in the darkness? It took all my will to dash away from them and in the direction of Watson Hall. Hayden was counting on me.

From the corner of my eye I caught sight of two silhouettes emerging from the tree line. Whoever they were, we would converge on the upper girls' dorm at almost the same moment. Pulling the smoke grenade from my pocket, I jerked out the safety pin before yanking on the pull ring. There was a four to five second delay to detonation, so the grenade had to land where the intruders would be in the span of a few breaths. Aiming for a spot roughly fifty feet ahead of the first guy, I let it fly.

A loud popping noise preceded a couple of frightened yelps and a spate of coughing. Running until I practically slammed into the side door of Watson, I reached for the handle, but a horribly familiar sound, like the noise a bullet makes when it whizzes by your head, caused me to hit the ground. Looking up, there was a metal dart lodged into the wooden doorframe, still quivering from its flight. The bastard had shot a tranquilizer dart at me. That answered the question of how they planned to get Hayden to cooperate.

A figure dressed all in black charged in my direction. Scrambling to my knees and grabbing the throwing stars, I flung one at him, followed by another and another. I'd only ever thrown at stationary targets, so I waited in terror for a dart or bullet to come flying out of the darkness.

Instead the man stumbled and let out a roar of pain. A gun fell from his hands as he clutched at his thigh. He howled again as he wrenched out the star.

"End them before they end you," I whispered, Benson's voice spurring me on as I leapt to my feet and hurdled headlong at my attacker. His head snapped up at my approach, and we both started in surprise as we recognized the other. The man with the horn-rimmed glasses forgot his wound and lunged toward his weapon. Somewhere in the back of my brain I realized my life depended on not allowing him to reach it first.

Hit 'em where it hurts flashed through my mind as I launched into the air and aimed a strike at his bleeding leg. His blood-curdling scream didn't quite mask the crack of breaking bone as his leg folded at an unnatural angle. I tumbled on the soft grass but quickly regained my feet, dimly aware my knee hurt like hell but more concerned about the other man emerging from the smoke cloud. It was Mr. Mustache dressed all in black, and he looked pissed.

Level the playing field. I dashed to pick up the discarded gun. Before I reached it, another dart went singing by, and I rolled empty-handed into the grass. He kept coming, loading another round into his weapon. I jumped back on my feet and whipped out the Taser.

Before he could raise his gun again, I fired. The prongs hit the mark and latched securely onto the front of his shirt. I pumped up the electricity and waited for the look of shock to cross his face. Instead he smiled. Tapping his belly with a thud, he grinned maliciously. "The new Kevlar vests are a marvel, wouldn't you agree?"

Dropping the Taser in panic, I turned and ran. Hope jolted through me when I spied Major Taylor standing directly in my path. Her face was so pale and cold, it could have been carved from stone. Then she raised her gun.

"Stop right there," she ordered.

"He's right behind me!" I shouted. "Shoot him!"

"I said stop, Riley." She pointed the gun at my chest.

I stumbled, shaken to the core.

"Shoot her!" Mr. Mustache yelled.

I met her unwavering gaze over the barrel of her weapon. "Benson trusted you!"

At the mention of his name, something flickered within the lifeless depths of her eyes. Suddenly she yelled, "Down!"

I plowed into the dirt at her feet as the gun roared over my head. I looked up to see her locked in a firing stance, a trail of smoke curling up from her weapon. I followed her gaze to the man clutching his throat, disbelief crossing his face as his life poured out between his fingers. Slowly he collapsed on the ground.

The side door to Watson Hall banged open, and Major Taylor and I both jumped. Hayden stood on the threshold, her face white with fear. A man stood behind her with a gun jammed against her cheekbone. Dressed in black like his companions, he had a frenzied look about him, as if he knew the mission was falling apart. *A desperate man is a dangerous man*, Benson would say.

Major Taylor aimed her weapon at him.

"What are you doing, Taylor?" he sputtered. "Put the gun down."

"I can't," she said, seemingly as surprised as he was. "I made a promise."

He darted a glance between the Major and me, tightening his chokehold on Hayden before cocking his gun and taking aim at my heart. "Drop your gun, or I pull the trigger."

After a second's deliberation, Major Taylor let it fall to the grass.

"You, girl," he said, "kick it over to me."

Rising to my feet, I shot a look at Major Taylor and hoped she got the message. No matter what she'd done or what price we had to pay, whether it was forfeiting her life, my life, or even Hayden's, we couldn't let him take Stephen Frasier's daughter alive. The damn software program should probably never see the light of day, but it wasn't getting handed over to someone who would kill to get their hands on it.

Show no fear. Absurdly I tried to remember if that was Benson's rule #5 or #15.

I slowly nudged the gun over, stopping directly in front of Hayden. Her teeth chattered from fear or cold, or maybe both. Her feet were bare, and she wore only her long T-shirt and sweats. Her wide eyes met mine.

"Stop," the man ordered. "Now pick it up by the barrel, and give it to me." Once he had both weapons, there'd be nothing to stop him from killing us and taking Hayden.

Here it was, the moment of truth. The one I'd trained for all my life, and the one I'd hoped would never come... but Benson was there. I could hear him over the blood rushing through my veins, and over the pounding of my heart. *Fight fair if you can, dirty if you must.*

I leaned over, pretending to reach for the gun barrel, and then I dove straight into Hayden's mid-section. The gunman's grip was no match for her reflexes, and she whipped out of his arms. They both lost their footing, and all three of us went down hard.

Major Taylor was there before we hit the ground. She grabbed for the gun still gripped in the man's hand, and he yanked her off her feet as well. We were a tangle of bodies locked in combat as the two of them wrestled for the gun. I wriggled out from under Hayden, who had collapsed, her breath coming in painful gasps. Crawling behind our attacker, I threw an arm around his neck and pulled. If Major Taylor could hang on another thirty seconds, he'd choke out.

The three of us struggled for several seconds, and I could tell he was weakening. Only a few more moments, and this would be over. With last burst of desperate energy, the man almost wrenched the gun out of Major Taylor's grasp, but she held on. I could hear people running toward us, calling our names. I even heard a bark and hoped it might be Scout cheering me on.

And then the gun went off.

The man in my arms slumped. I relaxed my grip, but I was strangely light-headed. Looking down, I grimaced at the exit wound in the man's back but was bemused to see blood gurgling from my shoulder. Concerned faces crowded around. Some I recognized, others I didn't.

At a familiar voice I glanced up to Karen shouting for an ambulance. Von and Sam popped up behind her with twin expressions of horror on their faces. I opened my mouth to warn them about Major Taylor, but with a sigh I slipped into oblivion.

BENSON'S RULE #27

LIVE TO FIGHT ANOTHER DAY

My heartbeat had never been so loud, nor so mechanical. I swam toward the sound and woke up in a room with pale green walls and white plastic blinds on the window. Sunlight filtered in through the narrow slats, illuminating a small table overflowing with flowers. A cluster of balloons urging someone to "Get well soon!" was tied to a nearby chair.

Curious about the source of the audible beats, I tried to move, but my limbs refused to cooperate. I lifted my head to find my upper body cocooned in snowy white gauze, and the rest of me tucked so tightly into bed I could count the ridges of my toes.

The door swung open, and a cheerful woman in pink scrubs marched in. She wore a stethoscope around her neck, and a picture I.D. badge clipped to her shirt introduced her as "Ana Garcia, R.N.".

"You're awake," she exclaimed. "There are a lot of people who will be glad to hear the news." She leaned in for a closer inspection. "How do you feel?"

"Thirsty," I croaked.

"That would be from all the meds." She shrugged it off as no big deal and grabbed a pitcher from a bedside table. Over the running water she called, "Do you remember what happened?"

"I think... I was shot?"

"We don't get as many GSWs as they do down south, and never so many from a fancy boarding school, I can tell you that." She poured a glass of water and offered it up. We stared at each other a beat before she realized I needed help. "Oops, hold on." She grabbed a straw, loosened the bedcovers, and freed my right hand.

I sucked down the water as she filled in around the edges of my memory. "They brought you in with four other patients, and let me tell you, the cops were on them like white on rice." Her eyes widened in excitement, relishing the opportunity to recall the event. "One guy was shot on the left side like you, two of them were busted up pretty bad, but the fourth..." She shuddered in distaste. "One of the nastiest compound fractures I've ever seen. That man's leg is going to be more metal than bone."

I winced at the memory of the man in the horn-rimmed glasses screaming as his leg collapsed like a Jenga tower.

"Wait," I said, recalling more of last night's events. "Two guys got shot." Major Taylor took down Mr. Mustache before confronting the guy who had Hayden.

Ana shook her head. "Sorry, only one other GSW came in through the front door. Maybe the other guy came in through the back."

"What's in the back?" I cleared my throat, still feeling dry as a Cairo summer.

She stalled a moment, as if realizing she'd said too much. "The morgue."

I guess it didn't matter which one survived, but Mr. Mustache had tried to kill me more than once. If he was still breathing, I wanted to know about it. "The guy who got shot, is he still here?"

"Now don't you worry," she said, misinterpreting my concern. "They are in a whole different wing, and there must be fifty cops keeping watch, which means fifty chances that one of them is hot and single." She fluffed her short black curls with a throaty laugh.

Someone knocked at the door, and I sent her a look of terror. "Don't let anyone in! I must look horrible!"

"Honey, I should look as horrible as you on my best day," she said. "There've been people sitting out there since you were brought in last night, and I don't think we can hold them off any longer." She strode to the door and threw it open.

A worried-looking Von stood on the threshold, holding a potted plant. "Is she okay?" He glanced past Ana, and visibly relaxed when he saw me. Needing no further encouragement, he rushed through the door, setting his gift on my nightstand.

He hovered over me. "How do you feel?"

"Not too bad, actually." There was an ache somewhere in the vicinity of my left shoulder and collarbone, but I'd have thought being shot would be far more painful.

"Of course it's not too bad," Ana huffed. "Do you think I run a torture chamber here?"

Von grinned at her. "So all these pain meds... will she remember this conversation later?"

Ana winked at me. "She won't remember a thing, so here's your chance to pour your heart out, honey."

Another knock announced the arrival of Sam, who strode through the doorway clutching a bouquet of at least two-dozen beautiful red roses. I'd gotten used to Sam's pretty boy looks, but Ana stared in appreciation as he came around the other side of my bed.

"Too late, Romeo," she muttered to Von.

Sam laid the flowers at the foot of the bed and smiled, making me wish desperately for a mirror and hairbrush.

"I guess you don't owe me any more secrets. That last one was pretty over the top." He laughed softly. "Are you going to be all right?"

"I'm fine, but what happened with you guys?" Neither of them seemed to have physically suffered from the experience.

"Last night was totally awesome," Sam said excitedly. "I wish you could have seen it. I have got to get one of those wicked batons."

Von glanced at Sam with disbelief. "In case you hadn't noticed, it wasn't totally awesome for Riley."

Sam's face clouded over. "I didn't mean to make it sound like..."

I waved away his apology. "It was a group effort. Is Hayden okay?"

"She and Stef were both removed from Harrington late last night," Von said. "I think everyone was finally convinced they needed to be kept in a secure location until the project is delivered, which should be in the next few weeks."

I breathed a deep, albeit uncomfortable sigh.

"So are you coming back to school, or what?" Sam spared us each a glance. "Are you guys even real high school students?"

"Riley is," Von said. "I graduated over a year ago, but the government promised full tuition at the college of my choice if I took on this assignment."

"How did they find you?" I wondered. "Were you in trouble with the Taliban, too?"

"Nothing quite so colorful," he said. "ROTC, valedictorian, that kind of stuff." That explained his amazing scores in calculus. "The State Department recruited me the day I graduated. They gave me three months of training, then sent me right back to high school. Like I told you, it was the seventh circle of hell."

Sam pulled over the chair with the balloons. "So do we call you Devin now?"

He pulled a face. "God, no. I've always been Von."

Sam casually reached over and placed his hand over mine. "Well, we'll miss you at Harrington, Von." Ana had been pretending to fuss over a monitor, but now she dropped the pretense that she wasn't avidly following our conversation.

Von glowered. "Riley does have other options, you know. There's a place for her in the State Department, that's for sure. Or she could graduate early and go to college, or maybe she wants to live in Paris." He turned to me. "I heard Karen talking to your dad this morning. He just got the Paris posting."

"Paris?" I was stunned. No one got that post without a lot of strings being pulled. "But how?"

"My guess is you've got a very grateful Stephen Frasier to thank," Von said.

"And what about Stef?" I asked, suddenly dying to know his reaction to finding out he'd been living with a secret agent for the last year. "Does he know you were there for his protection?"

Von nodded. "He knows people put their lives on the line for him, but will it make a difference?" He shrugged. "Maybe a close call will finally get his dad to realize that getting to know his son is a limited time offer, but I'm not holding my breath."

Even if Stephen Frasier never figured out what a wonderful person his son was, I suspected Hayden was coming to understand the value of knowing there was always someone who had her back. She and Stef would be okay.

"Gentlemen, may I speak to Riley please?" We all turned to see Karen standing in the doorway, taking in the scene. She wasn't happy. Von had probably questioned her loyalty with the ammunition I'd provided.

Sam sent me a sweetly questioning look. I nodded, suddenly realizing Hayden no longer stood between the two of us. If I chose to go back to Harrington, Sam would be waiting there for me. He squeezed my hand and headed out the door.

As Von rose to leave, I caught the scent of something wonderfully familiar. I breathed it in, suddenly realizing what it was. My eyes darted to Von in astonishment.

He grinned, reaching to move the plant closer to my bedside. "Arabian jasmine... so you'll always feel at home."

"So all that flirting," I asked, suddenly unsure, "was it just an act?"

He smiled shyly. "Only in the beginning."

I followed him with my eyes as he walked out the door.

Ana had taken up permanent residence in front of the monitors and showed no sign of leaving.

Karen cleared her throat. "Nurse, if you wouldn't mind?"

Reluctantly, Ana gave in. "Okay, I'll go," she said, turning to me, "but you'll let me know which one you choose, right?"

When we were alone, Karen sat stiffly in the chair Sam had just vacated. After a few moments of charged silence, she said, "I'm sorry."

"What?" I'd heard her fine, but it was completely unexpected.

"I said I'm sorry. I should have told you Rose worked for us. You trusted me, but I didn't return the favor. Maybe if I had, you would have recognized that guy at the nightclub, and we'd now have Grace Taylor in custody."

My mouth fell open in surprise. "Major Taylor is gone?"

She nodded. "By the time we realized a couple of the guys in the ER were men from her security team, she'd cleared out."

"Why did she do it?" Even though Major Taylor had played me, like how she'd tricked me into installing the GPS program on Hayden's phone to use for her own purposes, she'd honored her promise to Benson. He'd be both grateful and heartbroken when he learned of her betrayal.

"It's early days in tracking her movements, but money doesn't appear to be her motive. We're following up on a lead that it may have been extortion, that the safety of her son might have been threatened."

"What?" I gasped. "She didn't have any children."

Karen regarded me curiously, as if she thought it odd I would presume to know such a thing. "She's got a sixteen-year-old at a school in Switzerland. His name is Ben, I believe."

My body went cold. Was it possible Benson was the boy's father? The timeline sure fit. "What about his dad?"

She shrugged. "I'm sure he'll be contacted, or I imagine the boy will become a ward of the state. It's such a shame," she mused. "I can't understand why she wouldn't have gone to the authorities if her family had been threatened."

Whatever the reason, I bet it was a good one. Major Taylor had sacrificed everything for her son, for me, for Benson. Even if they never found her or discovered the true reason for her actions, I would always believe she had acted out of love.

Visiting hours were over, and Ana's shift ended. She'd made sure my phone was charged before she left, but it sat mutely on the bedside table. I'd called both my dad and Benson, but neither had answered their phones. Listlessly scrolling through the hospital's basic cable channels, I felt neglected and unloved. How often did a girl get shot? You'd think at least one family member would be on Skype fussing over me.

Snatches of giggling conversation from the nearby nurses' station confirmed Ana's hope that a few of the police officers standing guard were eligible bachelors. Down the hall, an orderly worked his way around the floor, knocking on doors and grandly announcing dinner was served like he was doling out dishes from a four-star restaurant. Everyone was busy while I was stuck in here all alone. I grumpily curled onto my good side and closed my eyes.

A knock came on my door.

"I'm not hungry," I groused.

"Not even for Nadira's walnut baklava?" My dad stood in the doorway holding up a rumpled paper bag that looked as if it'd been run over by a truck, but truth be told, he didn't look much better. His clothes were wrinkled, his hair was a mess, and he desperately needed a shave.

My tears began to fall. "You couldn't have called?"

He rushed to my bedside with a relieved smile. He always said I waited to cry until the worst was over, so if he saw tears I was in one piece.

"As soon as I heard, I jumped on a transport." He waved the bag in his hand. "Nadira chased me out of the embassy with this."

I sniffed, reaching for the pastry. "I got shot, you know." I still felt maltreated, but it would be a damn shame to let good walnut baklava go to waste. "I could have died, you know."

"I know," he said, his voice full of emotion, which made me feel a little better. "I never would have let you go if I'd known it would be this dangerous."

"I know, right?" I said through of mouthful of flaky filo. "But, Dad, you haven't heard the rest of it." I glanced toward the open doorway, searching for the hulking form that should be there. "Where's Benson?"

It wouldn't be right if he got a cold call from some government drone informing him the woman he'd loved had kept a heartbreaking secret from him all these years. The news should come from me.

He collapsed in the chair. "He's on his way to Switzerland."

My hand hovered over the next square of pastry. "So it's true then? Benson has a son?" With those two parents, the kid was probably a terror.

He nodded. "The school had his information on file in case of emergency. It was difficult, as you can imagine, that Grace never told him, but if anyone can find forgiveness, it's him."

"So do I have a sort-of cousin now?"

He laughed. "We are an odd assortment, aren't we?"

My phone chimed, and Dad passed it over. "Well-wishers from school?"

It was a photograph of a beautiful sandy beach, deserted except for two lounge chairs with a bamboo table set between them. Two cans of Coke on the table sweated in the heat. A pair of Prada sunglasses, identical to the ones Hayden picked out on our trip to Soho, had been placed alongside. A caption on the photo read, "This *does* make us friends."

"Yes," I said, with a smile. Hayden and Stef were someplace far, far away, and I hoped the sodas were Stef's way of letting me know that maybe he was ready to try life sober for a change.

"So you heard about Paris? There's an American School there." There was no mistaking the excitement in his voice.

"Congratulations, Dad. You really deserve it." I licked my fingers, gooey with honey, and thought it was all turning out pretty sweet.

He leaned in. "Well? What do you think? What do you want to do?"

Before I could answer, his phone rang. "It's Benson." He punched the key to put the call on speaker. "Need some fatherly advice already?" Dad winked at me.

"Joe, I need your help." Benson's voice was so ragged I barely recognized it. "My son is missing."

ACKNOWLEDGMENTS

This book wouldn't be this book without my brilliant big brother and story editor, Robb Sullivan. By day, he edits blockbuster movies and television series. By night, he makes me a better writer. You know you're stuck with me for life, Bro, right?

I also owe a huge debt of gratitude to my agent, Dawn Frederick of Red Sofa Literary, who believed in my vision of writing smart books about smart girls. It's inspiring to work with someone who leads instead of follows.

There are a number of friends and fellow writers whose insights were invaluable in writing this book. They include the amazingly talented Jennifer Hawkins, who lets me text her for no particular reason at all hours; Fiona McLaren, whose notes transformed my work; Quinn Wynes, whose sheer enthusiasm for Riley kept me at the keyboard way past my bedtime; Dete Meserve, who has unstintingly shared her joy and wisdom as I follow her down the publishing path; Annie DeYoung, who inspires me; and Jan Wieringa, who has held my hand every step of the way.

I must also give a shout out to the Pitch Wars team, and in particular Lindsay Currie. If I could bottle the support and encouragement this amazing group of writers provides, the world would be a better place. Thank you to the great team at Curiosity Quills, especially Andrew Buckley and Mollie Weisenfeld.

Lastly, this book would never have been written without the love and support of my amazing husband.

ABOUT THE AUTHOR

A native of Los Angeles, Kes Trester's first job out of college was on a film set, though the movie title will remain nameless because it was a really bad film.

Really. Determined to combine her love of reading and writing with the excitement of Hollywood, she became a film development executive, working on a variety of independent films, from gritty dramas (guns and hotties) to steamy vampire love stories (fangs and hotties) to teens-in-peril genre movies (blood and hotties).

Kes produced a couple of indie films, both award-winners on the festival circuit, before seguing into television. As head of production for a Hollywood-based film company, she supervised the budgeting and production of national television commercials (celebrities, aliens, talking chickens!) and award-winning music videos for artists such as Radiohead, Coldplay, and OKGO (more celebrities, aliens, and talking chickens!).

In an attempt to raise YA's who could actually pick their mom out of a line up, Kes turned to writing fulltime. Her contemporary novels for young adults are cinematic, fast-paced, and above all, fun. Add a pack of rescue dogs to the mix, and that's also an apt description of life in the busy Trester household.

Thank You for Reading

Please visit http://curiosityquills.com/reader-survey to share your reading experience with the author of this book!

Bleed Through, by Adriana Arrington

Twenty-five-year-old schizophrenic Liam witnesses a murder. He worries it's a hallucination, but becomes convinced that his medication has given him the paranormal ability to see past events and that the murder actually happened. Burdened with secrets he doesn't want to know, Liam tosses his pills. He spirals into a relapse and captures the killer's attention as he bumbles through investigating the crime. Hunted by a possibly imaginary murderer, and haunted by self-doubt, Liam must distinguish between hallucinations and reality.

The Dollhouse, by Nicole Thorn

Four girls were kidnapped seven years ago, and they've finally broken free of their prison. They were taken by a man who spent years perfecting them. Making them his little dolls, meant to love him and nothing else. They find themselves thrown back into society. Now nineteen, they have to acclimate to how the world around them has changed. Riley meets the broken boy next door. He seems to be the only one who treats Riley like she's more than a china doll. Riley just wants to feel human again, and she's willing to do anything to get there.

CPSIA information can be obtained
at www.ICGtesting.com
Printed in the USA
LVOW07s1156180917
549111LV00002B/552/P

9 781620 079072